Enthusiastic reviews for Lior Samson's

The Intaglio Imprint (Hoff

> "Super-realism, compelling rational, ethically probing, ... an intricate and incisive creation." —*George Church, geneticist*

> "[U]nanticipated but logical twists and turns, ripe with conflict, tension, and suspense." — *Hoffer Award, U.S. Review of Books*

The Rosen Singularity

> "The plotting is ingenious and the characters come through strongly. " — *Rebecca Goldstein, MacArthur Fellow, author*

> "Vibrant and distinctive characters,... an exciting, pulse-pounding story." — *Laurie Jenkins, book blogger*

The Millicent Factor

> "A solid page turner. The author keeps the pace just right with action and chases ... and backroom dealings. " — *RJ Beam, author*

The Four-Color Puzzle

> "[A] thinking person's ideal mystery; an eloquent feast of words and an excellent story." —*Jeanie B. Clemmons, author*

> "[A] fast-paced crime story that had me rooting for the hero. The story challenges the reader." — *Patricia O'Sullivan, author*

The Homeland Connection Novels

Bashert (Hoffer Award Winner)

> "Samson writes with a crisp elegance, like John Le Carré, and weaves his plot magically." —*James A. Anderson, author*

> "[M]oving with the speed of light between interconnected events, three continents, and a group of unique and memorable characters." - *Avraham Azrieli, author*

The Dome

"Suspenseful and timely, ... I cannot say enough good things about this novel." —Alan Caruba, critic, BookViews

"An excellent read, and very highly recommended."
—Midwest Book Review

Web Games

"An outstanding tech thriller—better than Tom Clancy.... one of the best [thrillers] I've read in 2011." —James A. Anderson, author

"This extraordinary author has the ability to anticipate events. ... You will not put it down." —Alan Caruba, critic, BookViews

Chipset

"[A] multi-dimensional thriller ... populated by flesh-and-blood characters." - Avraham Azrieli, author

"Lior Samson hits another one out of the park. ... a gripping story." —James A. Anderson, author

Gasline

"[A] high-energy plot and ... perfect mix of techno thrill and human conflict.... Excellent!" —Avraham Azrieli, author

"[A] great novel ... [It] will raise your blood pressure and make you think." —Columbia Review of Books and Film

Flight Track

"Well plotted ... compelling and entertaining.... kept me turning pages." —Harrison Jones, airline pilot, author

"Stunning, compelling, thought-provoking... [with] three-dimensional, engaging characters." —M. Thornburg

Distant Sons

Also by Lior Samson, from Gesher Press

The Rosen Singularity
The Millicent Factor
The Intaglio Imprint

The Four-Color Puzzle
Avalanche Warning

Requisite Variety: Collected Short Fiction

The Homeland Connection novels:

Bashert
The Dome
Web Games
Chipset
Gasline
Flight Track

Available from Amazon and other booksellers.

Distant Sons

a novel by Lior Samson

GESHER PRESS

Gesher Press
Rowley, Massachusetts
Author site: www.liorsamson.com

5 4 3 2 1

ISBN 978-1-7326091-0-5

Cover and book design: Larry Constantine
Set in Scotch Text (Positype)
Cover photos: Wikimedia;
Österreichisches Jüdisches Museum, Fotoarchiv

To my Ashkenazi Levite ancestors, with whom I am forever linked, and from whom I am ever disconnected

Every generation revolts against its fathers and makes friends with its grandfathers. – Lewis Mumford

ONE: Framework

That is what we are supposed to do when we are at our best — make it all up — but make it up so truly that later it will happen that way.

— Ernest Hemingway

Chapter 1
Without Preface

Twin Cities, Minnesota, yesterday

I imagine you, and often. Memories fade. Images of such clarity can only be of my own invention, yet they return, always unchanged.

You are coming up the back stairs wearing that silly cap that my mother insisted upon. You look up to see me above, and your expression changes, your eyebrows form gentle slopes with the faintest crease between — a question, wondering. What did I want? Yes, what indeed did I want. As if you didn't already know.

Or you are walking on the path by Lake Como, your auburn braids coiled at the back. A late June breeze that is at once both cool and warm plays with stray wisps of hair around your face. You catch me studying your profile against the bright gray of a morning fog that has not yet burned off, and you turn, flashing me a smile,

3

enigmatic, as if you withheld a secret from me but already burned to share it.

And, of course, there was that first time, and then, too, it was your hair —

With these words, without preface or introduction, my father's father began. I never knew Jakob Oster. The same was the case with my grandmother, but my grandfather was the deeper enigma. At least I had her name from court documents and could trace a few fragments of what might have been her story. It was Jakob Oster who was the greater mystery and who would blaze the path to the rest.

His words arrived in the form of a stack of faded gray-green chapbooks, each cover hand-lettered with Hebrew dates, the top one marked 5669-5674, over a century ago. How I came to read them is itself a long story, one best set aside for later when it will not get in the way of his story. In one of his many asides, he seemed to anticipate my own too often linear impulses.

All stories begin somewhere in the middle. Endings are real, beginnings are fiction. All things end, but something always came before, and better storytellers recognize this truth. The sketch of whom we might become was drafted before we were conceived, and, by that conception, an outline completes, the future is already circumscribed. When we are each ready to declare ourselves grown — by which we most assuredly demonstrate we have not yet arrived — the arc of the story is in place. At best, we each annotate some middle chapters in an extended saga.

We would like to think there are choices along the

*way, like whom to marry or whether to marry, whether
to cling to an old faith or cast it aside. Some decisions
that seem inconsequential are not, such as, whether to
descend a staircase or remain on an upper floor.*

What follows here is not Jakob Oster's memoirs. I thought,
briefly, about publishing an edited version, but the story he
wrote is incomplete and often disordered, as if he were unsure where next to go, whether forward or back. Not a problem. I am, after all, a novelist. Making things up is my profession. I deal in deftly filled detail where there was none. I
have extensive practice in creating something from nothing,
and this is another product of that craft.

For reasons that should need no explanation, names of ac-
tors have sometimes been changed, players appear from
behind a scrim of imagination, and incidents are interpo-
lated, but that in no way changes the essential truth of the
narrative. No one now knows exactly all that happened back
then, except that I am here to write this, so we can fill in
many of the missing pieces.

Jakob's voice as a writer is sometimes archaic and often
an eccentric concoction of the casual and formal, as if he
were writing an undeliverable letter or a private journal
even as he seemed to address some distant, unknowable future reader. He was, I am convinced, ever conscious of his
audience. This is a hallmark of genuine writers — a faith in
the arc of destiny — as if he somehow knew his works would
survive and pass to someone. In this case, I am that someone.

But there I go, injecting myself into the narrative. I had
promised myself at the outset that I would not intrude, that
this was not my story and I would let it tell itself. But it is,

after all, also my story, in a perversely impersonal and re-moved way. I am but a *shamas* to Jakob Oster, as he is to me.

Shamas: this is how Jakob Oster headed the entry that be-gins his notes, an entry that opens without prologue or pref-ace. *Shamas* means servant in Hebrew. To many Jewish families, the most memorable use of that word is as the la-bel for the candle used to light the succession of other can-dles during the eight days of Hanukkah, the Jewish festival of lights.

Taking my cue from Jakob, I begin in the middle. I am the narrator of the story, even though I was at none of these events. The italicized blocks are Jakob Oster's own words, unapologetically cribbed from his notes.

And yes, this is a prologue disguised as a first chapter, but if it had been honestly titled, you might have skipped it, so the deception is justified — or at least rationalized. Then again, this deception is only the first of many, but that is the task of the novelist.

Chapter 2
Shamas

St. Paul, Minnesota, 1909

Can a house be at once modest and pretentious? Ours in St. Paul was both: like its neighbors, a simple cube clad in white siding, but with black shutters decorating its windows, fluted wooden columns guarding the stoop, and sidelights flanking the front door. Early spring sun cast long rays through the panels of leaded glass beside the door. It was your hair, haloed by the sunlight, that I first noticed: thick, like the fur of some arctic animal, defiantly wavy, strands of it escaping all attempts at containment. You stood in the vestibule, your gaze lowered just enough to be respectful, your hair pulled back, emblematic of your readiness to work with deference and efficiency. These traits, I would learn, would abide through all your days.

You were speaking with my mother as I descended the front stairs, the lower flight with their precise parade of photographs from the old country mixed among miniature oils that my deceased uncle Rueben had painted. The display was chronological, reflecting the pursuit of order that was my mother's unflagging preoccupation. One could march back in time in descending those stairs, go forward by climbing them. It was not by accident that the most venerable images greeted any visitor at the foot of the staircase. The bottom-most of these, a portrait of a stiff and unsmiling family posed in front

7

of a modest wood-frame house in Austria, strategically covered a stain in the wallpaper. The babe-in-arms at the center of the photograph was my mother.

As a young boy, I had studied the stairwell gallery until their stories were memorized, as now I studied your face, committing it to memory out of fear and anticipation, already reaching for the words by which I would later paint you in a miniature of my own. There was a strength about you that arose from some inner radiant core, so different from my mother's strength, which was an armor she wore, ultimately fragile, like the thin shell of a pullet egg. It was your silent strength to which I was drawn and from which I wanted to draw in order to paint you in my sketchbook of words.

"Ah, there you are, Jakob. Come, come." His mother's brow was creased, the lines of her unending annoyance at all things out-of-order etched deeply into what otherwise might be a pleasantly pretty face framed by light-brown curls that every morning were renewed and aligned with the aid of her curling iron. Even when Sadie Oster smiled, which she did at moments like this when she sensed a temporary triumph over unspecified opposition, even in pleasant repose, disapproval lurked in the shadows of those lines.

"Yes, Ma*ma*." It was always Ma*ma* and Pa*pa*, spoken with the accent on the second syllable, as if his family were descended from some European elite rather than merchant-class Austrian immigrants recently risen into American middleclass status.

"This is Maggie, our new domestic," his mother said, with the cadence of someone in authority. "She will be with us six days a week, except for the last weekend of next month, when she will stay over to look after you while your father and I are off to Chicago. Another of his dental conventions."

"Chicago?" There was a mix of apprehension and excitement in Jakob's voice. He was thinking that he did not need looking after but knew better than to protest. "How long will you be gone, Mama?" He was looking at Maggie as he spoke to his mother. The girl was so different from the rotund and homely Frieda Brecher, their last servant. This one was slim and a little younger than Jakob — sixteen or seventeen perhaps. She had been speaking with an accent that announced both rural Minnesota influences and more distant Germanic ancestry.

"We shall be gone six days in all." His mother was answering an already forgotten question.

Jakob nodded his head in a much abbreviated bow to the girl. "Pleased to meet you." He stepped down from the bottom riser and started to extend his hand. He was stopped by a quick look of disapproval from his mother.

"Maggie starts today, so we must begin her training. And I am sure you have schoolwork waiting, so we shan't keep you." She turned her back on him. "Jakob is studying at the University of Minnesota, studying law —"

"Pre-law, actually," he interjected. "I don't enter the Law program until next year."

"— so it is important not to disturb him. His room is at the top of the stairs. You can straighten it when he is at classes, but be careful not to move any of his books or papers." She turned again to Jakob. "You needn't let us keep you from your work, Jakob."

He knew he was being dismissed, given an order in the indirect manner that was his mother's custom with him, but he was still studying the girl's face and didn't want to leave until he had completed the mental photograph to be developed and enlarged later in the careful longhand of his journal.

She was not pretty in any conventional way, but the sun at her back gave her round face a sweet, almost angelic quality. He could imagine a Renaissance portraitist brushing in subtle hints of a halo. His eyes darted back to his mother and then to the chandelier in the hallway in a swift attempt to appear to be uninterested in the girl.

It was too late, of course. His mother always took note of his every move, every shifting expression. He was her sole investment in a coming generation, her hope for grandchildren and for comfort in her old age. She might have preferred to hedge her biological bets, but there had been so many miscarriages and such a difficult birth, then more miscarriages and the final decree of age that Jakob was to be both the firstborn and the last.

"Is there something else, Jakob?" Her eyes narrowed in impatience.

"No, Mama. I was just wondering . . ." He glanced back at the girl. "Your name, what is it really?"

"Magdalena." Without lifting her head, she raised her eyes to meet his. "Magdalena Samson. But Maggie will do, sir."

"Jakob, will do, Maggie." He let a half wink punctuate his thin-lipped smile.

"Master Jakob, to you, Maggie," his mother corrected. To Jakob she said something about unnecessary familiarity, but he was not listening. He was watching Maggie's breathing, how each breath pushed her breasts against the unstarched apron she wore over her dress, how the subtle impression of her nipples grew as he watched.

His mother cleared her throat. She took Maggie's arm and

steered her down the hallway. "Let me show you where your cleaning things are kept."

⇶ ⇇

By dinner the following night, Jakob's father had already grown unenthusiastic about the new servant. From the head of the ebony-stained mahogany trestle table, at the end of the dining room nearest the fireplace that never held a fire, he looked down along the linen-covered expanse and let his disapproval be known. "This new girl, she is too skinny, too frail. She'll never last. Why can't we get another mature woman like Frieda."

"We cannot get another domestic like Frieda because all the Friedas seem to be occupied with their own families, or they want too much for too few hours. That's why. Besides, this girl truly needs the money. She will work hard. Her story is such a sorry affair, poor girl." She paused as Maggie entered from the kitchen, but continued as if the girl were not present. "Mrs. Poferl told me all about it, but I will not bore everyone with how they came to be living with their aunt and uncle. It is, I am given to understand, somewhat crowded in that small house, and the older children are being expected to earn their keep. I am sure she will be fine in our employ. So far she has acquitted herself well. She is rather quick to learn. I only have to explain something once. Frieda was a dunce by comparison. Please pass the salt, dear."

Jakob, seated in the middle of the long table, stretched to retrieve the salt cellar, then leaned to his left to hand it to his mother.

"Thank you, Jakob, but you could have waited for your father to hand it to you. More brisket, dear?"

"Uh, sure."

"Yes, please, you mean."

"Of course. Yes, please, Mama."

"Maggie, would you serve Master Jakob some more brisket?"

"Yes, ma'am." She smoothed her apron as she turned to fetch the platter from the side table. Standing beside Jakob, she worked the fork and spoon held together in her right hand to pincer a slice of meat as she had been taught that afternoon. The meat slipped from her grasp as she maneuvered it onto his plate. Her face reddened as she straightened. Jakob grinned up at her. "Thank you."

Sadie sighed with impatience. "You shall have to practice more, Maggie. We can't have the brisket slithering onto our plates, now can we?"

"No, ma'am. I mean yes, ma'am. I'll practice."

"Practice makes perfect, Maggie. Practice makes perfect."

Jakob smiled up at her again. "I thought you did just fine, Maggie."

His mother stiffened. "Maggie, you may leave us now." When the swinging door to the kitchen closed behind Maggie, his mother pushed her chair back a few inches. "I will not have you undermining my authority, Jakob, not with the staff. You are a grown man and should know better."

"Don't you think it's rather silly to pretend we are lords and ladies of the manor and to act as if we don't know her. She lives less than a mile from here. I remember seeing her on her way to school before I started at the University."

His mother looked toward the head of the table. "And do you have nothing to say, Morris?"

His father — Morrie to everyone but his wife, who insisted on calling him Morris — took his time patting his lips with the corner of his napkin. He worked his mouth as if trying to figure out which page of the script held his next line. Over the top of his reading glasses, he looked first at Sadie and then at Jakob. He sighed. "You should respect your mother . . . your mother's . . . ways." He looked down again to spear the last bit of potato on his plate.

It was clear that this token support was not sufficient for his wife. "It is hard enough running this household on . . . on such a limited allowance. I do not need to have insubordination encouraged by anyone. It is difficult enough finding and managing the help. I know the brisket was dry, but the cook does not know, apparently, how to do a proper brisket. Nadya Zimmerman seems to have hired the last decent cook in all of the Twin Cities. The woman travels by trolley to St. Paul all the way from South Minneapolis. Every day."

Morrie chewed his bite of potato and swallowed. "And what a source of civic pride it is that our fair cities are now crisscrossed with such an extensive network of street railways. More evidence, it would seem, that a motorcar is not only a luxury, but a wholly redundant one." With that, Morrie had toted up unexpected bonus points in the ongoing contest over whether the Osters should own an automobile.

Unwilling to concede the point, his wife exhaled with deliberate force. "I was not requesting a testimony from the Chamber of Commerce, Morris, nor a promotion for the Twin City Rapid Transit Company. I was speaking of the brisket."

"I thought the brisket was quite acceptable. As for the Zimmermans, Mrs. Zimmerman runs a small millinery shop of her own on Washington to add to what Abe brings in as a partner in Stone and Zimmerman. I would guess that is how she can afford better help."

Jakob looked from his father to his mother, suddenly aware that he was in the line of fire between dueling parties.

"May I be excused, Mama, Papa? I have an essay due tomorrow that I need to finish and copy out."

"Of course, dear." She spoke to her son but with her glare still fixed toward the head of the table. "Best run along and get to it."

Morrie cleared his throat and nodded. He carefully refolded his napkin and pushed his chair back from the table. "I'll take my coffee in the parlor, dearest. I assume you have instructed our skinny *shamas* how I drink it." He did not wait for a response but carefully restored his chair and exited immediately by the far door at Sadie's back. As he passed, his hand rested on her shoulder so briefly that it might have seemed as if he were brushing something away. She stiffened at his touch.

⇛ ⇚

The tap on Jakob's door was almost too light to be heard, but he had been staring in silence at the blank page in his journal. He laid the black satin ribbon back in place to mark his spot and closed the book. "Yes, come in."

"She sent me with coffee. She said you might need it." Maggie carefully set the small red-and-black japaned tray to one side on his walnut secretary, edging it in place so as not to bump the book lying open there. She stole a glance at the engraving on the right-hand page, a lettered line drawing of some machinery.

"Patent law," he said. "Very dry material unless you are an inventor or a patent attorney. I have no aptitude for the former but ardent hopes for the latter, or at least my mother and father have such hopes. As for me, I could more readily imagine myself a writer, perhaps, but then . . ." He noticed that her eyes were red from crying. "Are you quite all right, Maggie?"

14

She closed her eyes as her head drooped. "I am all right, Master Jakob." She started to back away from him.

"You live up on Van Buren, am I right? With the Hoffmanns?"

"Yes, sir. If you have no need of anything else, I'll . . ." She paused and shifted her eyes to the side as if trying to recall the next bit of protocol. "I'll take my leave."

"Not until you tell me about yourself. You're no longer in school?"

"I withdrew to earn my keep. The Hoffmanns have been very kind and generous, but with my brother and sister and myself added to the household, there are many mouths to feed. I have, though, been frequenting the public library whenever I can to keep up my studies. I should like to be a teacher someday."

"I see, but how will you manage that?" He pressed on, seemingly oblivious to Maggie's growing discomfort.

"I am not sure. I had hoped to apply to St. Cloud Normal School after finishing . . ." She licked at her lips nervously. "I really must get back downstairs."

"Yes, of course. We mustn't keep my mother waiting."

"No, and I have chores to finish before I leave tonight." She backed toward the door and curtsied a bit awkwardly. "Goodnight, Master Jakob."

"Oh, please, when we are alone, do not make me into a master. As yet I am master of nothing."

She smiled, nodded, and left the room.

Chapter 3
Working Class

It was no accident that we had so much time alone in those early weeks. Mother busied herself with preparation for the trip to Chicago, shopping for a new valise, searching out the downtown shops for just the right hat. She appreciated how attentive I was to inquire at supper about her day and her plans for the next, never failing to remark on my interest while facing down my father.

On those days when she was to trek downtown, I would announce that classes would be starting late. After seeing her off, I would seek you out under some pretense or another, and we would begin to talk: politics, trolleys, family, and death. We wandered the landscape of ideas without itinerary or guidebook.

It was thus that I learned not only the workings of your mind, but also of your heart. You were not quick-witted like my cousin Naomi nor sharp-tongued like Rachel Baumgarten, who seemed always to be straining to best me in classes at the University. Your intelligence was like the milk wagon that is never in a hurry but always delivers the bottles on time. You understood things. You figured them out, always at your own pace. The pauses in your paragraphs I came to understand were signposts of your dissatisfaction with uncertainty. You wanted to be sure of whatever you spoke:

each word, each thought. In this, you were so unlike my mother, for whom confident certainty was instantaneous, always ready at hand.

Sadie Oster expected her son to say goodbye to her before she left to meet Tova Goldfarb for lunch downtown, but she would not bring herself to yell up the stairs to let him know she was ready to depart. Instead, she took her white gloves from the table by the door, shouldered her purse, and left, closing the thick wooden door with extra force. At the heavy thud that carried through the balloon-frame house like a muffled earthquake, Jakob came bounding down the stairs. With flawless timing, Sadie re-entered just as he was reaching for the door handle. "Ah, there you are, Jakob. I realized, with the sun already so high, I would need a proper hat."

"Off shopping, then, Mama?"

"Lunch with Mrs. Goldfarb, as I told you last night. No classes this morning?"

"It's Thursday, Mama: a review session for the exam tomorrow, but I already know the material. I do hope you enjoy your lunch with Mrs. Goldfarb."

"I shall endeavor to, but it is, after all, Tova Goldfarb, and one can only endure so much tedium before the bile rises to spoil the appetite. In any event, I will return by midafternoon. I trust you will be at the University by then?"

"Long gone. And I have a late chemistry laboratory session, so there's no need to wait supper on me."

"I'll have Maggie set aside a cold plate for you. Well, I must be off or I shall miss my trolley."

"Goodbye, Mama." He gave her the mandatory peck on her right cheek and stepped back with his hands folded behind him.

"Yes, goodbye, son." She glanced up the stairs in a silent signal that he was being dismissed and should return to his studies.

He took two steps backward toward the stairs and nodded, then waited as Sadie retrieved her broad-brimmed blue hat with the feather flowers, adjusted it, and carefully inserted a pearl-headed hatpin. She left with a deep sigh as if he had somehow disappointed her. He leaned to the right just enough to observe her through the sidelight, his grin broadening as she unlatched the front gate and turned toward the trolley stop.

Maggie was not in the kitchen or the pantry. He found her in the fenced-in backyard, back turned, stretching to retrieve a clothespin to clip a monogramed hand towel onto the clothesline.

"And a good morning to you, Maggie." He was so close to her when he spoke that she collided with him as she spun around.

"I'm sorry, Master Jakob. You startled me. I meant to say just Jakob, as you told me. I forgot."

"What's in a name? Magdalena Samson. It sounds so biblical, with a name from each part of your scripture. Samson. Is it Swedish perhaps? But you look like no Swede I have ever known."

"My parents are . . . were Hungarian, but now it is called Austria. They came from the German-speaking borderlands of Austria-Hungary. And your name, Oster. It is Swedish?"

He laughed, one sharp syllable. "Hardly. Austrian, also. So, our families are from the same part of the world. Originally the family name was Austerlitz, but my father wanted to shorten and simplify it for the New World. I think it was also that . . . well, he felt it sounded too Jewish, too foreign. He was born in Vienna, to a family of rabbis and cantors and scholars, but it is my mother, whose parents were peasants, who extolls learning and speaks with pride of being Austrian. And Jewish."

"So, you are of the Hebrew faith?"

"We are Jewish, yes. But my faith is another matter. My faith is not in the ancient words of a parchment scroll. I believe we are living in the morning hours of a new day, a day brightened by science and study and industry, with a new philosophy placing humankind at its center and human reason as the route to a moral life." He smiled in triumph at his little speech, one polished from practice in classes at the University.

She chewed on her lower lip. "Begging your pardon if I speak out of turn, but how can there be a moral life without God, without scripture?"

"I said nothing of life without God or without the writings of the ancients, whether recorded on parchment or papyri or etched in clay. I refer to reason as the route both to understanding the wisdom of the past and to extending and elaborating and improving upon it."

"But the Holy Bible is the Word of God. How can anyone, any mere mortal, improve upon it?"

"As they have always done, by thought and by reason, by disputation and by written word. Who wrote down the words of the Bible? Who added the commentaries that explain and elaborate on those words? Mere mortals all, people such as you or I."

Maggie rocked up on tiptoes, as if to emphasize her words by gaining height. "But they were divinely inspired, guided by the Holy Spirit, and thereby they were empowered to record God's Word without human error." She paused, her brow creased in concentration. She shaded her eyes from the climbing sun with her small hand.

He hesitated in turn, then decided to plunge ahead. "So we are told. And who is to gainsay that? Only those who know that the sole sources of testimony on the matter are the writers themselves, long gone, or the followers who would accept without question such claims of divine guidance."

She shook her head. "I would not be so quick to blaspheme."

"Is it blasphemy to use the gifts of intelligence and discernment granted to us by our Creator? Is it blasphemy to read with care and note that this so-called inerrant Word of God is riddled with inconsistency and contradiction, that it bears everywhere the smudges and fingerprints of human hands, the intrusions, rearrangements, and redactions of human minds?"

She took a breath, but said nothing.

"I read the Bible," he said, holding out his index finger, "with the same respect and skepticism with which I read my economics textbook. If I believe the contents of either to be in error or the arguments to be flawed or misleading, then I am impelled by logic to confront them and, if need be, to reject them."

"Is this," — she inhaled sharply — "the nature of the Hebrew faith?"

"No, but it is the nature of mine. Or, then again, perhaps yes, for we are taught as Jews to argue and to bring reason to bear on our studies of the Torah."

"The Torah?"

"The Law, the Five Books of Moses. Do you read Hebrew?"

"No."

"Then I would say that you have not read the Bible. You

have read the writings of translators, more mere mortals, such as you and I."

"But they were divinely inspired and guided by the Holy Spirit."

"So say they, as do their apologists."

She stood there, confronting him, her gaze shifting from one of his eyes to the other, like hers, so brown and serious.

He waited. "And you have no response, no answer?"

"I do, Master Jakob." She lifted a shirt from the laundry basket and turned to pin it to the line. "I have work to do, as I imagine do you as well. That is my answer. Perhaps I will have more to say after I speak with Sister Mary Josephine, who is better at argumentation than am I." She twisted to be sure her face was not visible to him as she grinned in anticipation of an early rematch.

⇉ ⇇

Their morning debates quickly became a ritual whenever Sadie Oster was away or too occupied to monitor their whereabouts. Whether for Maggie's consultations with Sister Mary Josephine or for the accrual of practice, her arguments steadily took on ever greater sophistication, and her responses became more polished. By the time the extended weekend of his parents' trip to Chicago finally arrived, she could hold her own with Jakob on weighty matters from politics to philosophy.

It fell to Jakob to escort his parents to Union Depot to board the train for the thirteen-hour trip to Chicago. Morrie might have been content for the two of them to make it on their own by trolley on the Selby line to the station over on Kellogg, but Sadie insisted that they would have to go by motorcar and would need Jakob to assist with the luggage. Morrie had sent Jakob several blocks north to hail a jitney, one of the ubiquitous unlicensed drivers who plied the city for fares.

"And this, Morris, is why we really should purchase our own automobile," she told him as they approached the station.

"Why, so we can crank it into life once every couple of years for our son to drive us to the railway station?"

Sadie's terse reply was lost in the din as the driver maneuvered up to the depot entrance amidst a frothing tide of arriving and departing passengers. Motorcars mingled with horse-drawn carriages and pedestrians pushing handcarts, shouldering valises, and herding children. Morrie went to fetch a porter while the driver unloaded their suitcases. Jakob, with no immediate role to play, studied the elaborate façade of the station. Some ten years earlier, it had been remodeled from a squat and homely brick mélange into a taller, more ornate, but still ugly monstrosity.

Morrie arrived with a porter in tow and a mask of resignation on his face. "Thank you, son, for seeing us off. I'll settle with the driver and you can ride home in style."

"Thank you, Papa, but I will be fine taking the trolley back. Save the return fare for pocket money in Chicago."

Sadie looked from her husband to her son with disapproval deepening on her brow. "As long as you are here, Jakob, you might as well accompany us to the platform. Of course, if you have more pressing matters at home or at the University . . ."

"No, Mama, I shall be happy to see you off."

Once the train had chuffed away amidst steam and billowing smoke and the last goodbye waves from those left behind, Jakob turned and sprinted toward the trolley stop. It seemed to him as if all the trolley cars in St. Paul had suddenly stopped running. When the bright yellow trolley topped by its red-brown roof and fronted by its metal mesh "cow catcher" finally came in view, he held his arm aloft and waved impatiently to be certain the motorman saw him and stopped to let him board. "You're a determined young man. I saw you, you know," the driver greeted him. "I saw you."

In route, eager to resume his interrupted discussion of the nature of good and evil, Jakob bounced his foot in impatience each time the trolley paused for passengers to board or alight.

Like a horse sensing the barn ahead, Jakob ran the last blocks home from the trolley line, past the rows of white and gray and pale blue houses on narrow lots. He rushed up the front steps of his house with a grin that he could not suppress. The smile melted from his face as he searched and discovered the house was empty. Maggie, who should have greeted him on arrival, was nowhere around. On the dining table, he found a piece of notepaper neatly folded into a small tent.

"Master Jakob," it read, "the cook has left some porridge for you in the pantry. I must help at home today but will return tomorrow as agreed with Mrs. Oster. Warm regards, Maggie." It was disappointing news closing with a quiet note of promise. "Warm regards," he said to himself. The words warmed him.

⇶ ⇷

Returning from the University the following day, Jakob squeezed his way through the late afternoon crowd of passengers — workers and students and shoppers hurrying home for the weekend — and stepped off the noisy streetcar before it had squealed to a complete stop. He trotted down the street, his brown tie a trailing banner. It was nearly dark when he closed the front door and rushed into the dining room. He stopped so abruptly that the floral-patterned oriental rug bunched up and almost slid from underfoot.

Maggie was already standing at the table, twisting the second of two white tapers into the silver candle sticks she had retrieved from the glass-front mahogany cabinet at her back. She carefully aligned them together in the center of the table, then lit them with a kitchen match. She paused, spreading her arms, then circled her open hands three times above the candles before bringing them to her face and hiding her eyes. She held them there for several seconds before uncovering and opening her eyes again.

Jakob, entranced, stood where he had skidded to a stop just inside the doorway. "I . . . how did you know to do that? Did my mother put you up to it?"

"I don't understand. It's Friday night."

"Yes, I know, but the candles . . . Who taught you that?"

"I learned it from my mother. She didn't exactly teach me, but she always did that on Friday nights, just before sunset. I was not quite ten when she died, but I can still picture her doing this. Always two candles and circling her hands, her lips moving as she covered her eyes. I think she said something, like a prayer, but I never learned what. I don't know why she did it. It was just a family tradition — from the old country, or so I always imagined. And now I do it as a way to honor her, to remember."

"*Zachor et yom ha-shabbat l'kodsho.* Remember the Sabbath to keep it Holy. You know what this means, this thing that you say your mother always did?"

"No, I am sorry, Master Jakob, I don't know what it means. I hope I have caused no offense."

"Offense? No, to the contrary. We do this, too. Well, my

mother does, lighting the candles every Friday, just before sunset. The words she says over the candles are these: *Baruch atah, Adonoi, eloheinu melech ha-olam, asher kid'shanu b'mitzvotav vitsivanu l'hadlik ner shel Shabbat.*"

"It's that Israelite speech, not so?"

"Yes, it's Hebrew, a blessing, 'to light the candles of Shabbat.' *L'hadlik ner shel Shabbat.* So we are commanded."

"I always thought it was part of the Catholic tradition, something to do with the Friday fasting, when we do not eat meat."

"On Friday night? That of all times is a meal for meat, a joyous celebration of the start of the day of rest."

"But Sunday is the day of rest."

"For you, perhaps, but it is commanded in the Torah to rest on the seventh day, as God did when he created the world, not on the first day of the week."

"We believe in the Bible, not the Torah."

"We have spoken of this before." He sighed with impatience. "The Torah *is* the Bible. Genesis, Exodus, Leviticus, Numbers, and Deuteronomy: the first five books of what you call the Old Testament."

"I . . ." Maggie worked her mouth in frustration and confusion. "But why would my mother do this Hebrew thing."

"I don't know. Perhaps she was a Jew."

"No, that's impossible. My family are all Roman Catholic; we have been in the One True Church for . . . forever."

"How long is forever? Your German is better than mine. Maybe your family were Germans, German Jews."

"No, from Austria-Hungary, as I told you. My father and mother are . . . were from small German-speaking towns in the middle of the Empire. My father once told me that his town had two names, one in German and one in the language of the Magyar, the Hungarians. I remember only the German name, Halbturn, because my father spoke little of his past and my mother said even less. She was not one to speak of herself or her life. She carried with her a quietude that spoke, without words, of sadness and loss. She talked little about growing up, of her life there, as if her story began when she married. Of that world she would say, 'It was another life. We are here, now, in America. This is our life.' My father said little more."

Jakob nodded, encouraging her to continue.

"I know he was a builder of wagons in the old country. Here he became a laborer and then a mechanic working in the railyards, so also now my older brother, Jonathan. Where my parents came from was a borderland. There one might hear Hungarian and German on the same street. My father could speak some Hungarian, but my mother only German, I think. And, of course, the English she learned after coming here. She was good with languages, and mastered it quickly. Still, we spoke German at home and with many of our neighbors here."

Jakob nodded. "My parents speak German only by necessity. At home, they insist on English, which my mother describes as 'the language of your future' to me. What German I know is self-taught, picked up along with some Yiddish from those around me." He grinned. "I actually understand more than I let on, which has been useful at times when the adults switch languages in an attempt to exclude the younger generation from their conversations or to keep some secret from us."

Maggie waited a moment to be sure he was finished speaking. "Well, as I was saying, my parents grew up speaking German in villages that were only a few miles apart, each with its landmark, its claim to being special. My father lived within sight of a magnificent *schloss*, a castle on the crest; my mother was from Frauenkirchen, noted for its grand church on the square. *Basilika Mariä Geburt*, the Church of Mary's Birth, which is all that I know of the town, all I was told."

Jakob's eyes turned upward, toward the corner of the room, as he thought. "I have heard of that town, although I cannot recall from where. Ah, yes, now I remember. Frauenkirchen was one of the Seven Villages."

"Seven? Surely there were more than seven villages in all of the Austro-Hungarian Empire."

"Yes, but these seven, the *Sheva Kehillot* in Hebrew, were special because they had been designated by a prince of the House of Eszterházy as places for the Jews to live in peace and safety after they had been expelled from . . . from Vienna, I think."

"And Frauenkirchen was a village for Jews? I think not. There was a church there. It was a Catholic village, not Jewish."

"Maybe both."

Chapter 4
The Other

Frauenkirchen, Austria-Hungary, 1869

The approaching footsteps were almost lost in the soft flutter of the breeze sweeping across the flatlands surrounding the village and plying the slight rise at the edge of the field. Miriam stiffened.

Then he was behind her, speaking, just beyond the fieldstone wall on which she sat. "Your pardon I beg. I was alone, I thought. I shall leave."

He did not leave, though, but rather stood there, waiting for a response to his clipped sentences nervously spoken in stiff schoolbook German, as though he were a young student reciting before a class, trying to impress a teacher. Miriam kept her head turned in fear and modesty, as if focused in the distance, contemplating the weathered green of the copper-clad twin spires atop the gleaming white basilica for which the small town of Frauenkirchen was known. Without invitation, a smile began to soften her face. Still, she did not speak.

"I know you," he said. "I have seen you with your father, Herr Schneider, the tailor." She lowered her gaze and smoothed her gray apron, then folded her hands in her lap as her heart thudded in her ears. He continued. "I have heard you singing quietly to yourself as you escorted your sister. At the entrance to the *Judengasse*."

She twisted to look up at him, then quickly averted her eyes again as she tucked an errant black curl back under

28

her headscarf. "I must be going." It was barely more than a whisper. "Forgive me."

"No please, I am the one to be forgiven. I did not mean to interrupt."

She knew it to be a polite lie; he had meant to intrude. He had followed her, as he had on other days, watching her as she walked with her little sister Esterl after the market closed. Even though it was the Sabbath for them, Saturday would find some of the Jews of Frauenkirchen in the market alongside their Catholic neighbors. Often among them would be Miriam, who, even as a young child, was always exploring the limits of the allowed and disallowed. Though most of the Jews here were strictly observant, a few were less traditional and more informal in their lives.

It was different on the other side of the lake in Eisenstadt, the largest of the *Siebengemeinden*, the Seven Villages in which, under letters of protection from the House of Esterházy, Jews were allowed to live. There, before dark on Fridays, the entrance to the Jewish Quarter was chained shut so that nothing might disturb the peace of Shabbat. The chain was not removed until after the Rabbi had completed *Havdalah* on Saturday evening, the ritual marking of the end of Shabbat and the separation of the sacred from the ordinary. Frauenkirchen, though, was not a center of Jewish learning like Eisenstadt, with its yeshiva and visiting scholars. It was only a small market town amidst fields and orchards and vineyards.

Some seven hundred Jews lived in its Jewish Quarter, a village within a village with its own butchery to supply the community with kosher meat, and with a *mikvah*, a ritual bath, adjacent to the modest synagogue at the center of community life. The boxy whitewashed synagogue, imposing among the surrounding single-story structures of the Jewish Quarter, was modeled on a similar but larger one in Eisenstadt. It stood within sight of the monastery and the duly famed and much grander *Basilika Mariä Geburt* that overshadowed all.

Always before this particular weekend, the straw-haired boy-man who followed Miriam with his eyes had kept his distance, never had he spoken. It was a pretense, a delightfully terrifying game they had been playing all summer. As younger children, their paths had sometimes crossed when the headstrong girl would skip a stone in his direction across a pond or chase away pigeons that he was feeding scraps of stale bread.

Today, Esterl had insisted on asserting her own independence, skipping away early without her older sister. Miriam had let Esterl go, knowing that she herself would be the one scolded when back at home. Still, the game here with this boy was too seductive — forbidden and frightening, but also delicious.

He broke the silence. "I am Josef, from Halbturn. Josef Samson."

"Yes, I know. And I am still Miriam Schneider." They were both surprised that she had replied. Quickly she moved to explain. "My father tailored a suit for your brother when he was married. You came with him once."

"Oh yes, I forgot." But he had not forgotten, and they both knew it. She had then been unable to keep from stealing glimpses, drawn to the hazel in his determined eyes as he was drawn to the deep umber pools of hers. That day, she had kept finding excuses to return to the front room that was her father's shop while Josef and his brother waited for the final alterations to be completed.

At the time, Heinrich Samson had noticed his younger brother's interest. *"Eine schöne junge Jüdin.* Yes, she will be a most pretty little Jewess in a few years," he had remarked as they walked home. "Be careful, little brother. They killed Christ, remember. They are good for nothing save for a wrestling match in the hay loft. If you can ever get one of the girls alone, that is."

"Do they really have horns under their caps?" Josef half-whispered.

Heinrich winked. "No, at least the girls do not. That I know."

"And how do you know so much, Heinrich?"

"I told you what they are good for. How do you think I know?"

Josef's ears had burned with anger at his brother for being so crude and at himself for the thoughts that crept in unbidden, thoughts of the tailor's daughter, older and without her scarf, her bare head, hornless and covered in tight curls, her face mere inches from his own.

⇶ ⇷

Separated by the low stone wall and by a chasm much wider than the few miles between Frauenkirchen and Halbturn, Josef and Miriam now waited in silence. There were the years between them, but far more than that. Even their faces divided them. His, round, pale, and handsomely Teutonic, and hers, promising an angular beauty, with darker hints of distant ancestors to the south — Italy, perhaps.

"Here, I'll help you down." He reached out and took her hand before she could withdraw it, but she tugged it free. "Is something wrong?"

"We do not touch. Not boys and girls. I should not be here alone with you, not even speaking with you. At the synagogue, women and girls even enter by a separate door on the south side that takes us directly up to the balcony."

"I didn't know. I really know nothing about you ... about ... your people."

She laughed. "Well, we know about you." She tucked her legs under her and pivoted to face him.

"Is that so? What do you know about us?"

"You drink blood at your services, from a silver cup that the priest offers you."

"Where did you get that nonsense? It's not blood, it's ..." but he caught himself, realizing that he could explain neither Holy Communion nor the transubstantiation of wine into the blood of Christ, a mystery that repelled him as a child and that he had long since stopped believing. For just a moment, he thought of countering with what he had heard of the Blood Libel, of the stories of Christian babies stolen by Jews and killed to make the special bread for Passover, but he had never believed those stories. "It's just wine we drink, with little flatbreads."

Her eyes widened. "That's like at Pesach, the Passover. We drink four cups of wine and eat only matzos, the flatbread that is unleavened."

"Four cups?" Now it was his eyes that widened. "Even children?"

"Well, for the younger children they thin it with water, but I am thirteen. I am no longer a child."

Jakob, who had guessed her to be older, hid his surprise. "So, at thirteen a Jew is grown?"

"We become *b'nei mitzot*, children of the Laws. From that age on we are responsible for following the commandments given to us by our God."

"And what god is that?"

"The one God, the God of Abraham and Isaac and Jacob."

"But he is our God."

"Of course, you got him from us." She slipped down from the wall and faced him with a smile of success.

"Nonsense. Our God made the world."

"Of course, he did. And he chose the Jews as his people." She grinned in triumph.

"And gave his only begotten son to die upon the cross for our sins."

In the playful-serious rush of theology, they had closed the gap and now stood toe-to-toe. Looking up at him, clearly unsure what to say next, Miriam took a breath. Before she could speak, his lips were on hers. He quickly broke off the kiss and backed away, his face as red as the ripe apples in the orchard across the way. Without a word, he scrambled down the bank and was gone.

Miriam stood stiffly still, her heart pounding, shocked that it was not pounding in fear but from something else, something new that spread through her like the mulled wine of winter evenings, bringing on a warm and wonderful dizziness.

Chapter 5
Alterations

Frauenkirchen and Halbturn, Austria-Hungary, 1878

Saul Schneider was about to close the curtains on the shop window when he saw a man approach carrying a cloth-wrapped bundle. The man slipped through the door and quickly closed it against the blowing snow.

"And what can I do for you at this late hour, young man?"

"I am getting married. I need you to make this suit fit me. It was my brother's."

"Well, here, let's measure you and see what can be done. Miriam," he called, "please come back with my tape and chalk. And unwrap this package." A tall young woman with intense dark eyes strode through the far door of the room and stopped suddenly when she saw the customer.

Saul frowned. "This is my daughter, Miriam. Her brother, Zalman, is learning the trade from me, but she helps me at times. If she were a man, she would already be a better tailor than Zalman will ever be, but she is a woman and he is a schlemiel who puts the needle through his finger as often as through the cloth. Alas, I have only the one son. And a daughter who is too smart and strong-headed and should already be married." He paused. "Do I know you?"

"I am Josef, the wainwright, from Halbturn, Josef Samson. You made that suit for my brother Heinrich, but he left to join the cavalry and never returned. We still have not heard his fate."

"I am sorry to learn of that. But now you are to be married. That is a *simcha*, a cause for celebration. And the bride to be?"

"Zsófia Nagy."

"Ah, a Hungarian girl." His eyes crinkled with his smile. "Is she also from Felterony?" He deliberately used the Hungarian name for Halbturn, which, like nearly everything straddling the middle lands of the Austrian-Hungarian Empire, had two names. Here, in the mixing bowl between, families might mix languages though not religions.

Josef nodded. "Yes, she's Hungarian."

"Good, then *mazel tov*! Now, let's have a look at that suit." He fingered the fabric, a heavy black wool with a faint window-pane pattern. "This is a fine material, Italian perhaps. Some excellent dry goods now reach us here in Frauenkirchen. Ah, yes, now I remember sewing this. Your brother was very broad in the shoulders, wasn't he. And you? Not so broad. But we can take care of that. Here, take off your coat and scarf. Now, stand on this stool, and I will measure you."

Miriam turned her head and busied herself smoothing the jacket over a wooden tailor's dummy in the corner. Josef's eyes followed her every move as Saul measured and made notes on a scrap of paper.

"And when will you need the suit?"

"We are to be wed in two weeks."

"I see." Saul pursed his lips and nodded knowingly. Of hurried nuptials, he knew the story well and could imagine a first babe already crying in a newly made cradle before summer arrived. He looked from Josef to the suit and back again. "I can have it ready for you to try on Tuesday next, and then you can pick it up on Friday. Come to collect it as soon after midday as you can, please. The sun still sets so early."

Josef nodded. As he buttoned his coat, he caught Miriam looking at him. He glanced back one more time as he slipped through the door and into the blowing snow of January. There was sadness in her eyes — and something else.

⇛ ⇚

Josef's breath made tiny clouds in the April morning air, and frost still painted the fields at the bottom of the street. The sun inched from behind Schloss Halbturn, the grand white and yellow icon of brick and stone standing watch over the village, at once protector and oppressor. Josef fiddled with the bent cotter pin in the pocket of his coveralls as he paced in front of the house, his steps carving out a square, crossing the dirt road, turning and turning and returning in a ritual of banishment. The women would not let him in. His sister Mary should have been there with them, but she had married the Hoffmann boy the previous summer and they had left for America. Josef had spent the night at his father's house down the lane, sleepless, pacing and praying.

Now, every third or fourth crossing of the road, he would march to the small window to the left of the door and look in, but there was nothing to see save the drawn curtain and nothing to hear but muffled moans that came less and less often. The low grumble of words heard through the walls might have been Hungarian or German but were gibberish to Josef in his addled and agitated state.

Suddenly, the door of the house was flung open and Anna Poferl darted past him without a word, holding her gray skirt as she ran up the rutted street. He started back toward the house but the door was quickly shut in his face. "What is it? What is happening?" He put the side of his head to the door. "Zsófia, my Zsófia, what is happening?" There was no reply. He sat down on the ground in front of the door, his hands over his face.

The hurried footsteps startled him, and he realized he had drifted off into exhausted sleep for a moment. He looked up to see Anna returning with the priest.

"No!" It was a scream that surely awakened anyone in the street who might not have already risen. He turned to the door. It was unlatched and swung aside at the touch of his palm. The door to the back room was open, and he could see his wife propped up with pillows and blankets in the small bed. She was looking at him. In the crook of her arm rested a tiny bundle wrapped like a package of sausages from the butcher. "Zsófia!" He pushed past the stout Maria Hafner, who had midwifed half the children in Halbturn. She tugged at his shirt as he passed.

He leaned over Zsófia and smiled. "My Zsófia, my beautiful wife. There will be other children, God willing." Suddenly he realized she was not looking at him, not looking at anything. Her dead eyes were fixed on distant emptiness.

And then the priest was there, entering the small room, the Latin of the prayers for the dead and dying already on his lips. Josef backed out of the room and walked stiffly from the house. Several neighbors had already formed a ragged semi-circle in front of number eleven. He pushed past them, not hearing their words of sympathy and not feeling their hands on his arms and back.

He walked to the end of the lane and turned onto the road toward Frauenkirchen, without thought to where he might be going, but shuffling on, his eyes fixed on the reed-choked shoreline of the Neusiedler See, a shallow lake far too distant to actually be visible.

He returned the next day to bury his wife and his unnamed and unbaptized son and to finish the interrupted work on Joachim Hafner's wagon.

Chapter 6
Markets

Frauenkirchen, Austria-Hungary, 1878

The wooden carts arrayed around the plaza were filled with rust-red apples and bright purple cabbages. On a long trestle table, meat pies, no bigger than a boy's hand, steamed a spicy perfume into the autumn air. Dry leaves tumbled past the yellow pumpkins and misshapen gourds piled in pyramids in front of a one-eyed man whose military boots were scuffed and battered.

Josef, winded by the trot from Halbturn, rolled the pushcart into the square just as the bell in the *Basilika Mariä Geburt* struck eight. The cart was empty. It had been made for a farmer whose barn had burned to the ground and who had died trying to save his cow. The cow, traded to the butcher, would briefly feed his widow and four young sons, but there was no money to pay for a cart and nothing that Josef would accept in trade. He hoped to sell the cart in Frauenkirchen, or at least to draw attention to his craftsmanship and perhaps win a new order.

The turn of another year was approaching. Already the autumn nights would send chill drafts whistling through the cracks around the windows of Josef's house, the house so tiny on the outside, but so vast in its empty interior. In a single year, Josef had left young bachelorhood behind to become married, then a widower, and now an orphan. His ties to Halbturn, to the rolling flatlands to the east of the Neusiedler See, were becoming ever more tenuous. There was nothing here for him. Perhaps beyond the water might be something. Perhaps in the city, in Eisenstadt, a life might await. But here, here he was surrounded by death and loss; here he labored in resignation. Not even the satisfaction of completing a job could awaken him from sleepwalking through his days.

Suddenly the sun, too, was lost, as the shadow of a woman fell across him and his empty cart. "And so, my good sir," she said. "you are selling air? Or is it sunshine you have to offer?" She pointed to where the climbing sun brightened a corner of his cart.

Josef, whose thoughts had flown away even farther than Eisenstadt, looked up. Above him stood an angel, a dark-haired young woman, the sun at her back turning her cap into a gauzy halo.

"It is the wagon I hope to sell. The air and sunshine are free, God's gifts to us all."

"And which God might that be? And for whom are his gifts?"

Josef's mouth opened in a round smile of recognition. "Why the God of Abraham and Isaac, who blesses His children with the sun and the air and the stars and moon."

She laughed lightly. "A long interrupted conversation between two country scholars. I see you remember."

"And you as well. Is this not heady dialogue for a tailor's daughter?"

"And what of a wainwright's son?"

"Would your husband approve of a conversation with a maker of wagons, a Catholic from another village?"

"No."

"Then perhaps you had better return to your husband's side."

"That I cannot do."

"And why is that?"

"Because there is no husband. I was betrothed, it is true, but the young man, the grandson of a Rabbi, could not swim. He is now of blessed memory. Of course, we never met, so my memories of him are rather thin. As was he, I am told, a thin and ascetic young man who fell from a boat as he was ferried across the Neusiedler See." A blink of a smile told him precisely how serious the grave matter was to her. "It would be unseemly to marry too soon after my tragic loss. You understand, I am sure."

"I understand. But, although the lake is full again, it is not so deep that one could not stand to raise the head above water. He must have been not merely thin but also short."

"So it would seem, but then the bottom is muddy and choked with weeds. A tragic loss, that young scholar, but one that leaves me now more time to learn and converse with other would-be scholars. And wainwrights. But what of your good wife? Would she not disapprove of your discourse with an unmarried woman, so open and so public?"

"No. Unless the departed can disapprove from the beyond."

"Oh, I am so sorry." She put her hand to her mouth. "That is right. I heard of this. And a child?"

"Yes, a boy, but he died unbaptized, so he is not ..." His voice choked off and his eyes began to sting.

She cocked her head and waited several seconds before speaking. "And so, we have both been left alone, even as we were when this conversation began so many years ago." Suddenly emboldened, she reached a hand toward his to hold it.

He looked down. "I thought we could not ..."

She glanced around. "No one watches." She gave his hand a brief squeeze then quickly brushed at something unseen on her dress.

He looked at the dusty ground at her feet. "I would like to ... to talk more of these things, as we did by the wall when we were young."

"By the wall, then, after the market is over and you have sold your cart full of nothing." She pivoted away from him so smartly that the hem of her long dress brushed his leg. He stood and watched her as she moved from cart to cart. His hand had not yet lost the shape of hers. He raised it and studied it as if seeing it for the first time, as if the imprint of her touch might still be visible as some faint shadow.

⫸ ⫷

She waited in the growing shadows of an oddly warm afternoon, already perched on the stacked stones, her dark blue dress carefully arranged beneath her. She posed, turned away, staring into the distance, conjuring a mental picture of that long past autumn day so many years before, so many times revisited in waking dreams. The basilica was no longer visible from this corner, and the entire field was now an orchard, the saplings full grown and heavy with late-ripening apples waiting to be harvested. She was no girl, but a young woman, still headstrong, still eager, chasing words now shared each week, the broken dialogue of many meetings, no longer chance encounters but foreshortened ritual as regular as the blessings of Shabbat. As she waited, her cheeks reddened, not alone for the chill of coming winter.

As Josef approached, she turned to smile warmly and to gesture for him to sit with her on the wall.

"I told my sister Esterl that I would be home late. She suspects something but is good-hearted and inventive. She will tell some story that my father will believe. So, we have the afternoon."

Those words sent Josef's heart racing. The afternoon. It was a lifetime.

He sat where she pointed, and she started talking without waiting for a response. As she spoke, he studied her face, its symmetry and depth, like the sculpture he had seen when he had returned the repaired coach to Schloss Halbturn, her skin as smooth as the polished alabaster of those statues but almost as dark as a field of ripe rye. And her eyes, so brown, dark whirlpools of intelligence.

"Don't you agree?" she asked.

"Yes, of course." What was he agreeing to? He quickly re-played in his mind the sound of her voice. "But ..." — his thoughts raced to catch up with his words — "I am no priest. I am not a — what is it you say, a student of the Talmud? — only a maker of wagons. Still, I do not think God made us Catholic or Jew or even Musselman. We are his children. Is that not so?"

She smiled indulgently. "Yes. That is what I said."

"Well, yes. And that is what I am agreeing with." He wanted to keep talking, to keep her talking, anything to stretch out the afternoon and the luxury of being so close. Turned as she was, her knee was mere inches from where his hand rested on his own leg. The slightest shift, and his hand could be atop her knee. He thought of times with Zsófia, of slip-ping his hand beneath her skirt, sliding it toward the hidden warmth between her legs. It all seemed now so distant.

It was soon her turn to watch as he spoke. From theology, they had turned to talk of apprenticeship and trades and commerce. These were not as interesting to her as debates about the meaning of scripture or of life, but his growing confidence gave her a chance to study him. Over the years his face had grown less round, less boyish. At twenty-eight, his skin was already sun-wrinkled from work outdoors, and his hands were calloused from wielding spoke shaves and awls and mallets. She watched his lips as he talked of Eisenstadt, with its bustling commerce. She remembered those lips on hers, for only split seconds, nearly a decade earlier. She wanted them on hers again, not for seconds but for hours. The thought buzzed like a bee in her head.

"You were married," she said, interrupting him.

"What?"

"I said, you were married."

"Yes, for a while. Of course. Yes. But I was saying that I think Eisenstadt has so many opportunities."

"What is it like?"

"Eisenstadt? I don't know. I have only heard. I —"

"No, I mean being married. I mean . . . I am a grown woman and I have never . . ."

"I remember you told me you were grown when you were only thirteen."

"At thirteen, so I said. Now I know." She leaned toward him, her gaze shifting between his gray-green eyes and his full lips.

"Oh!" It was an exclamation of discovery, as though he had finally figured out the real topic of their conversation. As he shifted to kiss her, his hands began to touch and stroke, first on her thigh, then her waist, up to her breasts and down to her knee, a rehearsed and hurried exploration now remembered.

She pulled back and slid off the wall. It had once been part of a foundation, and on the side away from the orchard and the village, the ground was depressed, a shallow fossil of a long-gone cellar. She lay back in the weedy hollow and held out her arms to him. "Teach me. Teach me what you know."

"What I know? I know you are beautiful." He spread open her coat, tugged at the buttons of her bodice, and slipped his hand inside. She closed her eyes as he played with her nipple, sending sharp pangs of pleasure through her. He opened her dress farther and kissed her breast, then lay atop her and planted kisses all over her face.

"Teach me how to please you," she whispered into his ear.

He lifted her dress high and planted a kiss on her belly. "You please me. You please me with your words and with your eyes." He wedged a hand between her legs and she opened to him, wrapping her legs around him. Then, as he entered her, he ran his fingers through the tight curls on her head, reassuring himself that he was not consorting with some horned she-devil.

Her defiant panting did not cease when he finally stopped. For a moment, he wished he had taken more time, but she hugged him and kissed him as if he had given her some great gift.

"A *sho'o in gan eden*," she said.

"What?"

"An hour in the Garden of Eden, in Heaven. That is what you have given me."

"What speech was that? What language?"

"It is Yiddish. We speak it at home. It is close to the German we all speak, but there is also much from the Hebrew of the Bible, and it is written in the letters of Hebrew."

"I would learn this language, but only if you are to be my tutor."

"And I will teach you, but only if there is the time."

"Then I will find a way to buy the time, whatever the price."

As she kissed him again, she was thinking about what price that might be.

Chapter 7
Turning

Frauenkirchen, Austria, 1878

Miriam approached the stone wall of the old foundation, her heart hammering with anticipation and from the effort of racing along the trampled path through the field, already splashed with spots of snow. Josef was waiting, both feet up, his head on his knees, a silly smile on his lips as though he had drunk too much at the *Bierhaus*. "I am late, I know," she said, "but I could not get away from my father, who I think suspects us. He interrogates Esterl rather than me, because he is uncertain and thinks he can outmaneuver her more easily with words. And what is it that makes you smile so?"

"Because I know what is coming next."

"Oh, do you now? I am afraid there is nothing coming next save for a hasty hello and goodbye. I must hurry home."

"Well, perhaps there will be no need to hurry back, at least not alone."

"No, you cannot accompany me. People will see and talk."

"Already they see. Most likely they talk."

She shushed him, "I hope you are wrong."

"I do not care. I am going to ask your father for your hand in marriage."

Miriam froze. It was a dream, a dreaded and desired dream.

"What? No words," he said, "no squeals of joy, no embrace for your future husband?"

She shook her head gravely. "How I wish. Still, it cannot

be. I am a Jew and you, you are not. The Rabbi will not marry us."

"Then the priest will marry us. It has happened. It can happen."

She drew a long slow breath of chill air. "There is a ballad from Deutchkreutzer, another of the Seven Villages. The women there sing it. It is very old, '*Es war einmal eine Jüdin*' —"

"Once there was a Jewess. Yes, I think I have heard this song."

"Have you? It is about a Jewish woman and her beautiful daughter, a daughter who longs for a scribe, a Christian man. It goes like this." She sang the first verse.

Es war einmal eine Jüdin,
Ein wunderschönes Weib,
Die hatte eine Tochter,
Zum Tode war sie bereit.

"It has many verses and many versions, but, in the end, the scribe tells the daughter she should be baptized and marry him. She would rather die than deny her faith, so she throws herself in the water and drowns."

"Ah, but I have heard another version. In this one she is baptized and changes her name to Mary Magdalene, and they are married."

"It is a ballad, a fiction. I am Miriam, a Jew. I cannot become Mary, a Christian."

"Why not? Surely you know by now we worship the same god. That is, when we worship at all. I love you, Miriam, and you love me as well, if I can presume what has never been spoken aloud."

"You can presume as you wish, my Josef, but it is not a matter of love but of family and faith."

"I have no family, no parents, no wife. My brother died a soldier and my sister is gone to me and writes no more."

"I have a family, a father, a brother, a sister, and many, many cousins. None will let me convert. It is forbidden, apostasy."

"How can they stop you? You are a grown woman, with a mind of your own — and a fine one it is. Listen to it, and it will tell you that I am right, that we can make a life together, that we can be happy."

She had no answer for him. "It is getting dark. I must leave now."

"Then I will go with you. I will talk to your father."

"No." It was said with such quiet force that it drove the words from him. Before he could find them again, she was running away, a gray shadow in the dusk.

⇛ ⇚

There were no more trysts at the stone wall, no more stolen touches at the edge of the square in Frauenkirchen, no hurried exchanges as they passed along the road between the towns. Josef was devastated and distracted. His work suffered. He cut his hand sharpening the blade of his jack-plane and struck his thumb and forefinger with a mallet that should have driven home a wedge. And then, as he trudged home one evening, pulling a milk cart that did not track true, she was suddenly beside him.

"Is the cart new?" she asked.

"Yes."

"Are the wheels supposed to roll like that, like an old man after too much wine?"

"No."

"Do you still yearn to end your solitude?"

"I do."

She walked beside him until they reached a bend in the rutted road. A woman approached in the distance, carrying a baby on one hip and a woven basket on the other. Miriam slowed and slipped a few paces behind Jakob, hiding a smile as she did.

"I would talk to your father." Jakob spoke quickly and quietly into the growing space between. "I can craft more than wagons and barrows. You know my words can persuade."

"No. I will talk to him first."

He turned to face her. "Then you have decided?"

"I have decided only that I will talk with my father, nothing more."

"But . . ."

"But you were right about one thing, perhaps only that one. I do love you. You listen to me and you speak to me, not as a lesser being but as a person. That is worthy of sacrifice, and that is worthy of my love." She took his hand and repeated the pledge with her eyes, then left the road to cut across a fallow field, now a tangle of browned growth through which she could avoid an encounter with the approaching woman and her baby. In the distance, the domes of the *Basilika* beckoned, and just beyond lay the Jewish Quarter. She hastened, propelled by a mix of hope and dread and by the secret she now carried.

Chapter 8
Footsteps

St. Paul, Minnesota, 1909

I heard your hurried footsteps up and down the back stairs. You were behind on your work, as I was on mine — too many hours spent in deep dialogue or the pleasures of simple gossip with our few days rushing by like a vernal stream swollen by fresh showers. My parents were to return on Wednesday and it was already late on that Monday. That Monday. So it will always be marked in my memory, the Monday after the Sunday you had spent with your family, at Mass and with the Hoffmanns, with that terrible cousin of whom you spoke so scornfully.

I had spent Sunday consumed by longing, jealous of him and his proximity to you. I had not yet understood the full measure of your feelings about him, only that you spoke of him with an angry sentiment that seemed so discordant with the quiet soul you had become to me. I was filled with intense dislike for a boy I had never met, and flooded also with an emptiness that only you could fill.

It was no accident that we met in the stairwell. I stood at the top, listening as you ascended, timing with precision my own downward rush.

In the waning light through the small octagonal window at the landing, Maggie had to watch her step as she took the series of wedge-shaped treads where the backstairs turned sharply. She looked up too late to avoid colliding with Jakob, who was coming down. Struggling to keep her balance, she let out a cry. "Aaah!" Only his extended arm kept her from falling. "You startled me. I am so sorry Master Jakob. I expected no one on these stairs." She looked up at him, a quizzical look on her face as she tried to make sense of the situation and to guess what he wanted. "Is there something . . . ?"

"I fear it was my fault. I was taking a shortcut to the pantry and had my mind fixated on some bread and cheese. I am quite famished."

"Oh, I am so sorry. I had lost track of the hours. I will fix you a supper."

"There is no need. You have been working so hard all day. All I desire is some bread and a wedge of cheese, maybe a glass of claret to make the remains of the day go easier."

"I will fetch them for you."

"You will do that only if you bring two saucers and two glasses of wine. No, how will you manage that without the help of a dumbwaiter. Alas, the house was not built for nobility, only for peasants such as we."

She laughed at his sarcasm.

"So then, I will join you in the pantry, the place for us peasants. And we'll eat before we each get on with the rest of the evening." She started to protest, but he gently turned her around and steadied her as they both descended. "Oh, I am afraid I knocked your cap ajar." He tried to adjust the frilled white cap from behind but only knocked it more askew. "Silly thing." He lifted it from her head. "I do not know why mother insists on such out-of-fashion nonsense."

Maggie reached to straighten her hair just as Jakob's hand brushed across her head. As their fingers touched, they both stopped, standing without moving for several breaths made louder by the bare walls of the narrow stairwell. Maggie dropped her hand, and Jakob watched as she took the last steps down into the pantry.

→» «←

Her protests could not sway Jakob from his agenda. They sat on stools pulled over to the maple-wood chopping block and ate rye bread with fresh butter and a pungent cheddar. When they finished off the bottle of wine, Jakob went to the dining room and returned with a decanter of port and two small glasses.

"*L'chayim!*" He raised a glass of the ruby liquid. "And to Maggie, who brightens my dreary life."

Embarrassed and pleased, Maggie looked down at her hands before raising her glass to him. "What is that you said at first?"

"*L'chayim*, to life."

"Well, then, to life. And to love."

Jakob held his glass without moving it to his lips, but he was seeing only her face as she kept his gaze for long seconds before casting her eyes demurely down. He did not know whether to trust his ears. Perhaps he was reading far too much into her words, a simple toast, even trite. To life and love. It could have been said by school friends as they raised their beers at a late-night celebration. But it was not. It was spoken by Maggie in a quiet moment, to him and to no one else, with only a cutting block separating them. His heart pounded as he waited for her to look again toward him.

When she didn't move, he set down his glass and reached across to place his hand on top of hers. She turned hers upward and grasped his hungrily as she leaned forward. He rose, pulling her to him, kissing her with a thirst to match hers.

They said nothing as they left the pantry, hands still clasped, and walked around to the front stairs and climbed its broad steps side-by-side. In his room, they undressed each other in silence, a slow pantomime of the pleasure they took in each other's bodies. She seemed surprised by the sight of his erection, and he seemed surprised by how easily he entered her as she lay on his narrow bed.

Jakob struggled to sustain a gentle rhythm, but his body urged him on to frenzy and he climaxed sooner than he wanted. He wanted to apologize, to offer a litany of love and comfort, but, for once, the sentences would not form. Not a word passed between them until morning.

⇒≫ ≪⇐

He awoke to find her sitting on the edge of the bed, lips moving in near-silent recitation as her fingers stepped along the beads of her rosary. He strained to hear the words, catching fragments and phrases as her whispered voice rose and fell: "hallowed be thy name"; "as it is in Heaven"; "Hail Mary, full of grace, blessed art thou among women." He waited with patience and curiosity until she had completed the cycle of prayer.

"You know, we even pray the same. Well, some at least. You say 'Our father, who art in heaven.' We say *'Avinu sheba-shamayim'* — our Father in Heaven. 'Hallowed be thy name' — *'Baruch shem kavod.'* Well, it's very close, anyway."

She looked over at him and smiled, but there were tears in the corners of her eyes. "That is beautiful, but I have . . . we have sinned."

"How can anything so beautiful be sin? Whatever the Rabbis and the Torah say, I cannot accept that we were wrong."

"Perhaps that is a difference between us. You are so ready to question and reject. It is not so easy for me. I feel pulled, as if my insides were being tugged apart. There is you and your words, your inviting words, and there is God and the Church, my family. Perhaps you are the Devil in human form. There are those in my church who would say that of all Jews."

She still held the rosary. He took her free hand in his. "Would the Devil fall in love with you?" Both of them fell into silent shock at the sound of their secret longings spoken aloud.

She closed her eyes and lowered her head. "It is true, Jakob. You have spoken for both of us, and we are without hope."

"There is always hope. We —"

"You do not know me. You do not know who I am or what I have known, only these wonderful interludes of ideas and arguments . . . and last night, that . . ."

"I love you. Yes, there I have said it plain. I love you and I would marry you."

Her teeth closed on her lower lip as tears flooded her eyes. "That is impossible. It is not just this chasm of faith that lies between us. I am not who I seem to you. You see light but not the shadows. Even were I a Jewess, I would not be worthy."

"You think I care about your past, what class you are a part of, that your family is impoverished? These things matter less than dirt on the path. If it means nothing to me that you are a gentile, then none of these other things are of even the remotest consequence."

"But you do not know —"

"Then enlighten me. Tell me who you are, the bright and

the dark, all of it. I want nothing less than the sum, the total. And, I would marry you, whatever the tally."

She laughed. "You can sound so literary, especially when you are most serious."

"Then answer me that one question that has arisen and now floats above all others: Who are you?"

"Lena. I am Lena. That's what my father called me when I was a little girl. It is special to me. I want you to call me that, my secret name."

"Lena it shall always be. Now, my Lena, tell me everything."

She took a shuddering breath. "First . . . first I want you to help me forget other things. Before we talk, I want us be together again." She twisted around and kissed him with an intensity that surprised them both.

Chapter 9
Shiva

Frauenkirchen, Austria, 1879

The quiet along the *Judengasse* was broken as Miriam's father cursed her. He opened the front door and pointed into the fading light. "Go. You are dead to me. Your brother and sister and I will sit *shiva* in mourning."

Miriam stood in the street, her hands spread in entreaty. "Father, I am not dead, I am here and asking your blessing. We are to be married."

"My blessing? I am being asked for my blessing when shame has been brought to our house and to our people. Married? Do the dead marry? And where would that be? Where would the wedding of the dead be held?" He stepped out of the house and looked up and down the length of the *Judengasse*. "Not in our synagogue, surely no. Where then? Perhaps in a graveyard, a wedding officiated by Satan." He turned and reached for the door latch.

"Father, please, look at me. I am Miriam, your elder daughter, who has listened to stories on your knee, who has loved you and baked bread for you. I am to marry Josef, Josef Samson, the maker of wagons from Halbturn, the very man who made the barrow for you not two summers ago and charged you less than its worth. We are to be married in the *Basilika*. Josef is a wonderful man and will be a good husband to me. He is strong and will provide for us.

"And he talks with me. He also listens to me, as I beg of you now."

Saul Schneider stood talking to the door, head bowed. "I hear a voice, but there is no one speaking. Alas, my first-born daughter is dead. My beautiful daughter has died. Now I have only Zalman and Esterl. I am grateful that my beloved Chaya, may her memory be a blessing, is not here to be a witness to this *shanda*, this shame." He reached up to the sleeve of his shirt, yanking it violently until finally the seam at the shoulder gave and was torn open to signify that he was now in mourning. "I am brought low. And now I will tell Esterl to cover the mirrors, and we three must sit on the floor for seven days and say Kaddish for the woman whose name we shall never utter again."

Miriam reached for her father's arm, but he pulled away and entered the house, closing the door slowly behind him. She stood in the street, not knowing what to do or where to turn. Up and down the *Judengasse*, candles appeared in windows and heads poked from doors but were quickly withdrawn when she looked their way. The front door creaked behind her. She turned in time to see her sister's small hand pulling it closed. On the entry step, a bundle tied with a scrap of cloth waited as the shadow of a face passed behind the front window.

⇛ ⇚

Amid the howl of the rising wind and rattle of blowing sleet, Josef did not at first hear the knocking. When it grew urgent, he opened the door to find Miriam standing there, shivering. "What are you doing here? How did you come?"

"I walked, of course. My family has neither a horse nor wagon. And now I have no family."

"What happened? Where is your family?"

"May I come in? Or must I answer all inquiries first."

"Please, I am sorry. Uh . . . do come in." He leaned out the door and looked up and down the street, but with the weather worsening, no one was about. "Here, stand by the fire and let me fetch a blanket." He shook his head. "Poor darling, you are chilled through. Let me find some of Zsófia's . . . something for you to change into. I was never able to . . . I still have some of her things."

He returned in a few minutes. "I laid out a dress and sweater for you on the bed. I am hoping they will fit. You are taller. But at least they are dry and will be warm. You can change in there."

After she had dried herself and changed clothes, they sat in front of the fireplace in the front room. When Miriam finally stopped shivering, Josef took up his questions again. "What happened? Why are you here?"

"I am here because I have no place else to go. My family has sent me away and declared me dead to them. No one in the Jewish Quarter would now take me in. I am banished, excommunicated. You would know about that. Your church does the same to those who break from their faith."

"But surely . . ."

"Surely what's done is done, Josef. In the eyes of my family and my people I am no longer a Jew, no longer one of them, no longer even among the living. My father entreated me, my sister begged, Zalman rose to the occasion and tried to dissuade me with logic, but he was never a scholar, and I parried his every point. And then my father demanded, ordered me. When I refused to renounce my course, he pushed me from the house and declared me dead. Only my little sister showed mercy or any kindness to me. In haste, she made up that bundle with some of my clothes and a piece of bread and set it out on the step for me. But I am dead, dead to all of them, and can never go back."

Josef rose from his chair and kneeled in front of her. "Then marry me. My people shall become yours, and wherever I go, you will be with me."

"You sound almost biblical, my beloved wainwright." She leaned forward and stroked his cheek. "Even still, you have it backwards. I am the one who should say 'whither thou goest' for I am now yours."

He rose and helped her to her feet. Saying nothing, he led her into the bedroom. "I will first bank the fire, and then . . ."

When he returned, she was already beneath the covers with her arms raised, eager for the comfort of him.

⇛ ⇚

With the first rays of sun brightening the dark interior of the small house, Josef shot upright. "You cannot stay here!"

Miriam rubbed sleep from her eyes. "But where will I go? There is no one else, nowhere else."

"But you cannot stay here. Perhaps such things are permitted among Jews, but we are not yet married, and it would never be allowed."

"No, such things are not permitted for us either. But you and I have already defied God's ways."

"It is not God's ways that concern me, but those of the neighbors and townspeople. Ah, I know what! You can stay with my cousin Elise. I am sure she would allow that."

"But I do not know your cousin."

"My cousin is a dear. She married Wilhelm, a farmer from Frauenkirchen, and now lives in a farmhouse at the edge of the town. You must have someplace to sleep, and she has the room."

"Does she know I am a Jew?"

"I will tell her that you are a convert, in the process of instruction. She will ask no questions, I am certain, and I will

60

offer no explanations. Besides, she may have already heard stories of you, of us."

"What will we talk about, this cousin of yours and I?"

"You two will talk little. She and Wilhelm work the fields and talk of the weather or the progress of crops and the laying hens. They have no children to entertain or annoy. You can sleep there and spend your days in instruction with Father Stefan and reading the bible, our bible, with the New Testament. And when it comes time, you will be baptized and we shall be married."

"Only that last word of yours brings any joy to me, but so be it all."

⟫ ⟪

Father Stefan belonged to the diocese of the dour. He was not a happy priest. He served God and his parishioners with a deep sense of duty but little joy. His heart was lifted only by the Eucharist, when he was holding the chalice aloft in the magnificent white and gold sanctuary of the *Basilika*. In those moments, he was once more touched by the Holy Spirit. The rest of his responsibilities were ritual without spirit, performed by rote as part of a lifelong journey from bitter origins toward an unseen and distant kingdom promised on high. It was the only path he knew. He had been a sad and isolated child, an orphan raised by nuns on a preordained course that took him to the priesthood without detour, without ever the distractions of pleasure. Now he was a skeletal man of middle-age, already counting down the days to his own end.

With dispirited indifference, the priest listened to Josef and Miriam tell their tale and attest to their sincerity. A soul would be gained, he credited, and their children would be raised in the Holy Mother Church, but he could see little to celebrate. "You will pledge to raise your children as Catholics, and you will convert, of course. I will personally see to your instruction and baptize you. Whatever you may have heard or wished, I will not marry you unless you are both Christian. Are you ready for that?"

Miriam looked to Josef for reassurance before nodding to the priest.

⇛ ⇚

Miriam felt engulfed by the dark wood shelves and leather-bound volumes of the priest's cramped office. "And how do we know the Pope to be infallible?" she said, leaning forward in her chair as she spoke, bobbing like a yeshiva student arguing interpretations of Torah and knowing she was causing Father Stefan discomfort.

"It was confirmed to be true by *Dei Filius*, issued in 1870 by the previous Pope, Pius IX. But of course, the Pope is infallible only when speaking *ex cathedra*, officially and to all the faithful."

"So it is the Pope who said the Pope cannot fail?"

"Yes, but speaking — that is by written declaration — *ex cathedra*."

"So we know the Pope is infallible because he ... some Pope, who died not long ago, told us so?"

The priest's sigh was deep and suffused with sadness. "It is not our place to question but to accept. And it is not your place to question but to learn, that you might join the community of the Christian faithful within the loving embrace of the Holy Roman Catholic Church. Do you not want to marry your betrothed, Josef Samson?"

"I do. I am only trying to understand this faith I am joining."

"It is not always ours to understand, but sometimes merely to surrender before mystery. Especially as you are a woman, I might add."

"I see." She spoke with resignation and what humility she could muster, but her heart still argued, as it always had, and her mind spun with debate, as she had learned from her brother and her father. What she did not say was that she was already familiar with the priest's dismissal of her and her entire gender. She had heard it before, from the men of the Jewish Quarter. Truly, God had made all men the same, endowing them with common arrogance.

⇛ ⇚

The wedding was a simple affair in an elaborate setting. Although she had been shown the main sanctuary as part of her instruction, Miriam was still overwhelmed by the grandeur of the inside of the *Basilika*, in such contrast to the simple synagogue that had been her spiritual home all her life. The interior of the sanctuary was bright with light through tall windows along the south wall. Ornate paintings filled the vaulted ceiling, and everywhere, columns and arches and statuary glittered with gold leaf. Saints and angels robed in gold flanked the altar and looked down on the long narrow sanctuary with its row on row of wooden benches.

Some, but not all, of Josef's relatives from Halbturn had made the trek to the *Basilika*. A few of the local parishioners occupied the back pews, more out of curiosity than from community spirit or affection for the bride and groom. Most had heard of such things happening in other towns but had never witnessed it among the townspeople. At least, they thought, it was a Jew finally coming to Christ and not a Christian soul being lost to atavistic unbelief.

None of Miriam's family or neighbors came near the

church. It was a Saturday, and the observant Jews of Frau-enkirchen were starting their day with prayers within their modest synagogue. At the appropriate point, Saul Schneider would stand with others who were in mourning or observ-ing jahrzeit, the anniversary of a loss, and together they would recite the Mourner's Kaddish, the Jewish prayer in Aramaic said in memory of the dead.

In the balcony, where the women were kept separated from the men, Esterl sat in silence, thinking of her sister. From where she was seated on the north side, she could see through the half-round window above the Ark to the tall spires of the *Basilika*, only a few hundred yards away. She did not join in the Mourner's Kaddish, but when the *mi she-beirach*, the prayer for healing, was said, Esterl whispered her sister's Hebrew name, *Miryam bat Chaya*, and entreated for her *r'fuah shleimah*, the complete healing of body and of soul. Over the following year, Saul would continue to mark his mourning by saying the Mourner's Kaddish at services, and then, as custom dictated, he would move on with life, in the futile attempt to erase his daughter from memory, even as Esterl kept her secret vow never to forget.

A short walk away, in the *Basilika Mariä Geburt*, Miriam Schneider and Josef Samson stood at the front, taking their own vows before the ever-serious Father Stefan, and when the groom bent to kiss the bride, tears were trickling down her face. Above them there was no *chuppah*, the wedding canopy of Jewish tradition which Miriam had dreamed of since girlhood. No wine glass would be wrapped in a ker-chief and broken underfoot. No exuberant party of revelers would follow to last late into the night as the newlyweds re-treated to the marital bed.

Outside the church, Josef helped Miriam up into a wagon

of his own making pulled by a horse borrowed from his cousin. After the short ride on the snow-clogged road to Halbturn, he would return the horse and in the following days try to sell the wagon in hopes of adding the proceeds to his savings, his investment in a nebulous dream of a better life somewhere. It was a dream he could entrust to Miriam, whose own rebellious spirit fueled his drive to escape, to go elsewhere, some elsewhere, to Eisenstadt or beyond.

That evening, as the couple prepared for their first night together as husband and wife, Miriam surprised Josef with an announcement followed by a declaration. "Husband, I have news. I am carrying your child. And henceforth to you and to all I am to be known as Mary, after the girl in the song who took a new name when she left an old life." Her voice was a mix of celebration and sorrow.

Chapter 10
Candles

Halbturn and Frauenkirchen, Austria, 1880

The smell of smoke lingered in the morning air, like on a still winter day when every stove and fireplace in the town was being fed, yet this was not the clean, salty smoke of firewood. An acrid accent, almost of burning garbage, assaulted the nostrils. The odor grew steadily worse as Josef marched on; by the bend in the road midway to Frauenkirchen, a thin column of muddy gray smoke could be seen rising above the town ahead.

His handcart began to bounce as Josef quickened his steps. The cart rattled with its assortment of miniature carriages and wagons, toys that he had spent frigid winter nights shaping in front of the fireplace in hopes of extra earnings in the spring.

As he approached the market plaza, Josef noted how sparse the crowd was for such a late hour on a warm spring morning. Those gathered there were clumped in scattered knots of animated conversation accompanied by much gesturing.

He approached a group of elderly men standing at the edge. "*Guten tag. Was ist los?*"

"Good day, you say. What is wrong, you ask. Look." Together the men raised their arms and pointed across the plaza to where lazy smoke could be seen rising above the Jewish Quarter, then bending to be blown slowly to the east as it rose.

"What happened?" Josef said.

A gray-bearded man dressed in black, from his black hat and coat to his black shoes, shrugged. "*Es brennt*," he offered in Yiddish.

"A great fire," a companion continued in explanation. "It started last night, just after dark, the start of Shabbos, and burned through much of the Quarter, even the synagogue. *Baruch HaShem*. Thank God it was still early and not worse. We were still at our tables and not asleep in our beds."

"How . . . I mean, does anyone know what started it?"

A beardless young man who had arrived after Josef and had been listening at the periphery spoke up. "It was the candles, I say. Always they do this thing with candles, the Jews. At Christmas they put so many candles in their windows, dozens. It is a miracle they have not burned it all to the ground before. Next time it could be the entire town."

The bearded one sneered. "You are a stupid boy and speak nonsense. We do nothing for your Christmas. We leave that to you. The candles in the window in midwinter are for Hanukkah, for the eight days. That is a miracle, yes, but we —"

Josef cut him off. "Was anyone hurt?"

"It was a fire that burned most of our houses — and the synagogue. What do you think?"

"Will you watch my cart if I leave it here with you?" The men nodded then shrugged almost in unison, and Josef strode swiftly toward the smoke.

The *Judengasse* and the other narrow passages woven through the Jewish Quarter were crowded with people and choked with furniture and other household goods that families had carried out to save from the fires. Josef approached a young man standing alone by a smoldering beam. "The Schneider family, do you know if they are all right?"

"Which of the Schneiders do you mean?"

"The tailor."

"*Herr Schneider, der Schneider*?" He laughed. "I don't know, I think . . ."

Looking around, Josef spotted Esterl down the alleyway and called to her. She turned, and her eyes widened when she saw who it was calling her name. She looked nervously to either side before starting to run toward him.

"Esterl! You are all right? Is your family safe?"

She looked to either side again, as if checking to see whether anyone was watching or could hear, then turned to face the smoldering remaining wall of a small house. Without looking at him, she spoke. "I cannot speak of her, but I . . . you must tell your wife . . ." Her body started to shake as she sobbed. "*Er ist tot*," she blurted out. "Zalman is dead."

"I am so sorry, Esterl. I will tell her. Your brother was a good man." It was condolence by formula. He had never met Zalman but had grown up with the time-honored expression that all the dead are pious.

"I wish . . ." She hung her head and spoke to the ground, here frosted with ash. "I wish he could have . . ." She paused to wipe tears from her eyes and cheeks. "He went back into the house to retrieve the new sewing machine of which he was so proud. We told him not to go. The roof collapsed. He . . ."

"And your father?"

"He is all right. His hand is burned, but it will heal. His heart may not. First my mother, may her memory be a blessing, then . . ." — her lips moved without sound — "and now his only son. I must go. I need to look after my father." She left Josef standing at the end of the street wondering what to do next. He spotted a shovel beside the road, its shaft blackened but still intact. Though his eyes stung from the lingering smoke, he joined a small group of men who were shoveling dirt over smoking embers and beating out spurious flames that here and there sprang from charred ruins.

⇛ ⇚

It was almost dark when Josef reached home. His face was smudged with soot and dirt, and his clothes smelled of smoke and sweat. Mary, who only a year before had been Miriam, came out and greeted him as he trudged up the street, a look of horror written on her face.

"I heard," she said. "The Hafners were at the market today and left early to spread the word. Are you all right? Where is your handcart? Are you hurt?"

"I am not hurt, only tired. I spent the day helping in the Jewish Quarter. Many of the townsfolk did the same. At first, some of the Jews only stood and watched because it was the Sabbath, but then the Rabbi explained that preventing the fire from rekindling or spreading to the rest of the town would save lives. This, no surprise, was followed by much animated debate in Yiddish that I could not always follow, but most of the Jews then joined in the work of recovery.

"Oh, yes, the handcart I left in the village. I reasoned they would have use for it now."

"You are a good man, Josef, and generous."

He took her hands in his. "But there is something I must tell you."

"Oh, no!" She shook her head and closed her eyes. "Not . . ."

"Zalman —"

"Not dear Zalman, not my poor awkward brother. And?"

"Esterl and your father are fine. I spoke with her, or with

69

the back of her head, I should say. Your brother was being brave and prudent, as were many of the Jews last night. A fire started in one house near the synagogue and quickly spread through the crowded Quarter. There was not much that could be done. The town is too small to have much of a fire brigade, and there is no pond near enough from which to draw extra water."

"Are there others, I mean, who died?"

Josef nodded. "Your uncle was alone in his house and was overcome by smoke. A few children also. Three I think, but I do not remember their names."

"And the synagogue? Does it still stand?"

"In a sense. The roof is gone, but the walls still stand, at least in part. There is talk of a temporary repair before rebuilding it entirely."

"You spoke with dear Esterl. How I wish I could as well."

"Then go with me tomorrow. Many of us intend to return to help. They will need our hands and our skills to rebuild as quickly as possible. You can bring the baby and join with the women there. Surely, with what has happened, your people will not shun you now."

⇛ ⇚

Josef proved to be wrong about the Jews of Frauenkirchen, as he often was when it came to people and peoples. Though Mary labored alongside townspeople and others who had arrived from Halbturn, no Jew from Frauenkirchen spoke to her, and none of the women would tend her baby girl. Only the Catholics offered to watch her Catherina and accepted her help preparing food for the men who took on the hard labor of clearing the rubble and stamping out lingering fires.

The fine weather of that spring and summer spared the workers, Catholic and Jew, and houses were handily restored or rebuilt. Few words, other than those needed to complete a job, passed between the two communities, but a wordless bond was gradually restored by shouldering a shared burden. At the edge of the Jewish Quarter, two houses belonging to gentiles had been badly burned, and the Jewish men started with those first, putting their backs and their tools to the job of restoring the roofs and then reworking the charred interiors.

There is a synchrony that sprouts from shared labor, a dance of necessity that takes over and needs no or few words. A man on a ladder looks to his left, then his right, and a saw appears in his hand, handle first, a saw with which he cuts off the end of an overhanging beam, the end of which has been steadied by the hand of yet another silent neighbor. These are practiced and known maneuvers of a manual reality that knows nothing of belief or doctrine. Working side-by-side, the Jews and the Catholics of Frauen-kirchen often lost track of who held the other end of a board or who brought a barrow of freshly mixed plaster.

By late summer, the Synagogue had a new roof and was usable for services, already well on its way to a complete restoration. Nearly all of the houses and shops of the Jewish Quarter were rebuilt or repaired or nearing the end of necessary work. By the last days of summer, the communities were once more two, once more separate but not quite equal, moving onward in an awkward accord, as they had for decades. Yet something had been mended even as something else was torn. The Jews were grateful to their gentile neighbors for coming to their aid, even as they resented them for that very aid. The Catholic majority, whose territory surrounded — engulfed — that of the Jews, their neighbors by decree, were grateful that the conflagration had not spread to the rest of the town and resentful that it had started with the Jews.

In all the days of labor, in all the encounters of that joint endeavor, not once did any member of the Jewish community speak to Mary or smile at her baby girl; not once did the parishioners of her adopted faith go out of the way to welcome her. Many times, Esterl and Mary spotted each other across the square or on opposite ends of a table spread with bread and cheese and water for the tired workers. Many times they turned their gaze aside, and never did a word pass between them.

TWO: Translation

There are always antecedent causes. A beginning is an artifice, and what recommends one over another is how much sense it makes of what follows.

— Ian McEwan

Chapter 11

Separation

Halbturn, Austria, 1882

Josef caught Esterl with her hand on the small basket, his rough fingers closing about her wrist. She recoiled and tried to pull away but said nothing. Startled, a mourning dove fluttered up from the gutter and vanished into a pre-dawn sky of tarnished-silver, the same color as its feathers.

"Still the silence, Esterl? Our little Catherina is already three years old. She favors her mother, you know. Like your sister she is so smart, so serious. What if I told your father what you do every Friday?" She stifled a small inward cry with her free hand. "Always the two loaves, always before there is anyone in the street."

He looked along the narrow lane as far as the curve in the road that angled toward Frauenkirchen. The painted wooden doors still filled doorways with their bright colors, and the windows remained shuttered. A gray-and-black cat belonging to the Schultzes trotted along on some feline mission.

"We may be leaving for America, Esterl. I had always thought we would move to Eisenstadt before the new baby, but my brother-in-law writes from Minnesota, which is in America, and says there is work and my sister is with child again." Esterl looked up at him, keeping her small hand tightly against her lips as panic sparked in her dark eyes. Josef had to remind himself that it was young Esterl, not his wife but her sister, who knelt before him. Her face was already shedding the round cheeks of girlhood and taking on the elegant beauty for which the Schneider women were recognized.

Inside, still asleep, awaited Mary, his *schöne Jüdin*, his bride, the rebellious young woman once known as Miriam with whom he had, as a boy, chased crows and skipped pebbles on the pond at the edge of the orchard — so close, always, yet so distant and unobtainable. But he had obtained her, won her at no small price, and the price she had paid for yielding to him had been even higher.

"She is dead to me!" her father had screamed in front of the boxy synagogue in the Jewish quarter. He had torn the sleeve of his coat and the entire family had sat for a week on the floor of their tiny house on the *Judengasse*, not bathing, not shaving, only chanting prayers and mourning the loss of the elder daughter who was dead to them even as she was being married in the church only a few minutes' walk away. Not a single one from her community attended the wedding, and not a one had spoken to Mary since.

The Jews of her village no longer acknowledged her presence. They would study the ground if she passed in the market square or face a wall in her presence. The easy social intercourse that had for many decades marked relations between the Jews and their Christian neighbors in Frauenkirchen had turned cold. The community spirit that had followed after the fire in the Jewish Quarter and during the rebuilding had been extinguished almost as quickly as the flames.

Josef studied Esterl's unlined face as she averted her eyes. He saw in it echoes of the young woman he had married three years earlier, whose face was already now creased with worry and marked by the suffering of isolation and the pain of childbirth and the early death of her second child. She was pregnant again for a third time, and that was a strand of the goad that was taking them to America — the hope that this child would be born to a new life in a land where it mattered less from where they had come or who they had once been.

"Thank you, Esterl. Thank you for the bread. I know you are forbidden to speak to me, but I still want you to know that it means much to your sister. She still lights two candles every Friday evening before sunset and waves her hands above the flames as if to warm them before placing them over her eyes. I do not know all that this means — she no longer speaks of these things with me — but I know it is important to her.

"It is the same with the pause outside the church and the prayer she mumbles before she enters for Mass. I have strained to hear the words. *Shakets teshaktsenu* she begins, or so it seems to me, her lips moving almost without sound, but she will not tell me what it means and will not step across the threshold without first performing this ritual. I always stand beside her and pretend to be admiring the architecture. I nod as if inspired by thoughts of God and the

Savior, but I am shielding her, trying to keep others from noticing her hesitation."

Esterl closed her eyes, sending rivulets of tears down her smooth cheeks. She opened them again, then opened her mouth as if to speak, but all that escaped was the strained sound of a breath that carried more suffering and sadness than any words could convey.

"I know you love her still," he said. "And she loves you as well, all of you." He at last loosened his grip on her arm, and she withdrew it."

"*Challah*," she said, just the single word as she rose and took a step away, nodding toward the bread. Then she was gone, running down the street and around the turn. The Schultz's cat leapt aside as she passed.

Josef lifted the blue-checked cloth folded over the still-warm bread and inhaled the yeasty sweetness. How did she do it, he wondered. She must rise long before dawn. It was a mystery, one of many, but it was not one he was inclined to pursue. Bread-making was for women, and the ways of the Jews were still unfathomable to him. The history and language lessons that had fueled his early relationship with the young Miriam ended with her conversion when she became Mary. But he did not need to understand baking to savor the glossy braids of Esterl's bread, and he did not need to understand women to enjoy the brush of Mary's thick hair against his face. Or to appreciate Esterl's smooth skin or the burning heat of it as he had held her wrist.

⇒» «⇐

Inside the house, a tiny figure in a print nightshirt and hand-knit sweater waited, dark curious eyes silently questioning him.

"For tonight, Cathia, as always." He lifted the basket to the shelf by the door as Catherina reached, begging, with an outstretched hand. "No, please don't cry. Mama will feed you." He pointed toward the kitchen. "Go ask Mama. Papa has work to do."

Catherina lifted her arms to him and grunted a wordless demand. He sighed and picked her up one handed, swinging her onto his hip. She buried her red and runny nose in his armpit. "My skinny squirrel. You are one smart little squirrel, but when will you ever grow some. Let's go find something for you to eat."

In the kitchen, Mary was already at the stove, cooking up porridge in the large pot and caramelizing an onion in a small skillet. "See, my little squirrel, Mama will feed you."

Mary looked up from her cooking and greeted him with the same silent eyes as Catherina.

"She brought the bread again," he said. "This time in a basket. At least it was not those thin burnt crackers."

"Matzohs. I told you. It was Passover. We . . . they do not eat leavened bread during Passover. But Catherina liked them. She liked to suck on them."

"Yes. At least she was eating. Can you feed her? I have to hike over to the Schmidt farm to fix a plow."

"And now you are become a ploughwright?"

"I am whatever I am asked to become. I have a growing family." He nodded toward his wife's belly. "And that is why we are going to America."

Mary hammered the wooden spoon on the edge of the pot, more times than were needed merely to shake off the sticking porridge. "I thought it was not yet decided."

"It was not. Now it is decided. I have already made inquiries."

"It is decided." She banged the spoon for emphasis. "You

have made inquiries." Another strike of the spoon. "Once, not that long ago, we would talk. We would talk of many things, certainly of the things closest to our lives. And now? It is decided. Inquiries have been made."

Josef scowled. "Now we are married. It is different. I made inquiries to learn what we need for passage. We can sell the house and auction my tools."

"This house, sell this house, our home. What of my family, my father and sister . . ."

"Your family has disowned you. You are dead to them. Even here, the neighbors barely speak to us. I have ever more trouble finding enough work. There is no place for us here, Miriam."

"Mary."

"Then let it be Mary. By any name, we no longer belong here."

"We were born here. My family is still here."

"Your family denies you. Your sister leaves loaves of that bread on the doorstep on Fridays, but has not spoken to you or of you in years. In America there is work. In America we can start over, just Josef and Mary Samson, late of Austria-Hungary. My sister says there are many Germans and Austrians where they live. The Hoffmanns will help us find work and settle in."

"But they speak English in America."

"They do, but many speak German as well. You can learn, we can learn. Our children will go to their schools and will learn to speak English and be American. How would you like that, Cathia, my little squirrel?" He gave her a tickle bringing a giggle to her lips.

"If we leave soon enough, the baby will be born in America and will already be an American. That, my sister says, is how it is in America. Her children are already Americans, American citizens."

Mary turned from the stove. "It is true, then, that America is . . . is more open?"

"It is different there. They have different laws that do not respect one religion over another. Jews and Catholics live as neighbors."

"Do they live as husband and wife?"

Josef exhaled slowly. "That I do not know. But it is hardly our concern, is it, as we are both good Catholics," — he paused —"and no one will know or can say otherwise in America."

-≫ ≪-

Josef rounded the corner of the house to where his wife and daughter were pulling up spring onions. He waved a sheet of paper as he approached. Cathia dropped her onions into the basket by her mother. "What is it, Papa? What is it?"

"Our future, my Cathia." He walked over to Mary and gave her a hand up. "I have booked passage, and this letter confirms it. We leave in two months from Hamburg; we shall take the train from Vienna."

Mary drew back. "Two months? So soon?"

"The Brauns have offered to buy the house for their youngest boy, Hans Peter, who is soon to marry. The bans have already been read. They are not paying what they should, but it is enough. My brother-in-law has already promised to get me work at the railyards in Saint Paul as soon as we arrive. There is a house that is empty, in the same street as theirs. Joseph has spoken to the owner, who is German. He will rent it to us at a reasonable rate. My sister jokes that it is so Catholic there that we will be Josef and Mary Samson down the street from Joseph and Mary Hoffmann in a neighborhood where Joseph and Mary can be found on nearly every block."

"This city, Saint Paul? It is a Catholic city?"

"It is an American city."

Chapter 12
Discoveries

St. Paul, Minnesota, 1909

Where does one world end and another begin? Austria, Hungary, the Austro-Hungarian Empire — were any of these ever real? So many of the seemingly important boundaries of human geography and timekeeping are mere artifacts of our measuring, our counting, like the turning of the century that our own lives had already bridged or the neighborhoods that were the separate worlds of our childhood. Those imaginary yet very real islands of identity were overlaid on the orderly grid of streets and avenues that defined most of the city of St. Paul, a city we had shared since birth and that divided us by unmarked borders which blurred and shifted over time, even as each remained centered by the centripetal forces of some focus, a focus made concrete and visible by constructions of brick and stone, monuments making manifest the invisible ties of faith and of origins.

For my family and its network, that focus was Mount Zion Temple at Holly and Avon, a building with a pillared entrance that always reminded me more of a bank or library than a synagogue. In that liberal shul, within a tradition emerging from the Reform movement of nineteenth-century Germany that had since taken root in America, I had become bar mitzvah, and from there I had begun the meander that would lead me ever further away from even its diluted conservatism.

Other than the High Holy Days, I had not been back since that day at thirteen when I was first called to the Torah, yet Mount Zion remained the origin of my coordinates, a point of reference in my steady differentiation as a believing being.

And for you, the pivot point was the Church of St. Agnes, in that other German-speaking neighborhood, to the north of University Avenue.

Curiosity breeds curiosity, even as familiarity reinforces itself until we are sated, taking things and people for granted. Surrounded though my community was by Catholics, I had grown up within what amounted to a ghetto of the mind. Even at the University, my friends were mostly fellow Jews, and I had made few attempts to reach beyond self-imposed fences. Now I longed to know more of this Catholic world from which you sprang, even as my hunger to know you deepened.

I could not get my fill of you. The more I learned of your deceptively simple self, the more subtlety I sensed. How could a young girl, so unassuming on the outside, contain such complexity? I wanted to be inside you, in your head and, of course, once more in that magical physical way. With the return of my parents, however, and the approaching end of the term at the University, it became ever more difficult for us to find opportunities for conversation, much less a reprise of our only night together. We began to clutch at every opportunity that drifted our way — or at least I did.

I remember it was midweek, and we were alone in the house. My mother was at a meeting of a women's group at the temple, my father was working late, and you had secured permission to leave early. As you completed your chores before leaving, I dogged your steps and used all the rhetorical acrobatics at my disposal trying to draw you into conversation or, better yet, to seduce you once more into my bed.

You would have none of it.

"We cannot, Jakob. Your mother could return at any moment, and I promised her I would finish before I left. Please let me finish my work." Maggie toweled off the last of the saucers and placed it gently in the stack beside the sink.

"Your dedication is admirable, as is your prudence, but my mother's meeting is not over for another hour, and she will gossip with the ladies for the better part of an hour afterwards. Leave this drudgery and come upstairs with me."

"Why are men always so single-minded?" She carried the stack of dishes to the pantry.

"Are we?" He followed just behind her. "Yes, perhaps, for my mind is almost always, one way or another, singularly occupied with one thing: you."

"Perhaps it is easier for men, then. For women there are ever so many more matters demanding our attention."

"Like, for example?"

"Like ... oh, never you mind. Just let me finish putting away the dishes so I can have time to stop in at St. Agnes on my way home."

"I would go with you. I have never been inside a church. You can further my cultural and religious education."

She closed the glass-fronted door of the china cabinet. "No, that would not be a good idea. Besides, I want to make confession."

"Tell me about that, confession."

"What is there to tell? We confess our sins to the priest."

"And how is that?"

"How? We just say, 'Father forgive me, for I have sinned.' Once we have acknowledged our sins, he tells us what we must do in contrition to earn forgiveness."

"What sins can a girl such as you have to confess?"

"Oh many, cardinal among them would be the mortal sin you want me to repeat upstairs."

"And you don't want that? You don't want me?"

"I do, my Jacob, I do. And that, too, is a sin, also a mortal one."

"Mortal? What does that mean? We are mortal, yes, but sins? What otherwise might they be?"

"Some sins are only venial, others endanger your immortal soul. It is . . . it is like the law as you explained it to me. There are misdemeanors and there are felonies. A mortal sin is, I suppose, like a felony. Were you to die with a mortal sin on your soul, unconfessed and unforgiven, you would be condemned to hell for all eternity. But many everyday things — coveting, white lies, bad language, a moment of hate toward a neighbor — are venial sins, still to be owned and in need of forgiveness, but misdemeanors."

"So many sins you Catholics have."

"And you do not, with your six hundred and something commandments?"

"Six hundred thirteen. But, well, that's different. What I want to know is why you confess to a priest? Why not just ask God to forgive you?"

"The priest is God's representative, he intercedes on our behalf. Is that not what your rabbi does?"

"No, no one stands between us and God. If we sin against others, we ask their forgiveness, and if we sin against God, we ask His. This we do during the High Holy Days, when the books of life are completed and sealed for a fresh start in the new year. Or so it is said, though I am no longer sure about the details or the truth of many of these matters. And I am no rabbi, only a pre-law student with more doubt than faith — and a deep, as-yet unsated longing for you, my Lena, my love. But I would learn. If you will not go with me, let me go with you. Show me your church and share your faith."

"No, this I do alone. Please, I am serious. Promise you won't follow me."

"All right, I promise. I won't follow you. And I will now retreat to the solitude of my lonely monastic room at the top of the stairs." He kissed her quickly before she could pull away.

⫸ ⫷

The Church of St. Agnes at the corner of Kent and Lafond served a large German-speaking community of Catholic immigrants from Germany and the Austro-Hungarian Empire. It was a work in progress. Under construction for years, the gray stone structure with its simple lines and baroque details mimicked the old-world architecture already familiar to its immigrant parishioners. It still lacked its long-awaited onion-domed bell tower, but its distinctive red-tile roof, a rarity in the Upper Midwest and visible around the area, served as a silent call to the faithful.

As Maggie approached, she noticed a lone figure seated near the top of the front steps. As she neared, she saw it was Jakob. "What are you doing here? You promised."

"I did. And I didn't break my promise. I didn't follow you. I slipped down the back stairs and out through the side gate and ran ahead." He smiled as if proud of a clever deception.

"Please go home, Jakob. It would not be good for you to be seen here."

"Why? Would anyone know who I am?"

"No, but they would know who you are not. You are not one of us. Now, I want to enter alone and make my confession." She climbed the last steps and stood to the side just outside the door, eyes closed, speaking softly. "*Shakets teshaktsenu, veta'ev teta'avenu ki kherem hu.*" She opened her eyes to find Jakob at her side, mouth agape.

"What was that? What did you say?" he said.

"It is a special thing my mother taught me, an old-world expression of piety, a blessing that she told me always to say before I enter a church." She repeated it.

"Do you know what that is? It's Hebrew, biblical Hebrew, from Deuteronomy, if I remember correctly."

"Hebrew? Are you sure?"

"Yes, I am sure. It means, 'You shall abhor it, for surely it is to be shunned.' Something like that, a commandment against idol worship. But for you it means far more than that. It means what I had begun to suspect before, that your mother was Jewish. Moreover, she never let go of her faith but held fast to it in secret."

Maggie, stunned into silence, stood swaying slightly.

"And, my beloved Lena — for that is what you will always be to me, my beloved, my Lena — it means even so much more than that to us. It means you also are Jewish. Everyone with a Jewish mother is considered a Jew. This means we could —"

"This means nothing. I am Christian, Catholic. I strive to be a good Catholic girl, even as you tempt me." There was the hint of desperation in her voice. "That my mother muttered something outside the church and taught me to do the same does not make me a Jew."

"That your mother entered a building with you does not

make either of you Catholics. That she recited a commandment from the Torah before entering means much. It means that her conversion, if that is what happened, was not truly by choice, and you, then, are of the *b'nei anusim*, the children of the coerced."

Maggie shook her head slowly but emphatically and turned to enter the church, leaving Jakob outside alone, at once discouraged and elated. Intensely curious, he wanted to follow her, but as he stepped toward the doorway, his discomfort grew to win over curiosity. He walked away, wondering whether he, too, should recite the passage from Deuteronomy.

Chapter 13
Irregularities

St. Paul, Minnesota, 1909

The tardy Minnesota spring, with its smells of earthy rebirth and late melting hillocks of dirty snow, gave way to the warm exuberance of early summer, the transition taking place almost beneath my notice, preoccupied as I was with the pressures of studies — and the presence of you. Yet, even as you filled so much of my field of view, I was somehow blind to so many of the most important matters, not the least your frequent reluctance to return home to the Hoffmanns, a hesitance which took time to rise into awareness and which, in that fashion so common among males, I at first misread as being centered on me.

Sunday was your day off from domestic duties, and the large park up at Lake Como became our favorite haunt on Sunday mornings. It was far enough away that there was little risk of being seen by anyone who knew us, but it was easy to reach by trolley, which ran through the park and all the way over to Lake Harriet in Minneapolis. While many would make the entire route an excursion in itself through the diverse neighborhoods of the two cities, we preferred to stroll around Como Park, which could become crowded on a summer Sunday afternoon but afforded quiet seclusion at many spots earlier in the day.

The entrance to Como Park came into view and the trolley slowed, jarring Jakob out of his reverie. Though the streetcar station was only a few years old, its nobbled exterior of local stones, like cobblestone roadway turned vertical, gave it the look of an ancient and oversized cottage from some Old World fairytale setting. For once unhurried, Jakob stepped off the trolley and began a slow stroll toward the lake. He was early, and a patchy low-lying morning fog still lingered over the water.

As he neared Cozy Lake, the small pond to the west at the north end of Lake Como, he was surprised to spot Maggie sitting on a wooden bench beside the flower-lined path. She stood as he approached and smiled warmly up at him as she took his arm. "You're out early on a Sunday," she said.

"And you. I was confident I would arrive before you."

"I went to early Mass at St. Agnes to confess and then take communion. Then I came here. I wanted extra time to think, some time to myself."

"Should I leave you to your thoughts and return later?"

"No, my silly scholar. Now that you are here, my thoughts are of you."

"Should we walk or would you prefer to sit?"

"I prefer only that we talk. We have had so little time these weeks, what with your mother hovering and you so busy studying for exams."

"Exams are now in the past, thank you, at least for the semester. My mother, on the other hand, remains with us. So, let us enjoy what intercourse we can." He gestured toward the bench, smiling at his own wordplay.

Maggie sat down again and smoothed the skirt of her flowered dress, looking down at her lap as if studying the pattern but saying nothing.

Jakob waited, expectantly, until he finally felt compelled to fill the silence. "My father wants me to continue my studies this summer, taking extra courses."

"And is that what you want to do over the summer?"

"I don't know. Maybe not. I have friends from the University with a sprawling old house on Lake Minnetonka that belongs to the uncle of one of them. They invited me to come stay at the lake for July and August. They assure me that it will be more bearable than the city."

A shadow of displeasure passed over her face. "What would you do there?"

"Swim, go boating, play pinochle, drink too much — you know."

"No, I don't know. There has been no time in my life for swimming and boating, certainly not for card games. Only once did I drink much at all, and that was with you, that first night."

"Really? I thought you drink whenever you take communion. And your mother lit candles on Friday night before dinner. Was there no wine for everyone?"

"At Mass, it is only a sip, as I once told you, and at home with the Hoffmanns there is only beer, sometimes, for my uncle and . . . for . . . for the Hoffmann boys."

"And how old are they, these boys?"

"Joey, Joseph, Jr. is . . . he . . . he's the oldest, nineteen. Then there's Michael. He's sixteen, though I have seldom seen him with any beer. The youngest, John, the baby, will be four next week." She laughed. "When John was barely a toddler, he was at a family picnic where he sneaked a couple of beer mugs under the table and finished off the dregs. He was one very happy little boy when he staggered back out into the open."

She cleared her throat. "And yes, there's also Frank, who is eleven, and George, who is six."

"All boys, then. I knew the Hoffmanns were a large family, but . . . five boys."

"Plus four girls: Anna, Marie, Beth, and Nancy, the baby. And my aunt is expecting again, in October. She hopes it is another girl. And she is not alone in that. I —"

"I confess to amazement. Ten children, in that house? It's hardly bigger than ours."

"Uncle Joseph built an addition at the back, so it is bigger than it looks from the street. But my brother and sister and I are there as well, don't forget. I share a bedroom with the two oldest girls. My brother and sister and I are saving what we can in hopes of being able to find a place, perhaps somewhere in the neighborhood, where we can live. Once Jonathan reaches his majority, we can, perhaps, be truly on our own. I am rather eager for that. I do not mean that my aunt and uncle have not been most kind to us, but . . ."

"I imagine you would be eager. It must be very crowded."

"Sometimes, yes. Other times not enough."

"What do you mean?"

"Only that . . . No, it is nothing." She drew in her lips as if trying to hold in some thought.

"Are you quite all right, Maggie? You look suddenly rather peaked."

"Not everything begs discussion, Jakob, even between us."

"I had thought otherwise. We are not mere friends. I love you, and we —"

Her face became suddenly stern. "And what exactly does that mean, that you say you love me? What does it entail? How far would that love stretch, what strain or stress could it endure?"

"Anything."

"Is that so? What if I told you that . . . oh, never mind." She shook her head as if to clear it. "Look, the park and day are so beautiful, and they are ours for a few hours. Can we not just savor what we have in these moments?"

"Surely," he pointed toward the brick-and-stone arch that bridged the channel connecting Cozy Lake and Como Lake. "Let's cross over and circle the long way around."

⇒⇒ ⇐⇐

Dusk was approaching and Jakob was in his room, immersed in a library book on Minnesota history, when he heard the knock on the front door. By the time he descended to the landing of the stairs, his father had already emerged from the den and was reaching for the doorknob.

"Why, Maggie, what brings you here on a Sunday evening?"

"I am sorry to interrupt. Might I speak with Master Jakob?" She tried to cover that she was out of breath. "I promise not to be long about it."

"I suppose. Jakob," he called up the stairs, only to be surprised to see his son already standing at the landing. "Ah, Jakob, Maggie Samson is here and wishes to speak with you. I hope nothing is amiss. I —"

"Nothing, I promise," she interrupted in earnest, "And I shall not take him from his studies for long."

Morrie looked from Maggie to Jakob and back with a quizzical frown. "I suppose. You may talk in the front parlor. Should I inform Mrs. Oster that you are here?"

"No! Ah, rather I mean, that won't be necessary. Thank you for your thoughtfulness. We shan't be long."

Jakob crossed in front of his father and gestured for Maggie to enter the parlor.

"You may leave the door open, son," Morrie said as he started down the front hall. "I'll be in the den with my newspaper."

In the parlor, Jakob gestured toward the divan and turned on the lamp beside it. "What brings you here?" In the light, he noticed her hair was mussed and a scratch marred her left cheek. "What happened? Are you all right?"

"I am. I just needed to get out of the house, and I didn't know where to go."

"The Hoffmanns? Your brother and sister? Everything is all right?"

"They are not yet back from their picnic. Except for Joey. He ... he stayed home. I didn't know that until I returned from Lake Como expecting the house to be empty. He ..." She turned away. "He tried again. I really don't wish to talk about it, only to stay away for a bit until the rest of the family returns."

"Did he hurt you? Yes, I see that he did. What could he possibly ... ?" Jakob's mouth opened in slow recognition. "Oh, no, of course. How could I not understand? Oh, my poor Lena. I am so sorry. We must do something about your cousin."

"We must do nothing. There is nothing to be done. I only need to be careful never to be alone with him."

"What about the Hoffmanns? Shouldn't you tell his parents?"

"To what end? I am not even sure they would believe me, and he would most certainly deny everything. Besides, the shame, the shame falls on me even though he ... he forced himself on me." She started to cry, then took a deep breath to stifle her tears. "Please, it's not something to be talked about."

"He is the one in the wrong, not you. You have done nothing wrong."

"Is memory so short, Jakob? How can you say that I've done nothing wrong? You do not know. Perhaps I didn't struggle enough, perhaps I somehow led him on. With you, there was no perhaps, and soon everyone will know, the world will know."

"What are you talking about?" He followed her gaze as she bowed her head. "Oh, oh no."

"Oh, yes."

"Are you certain?"

"I am."

"It . . . it's Joey's?"

"No, it is yours."

"How can you know?"

"Because I know. These things a woman knows. The timing . . . but men understand none of this, have no need, except when there is need."

"What will you do? I . . ." Jakob was already sorting scenarios in his head, wondering what might be possible, which direction to turn.

"I don't rightly know. I think we have much to talk about."

"I'll marry you, we'll get married."

"A grown Jewish boy and a sixteen-year-old Catholic girl, here in St. Paul. It would never happen. I am still Joseph and Mary Hoffmann's ward. My uncle, particularly, is very strict and quite old fashioned. And I am certain your parents would never approve of such a match. A poor Catholic girl — a domestic, no less, already with child — marrying their son, a Jewish lawyer."

"Not yet a lawyer. And soon I reach my majority and can decide such things on my own."

"But I cannot. And you are assuming that I would want to marry you."

"But . . ." — he was stunned and hurt — "you told me you were in love with me."

"I did. And I meant it. But love does not change circumstance, love does not change families, love does not change the worlds in which we live."

"Lena, please." He stood and reached down to take her hands and draw her to her feet. He stroked her hair and gently drew his thumb along her scratched cheek.

They both jumped at the sound of Morrie Oster clearing his throat. "Ahem, you two." He stepped into the parlor. "Perhaps you both should return to whatever you were doing before our evening was disrupted. Do you need someone to see you home, Maggie?"

"No, sir, I can manage on my own. I'll be leaving now, while it is still light enough. Please tell Mrs. Oster that I will be here in the morning as usual. Goodnight."

She slipped past Morrie and let herself out.

"Well," Morrie said as he creased the fold in his newspaper, "that was most irregular. What did she want with you?"

"That, Papa, is the question. When I learn the answer, perhaps we should sit down for a talk. In the meantime, I will return to my review of the plight of early settlers in our fair city."

"Well, then, perhaps you should see to that. I find no need to perplex your mother with any remark on the irregularities tonight. She finds anything irregular to be most distressing." He looked at Jakob over the top of his reading glasses and waited.

Jakob nodded with a wan smile and left to return to his room. Morrie watched until his son disappeared at the top of the stairs. "Most irregular," he said to himself. "Now I wonder just what our skinny *shamas* has brought into our house."

Chapter 14
Departure

Halbturn, Austria, 1882

The dissonant cadence of a sleepy cock who was late to greet the sun announced their imminent departure. The crowd of neighbors assembled to see the Samsons leave consisted of a few curious children and the Nagy's German shepherd, who sensed something novel going on but could not arouse himself to more than a few desultory sniffs at the wheels of the wagon that now blocked the street.

Josef tugged on a rope to tighten the lashing that held their luggage fast in the bed of the wagon, a cart he had rebuilt for the journey, with added room in the back for a straw mattress on which Mary and Catherina could rest for the forty-three miles to Vienna. The horse belonged to the Brauns, a gracious but easy loan to their departing neighbors, since their son would be living in the Samsons' house and the cart, once delivered back to Halbturn by Hans Peter Braun, would become a wedding present from the Samsons to him and his bride, a lavish but unavoidable gift to the soon-to-be-wed couple. The Samsons could hardly take the cart with them to America.

As is, Josef wondered over the wisdom of what they had packed, what they had not sold at an impromptu auction the Saturday before. The one large trunk and several smaller cases and bundles seemed at once a burdensome excess and yet meager provision for the start of an entirely new life half-way around the world. His brother-in-law's advice in a final letter, had been of scant worth: "Bring what you can manage."

Mary, whose anxiety over the departure had been escalating over recent days filled with sewing and sorting and packing, was already seated in the back, fussing over the contents of her hand luggage. "You are certain about the train and the tickets, Josef? There is enough time, you are sure, and we can purchase our tickets at the railway station in Vienna?"

"Yes." It was a word of frustration frosted with indulgence. "I talked with Father Stefan, and he told me all about it. He has traveled and even once took a trip by rail all the way from Vienna to Rome, although he had little good to say of either city. His brother still lives in Vienna with his family and sends letters regularly. So."

"But you, however, have never done this, never traveled. And now we are doing this, a trip so . . . such a long trip."

Josef reached over the side of the wagon and squeezed her hand. "Everything will be all right. There is no need to worry. It's all taken care of. Here, let me hand Catherina up to you." He turned to his daughter. "Are you ready, my little squirrel?"

The girl nodded and turned around to show off the sailcloth rucksack her mother had sewn for her. "See." She had slept with the rucksack ever since Mary had surprised her with it the week before. Catherina held up her favorite doll, the one with the porcelain head and a new dress Mary had also sewn to match the one that Catherina now wore. "Hannah is ready, too."

"I am glad to hear that. So, now up you go." Josef swung his daughter and her doll up beside Mary. "Then you and Hannah should wave goodbye to the house and the garden.

We are going on an adventure, an adventure all the way to America."

"Is it far away, Papa?"

"Very far. But your mother and I will be with you all the way to our new home. There we will start a new life, a good life. And you will meet your cousins."

"When? Today? Will we get there today? Will we meet my cousins today?"

"No, it is so far that it will take many days — by wagon, by train, and by steamship."

"How will we know how to get there if it is so far?"

"Today, we just follow the road, *Weiner Strasse*, all the way to the city, Vienna. And there, we will board a train that will know which way to take us to Germany."

"And when do we come back, Papa?"

Josef looked to Mary, pleading with his eyes. She tightened her arms around Catherina and stroked her head. "Our new home is in America," she said. "Maybe someday we will come back, but not for a long time." Catherina started to cry, and silent tears began to wet the cheeks of her mother.

Josef cleared his throat and circled the wagon for one last inspection, stealing only a glance at the house that had been his home for so many years. "Well, Hans Peter," he said, as he climbed to sit beside the young man, "it is time we were off if we are to reach the train station by early afternoon and you are to be back before dark." The wagon lurched and rattled as the horse began to pull slowly up the street. The Nagy's dog finally came to life with a barking sendoff. Josef turned in his seat to find Mary staring off, not back at the house they were leaving but into the distance, down the *Frauenkirchen Landstrasse*, toward the world she had left, a world that refused even to acknowledge her departure.

✧≫≪✧

Hans Peter had taken over the reins for the last miles toward Vienna, and they had made good time. The elaborate stonework of the *Staatsbahnhof* came into view as the clock atop the entrance showed just past one. The clock overlooked a balcony guarded by larger-than-life statues of four bare-breasted women robed in classic garb. As Cathia laughed and pointed at the figures, Hans Peter maneuvered the wagon as close as he could get to the curb, then hopped down from the seat to begin unloading luggage with Josef. Together, he and Josef slid the largest trunk to the edge and off the back, standing it on end on the pavement.

"There you go, Josef, that is the last of them. Are you sure you can manage from here?"

"I can manage, I'm sure. If not, I can borrow a hand truck or get one of the porters to lend us a hand. You best be off." Even with a strong fresh horse, the journey from Halbturn had taken all morning. "It is a long ride back to Halbturn, and there is only a sliver of moon tonight. What will you do if you cannot make it before nightfall?"

"That's my problem to face if I need. Take care of yourself and your family, Josef. That should be enough for you."

Mary now sat on one of the suitcases with Catherina already drifting into an afternoon nap in her lap. Their departure so early had taxed them all, but Josef felt it was necessary to be sure they reached Vienna in time to board their train for the overnight journey to Berlin. Once there, they would take another train to Hamburg where they would stay the night in temporary quarters provided by the steamship line before boarding the ship for New York.

Josef took Hans Peter's hand and shook it firmly. "Good luck. And congratulations to you and your bride-to-be. I am sorry we will miss the wedding, but I hope you both are happy in the house."

"I am sure we will be. And we have a fine new wagon as well. Thank you, Josef. *Auf wiedersehen. Viel Glück und eine gute Reise.*"

"Yes, goodbye and good luck to you also on your journey."

The Samsons watched as Hans Peter drove away, the wagon's iron-tired wheels rattling loudly over the cobblestones.

Josef exhaled sharply as if to punctuate the separation. "Why don't you and Catherina wait here with the luggage while I scout inside and see where we need to be."

The décor was more sterile and the columns were not sheathed in gold, but the grand entry hall of the station, with its high arched ceiling and baroque decoration, was oddly reminiscent of the *basilika* back in Frauenkirchen. In the midday crowds it took several minutes for Josef to find his way to the queue at a window selling tickets. When at last he reached the front of the line, the man on the other side of the barred opening looked up and said, "Yes?"

"The through train for Berlin, I need three tickets, for my wife and me and our daughter, Catherina, who is three. When does it leave?"

"It does not. I am afraid there is no train for Berlin, none in fact to the north. Only to the south and east. Do you wish to go to Budapest, to Trieste? Or perhaps all the way to Rome. For that I can sell you tickets."

"No, there is a train to Berlin, I know. We were told, from Vienna to Dresden and Berlin and then to Hamburg. We have booked passage to America by steamship in two days. We must be there. See," he removed a creased packet of papers from the pocket in his jacket and carefully unfolded them. "See, these are our passports, and here is the letter confirming our steamship passage. Surely you know of this train to Berlin."

"Of course I know of trains for Berlin, but there are no trains for Berlin from here. You are at the wrong station. You want the new station, the *Nordwestbahnhof*. I can't help you." He looked past Josef to the man next in line.

"But ... but how do we get there, to this other train station?" Josef pleaded. "We have our luggage. And our little girl. We have to get the train to Berlin."

"I don't know. Take a carriage. You'll see them in the rank opposite the station. Now please, there are people wanting to purchase tickets." He raised a finger to signal the man behind Josef.

Josef's heart pounded with panic as he pushed through the crowd to get back outside. Catherina was now standing atop the upended trunk, holding her doll aloft and pretending to dance like a monkey. "Papa, papa," she called. "Over here. Guess what we saw."

"I cannot guess, and I have no time for guessing games."

"But, Papa, I saw a monkey, a real one, who danced with music that came from a box this man carried."

"Look, be quiet. I must get us a carriage."

Mary cocked her head. "I thought we were going to Germany by train. Surely no carriage can take us to Germany."

"Surely. But the train we want does not leave from this station. I didn't know that. I still don't understand how there can be more than one train station. Is one not enough for a city? At any rate, wait here again with the luggage, and I will try to find a carriage that will take us to the right station."

⋙ ⋘

It had taken considerable time for all their luggage to be stuffed into and strapped onto the carriage by a driver who seemed none too happy with the prospect of taking on such a midday fare. The dappled mare in harness seemed even less enthusiastic. Indeed, their progress soon was slowed by heavy traffic, by people crossing the street on foot, and by vendors with carts narrowing the way. The city seemed to stretch on forever, and the trip to the far side of Vienna was taking much longer than Josef expected. He looked nervously at the sun, already high in the summer sky. With no watch in his pocket to check, he strained to count the bells of a clock tower in the distance. Was that two or had he missed one chime? What if they are late, he wondered. He had no experience with trains, and his life had never been one run by schedules. It was beyond him what might happen if they missed the train for Berlin. Perhaps he should have allowed more time, maybe they should have left days earlier. He was agitated and felt powerless. The Ring Road on which they now traveled took them around the densest heart of the city, but it was crowded in the middle of the day with carts and wagons and hansom cabs, none of which seemed to be moving as fast as he wanted.

Josef leaned forward to speak to the carriage driver. "How long will it take? Is there no other road to the station?"

The driver turned in his seat. "There," he pointed. "See ahead? Just there on the left is the road we want. That leads directly to the new station, the *Nordwestbahnhof*."

"Are you certain?"

"What, do you think I don't know my own city? I live here, on this side of town. I take people to and from the train stations all the time. Ahead is the new station, I tell you, with the train service you want, all the way to Berlin through Dresden. There is nothing to worry about. There is plenty of time. Besides, there is a train every day."

✦ ⟫⟫ ⟪⟪ ✦

More than twenty minutes passed before the vast bulk of the *Nordwestbahnhof* loomed ahead. Catherina pulled herself standing and held onto the edge of the carriage as she leaned out to peer around the driver. "Papa, I have never seen such a building. It is larger than *Schloss Halbturn*. Who lives there?"

"No one lives there, Cathia. It is the building for the train, the train that will take us to the far city called Berlin. Then we will go on another train to Hamburg."

"Is Hamburg in America?"

"No, my silly squirrel. Hamburg is where we will get on a steamship, an enormous boat that will take us to America."

"Always you say 'America,' Papa. I am tired of it. I do not want to hear any more about America. I want to go home."

"The train and the ship will take us home."

"I do not think so, Pappa. Hans Peter brought us to this place. He will take us home."

"Hans Peter is already on his way back to Halbturn."

"And that is where I want to go. I don't want to go to America." She held up her doll. "Hannah thinks America is a terrible place. She doesn't want to go there either." Cathia started to cry.

"America is a fine place, a beautiful place."

"How do you know? Have you ever been there, Papa?"

"No."

"Then how do you know?" She spoke between already fading sobs.

"I have seen pictures, and so have you. Your uncle has sent us postcards, remember? With pictures of St. Paul."

"But those were pictures of St. Paul, Papa, not America."

"St. Paul is in America, just like Halbturn is in Austria."

"I don't understand. But I already know I don't like America, and I will never go there."

"Okay, then, but instead how would you like to go for a fun ride on a train with us, a train with a big metal engine that can go very fast?"

"Yes, I would like to ride on a train. Then after that we can go back home to Halbturn."

⇛ ⇚

This time Josef had no trouble locating the ticket window from the length of its queue. When at last he reached the counter, he explained what he wanted to the agent, who told him how many gulden it would cost, much more than Josef had thought. Counting out the folded banknotes from the pouch he wore tied to his belt, he smiled and thanked the man, who slid the tickets toward him and asked for the next in line to step forward. As Josef was turning away, he fanned the tickets to read what was marked on them. "But wait, this is the wrong date. These tickets are for tomorrow. We want to travel today."

"They are for tomorrow because the train today is about to leave. There is no time."

"But the carriage driver told us there was plenty of time."

"What does a carriage driver know of train schedules?"

"But what are we to do? We must reach Hamburg. We already booked passage to America. My wife and daughter . . ."

"Give me the tickets back then."

"But . . ."

"I will change them for you, but I can do nothing about the train. It leaves when it leaves, at 2:30."

"But I thought it left at 3:30."

"That was the old schedule. Now it leaves," — the man glanced up at the big clock at the end of the hall — "in ten

105

minutes." He handed the tickets back to Josef. "You should waste no time."

Josef, whose life had never operated at this pace, was near panic. He stuffed the tickets into his pocket and edged his way through the crowd to look for Mary and Catherina. "Ah, there you are. I told you not to move, to stay with the luggage." His voice was harsh and impatient.

"I thought we might need a porter," Mary answered. "Our bags are already loaded onto his cart, and he is waiting by the left gate to the train hall. See? Over there."

"I . . ."

"If you have the tickets, we should board our train. The porter said it is about to depart." Her face carried something just short of a smile, a look of silent triumph that Josef recognized and remembered from their days of arguing questions of faith.

"Yes, then we should board, as you say." He gathered their hand baggage as Mary took Catherina's hand and led the way. At the gate to the great hall, Josef told the porter waiting with their bags that they were boarding. The man made no move but only stood beside his cart with his hand at his waist, upturned.

"Pay the man, Josef, so that we can be on our way."

"Ah, right. Uh, . . ." He fished in his pocket for some coins and placed them in the porter's palm. "We're going to Hamburg . . . I mean Berlin. Please be sure our bags go with us."

The man stole a glance at his palm before pocketing the money. "Very well, sir." His broad smile told Josef that the tip was too much.

Beyond the gate, the engine stood hissing, sending steady smoke up toward the glass and ironwork roof high overhead. Catherina clung to her mother's leg and looked around with fright. She jumped and reached up in terror when the train whistle sounded a warning blast. They hurried past the impatient engine even as the conductor was calling for all passengers to board. Josef nervously checked their tickets and scanned the markings on the sides of the train carriages. "I think we are in a car farther down, toward the back of the train."

With his arm held high, the conductor waved them and a few other stragglers toward the steps on the carriages. "Third class?" Josef asked as they passed the man.

"Second to last car. You must hurry." He opened his pocket watch. "The train leaves on time. This is Austria, not Italy."

Josef shifted the straps of their handbags and took Catherina from Mary to race toward their car. There he stood, one foot on the step, one on the ground, a futile gesture in attempt to prevent the train from departing until his wife caught up. She did her best, but she was heavy with child, and the train lurched with much loud clanking as the engine started to reverse to back out of the station. The drive wheels squealed, steel on steel, as the train began to inch backwards. Josef set Catherina on the top step at the end of the car and reached out toward Mary, who half ran, half waddled the remaining yards before he could grab her hand. With their combined strength, she was able to get a foot onto the high first step of the car. She clung with her free hand to the handrail while catching her breath. As the train picked up speed, Josef helped her up the rest of the steps.

"I hope the baby likes excitement," she said. "Perhaps he will be an equestrian. Posting to a trot will already be familiar after this."

Josef grinned down at her. "So long as he does not enter

the cavalry as did my brother. Come, let's find seats." Josef led the way up the aisle of the third-class car, with Miriam carrying Catherina. Only one of the slatted wooden benches was still completely unoccupied, and Josef hurried forward before a man in a leather jacket coming from the other end could reach it. "Here, Mary, we can sit here."

Catherina clambered over to the window and kneeled to look out as the train pulled from the station. "How long does it take the train to get to . . . to the other town?"

"Nineteen hours, or so I was told. We sleep on the train tonight, my little squirrel, and arrive in Berlin tomorrow morning."

Her eyes widened. "We sleep on the train? Where are the beds?"

"Right here, Cathia. Don't worry, we will be fine. Are you hungry? Mama has bread and cheese in her bag."

Chapter 15
Connections

Berlin and Hamburg, Germany, 1882

Announced by steam, smoke, and the screech of brakes as wheels reversed, the train rolled into Berlin's *Dresdner Bahnhof* just before ten in the morning, within a few minutes of its expected arrival time. Catherina was wide awake and watching with her nose pressed against the window. She, alone among the three of them, had slept more than short stretches during the long, noisy night, including a slow passage around the outskirts of Dresden in the early morning hours. "Oh, look, Mama, it's another castle for trains. Is this America?"

Mary rubbed her eyes. "No, *meine Liebchen*, this is Dresden. No, wait, not Dresden. We are now in Berlin. This is still the German Empire. Berlin is the capital city of Germany, like Vienna is the capital of Austria."

"Like Vienna? Will we ride in a carriage again, with a dappled horse and a driver with a tall whip?"

"I don't know. Perhaps your father will know. Josef, wake up. We are arriving in Berlin."

Catherina crawled over her mother and started pushing on her father's shoulder. "Papa, Papa. Wake up."

⇻ ⇺

The depot was disappointing, small and inelegant compared to the monumental stations they had left behind in Austria. It was crowded, busy, and already strained to capacity despite its short history. As they alighted, Josef looked around to get his bearings. This time he knew what to do. They had arrived at the *Dresdner Bahnhof* but would need to depart from the *Hamburg Bahnhof* on the north side of the city. First, they would need to collect their luggage, then he would have to negotiate transportation to the other station.

As they inched through the turmoil of arriving and departing crowds, Catherina tugged at her mother's hand. "I'm hungry."

"I'm sorry, but you already ate the last apple. And the nutmeats. I am glad you are eating so well, but we already ate up everything I brought."

Josef turned a full circle, craning his neck to scan the crowded station. "See if you can find something to eat, Mary. The people of Berlin must also get hungry. I'll try to retrieve our bags. Let's meet back here, by this lamppost."

"All right then." Mary reached toward her daughter. "Come, my little monkey, let's see what we can find here. Oh, look, over there. I think I see a vendor selling sausages. Do you think you might like to eat a *Berliner Bratwurst* for breakfast?"

"Is that like a *Würstl*, Mama?"

"I don't know, but we can find out whether a Berlin sausage is like a Vienna sausage. Just do not let go of my hand. There are so many people here, I would not want to lose my little monkey."

"And I will hold tight to Hannah. I would not want to lose her either." Cathia grew excited as they approached the cart with its charcoal brazier glowing. "Oh, look, Mama, he has a fire in his cart."

Mary smiled at the vendor and asked for three sausages. He wiped his hands on his apron and put three fat sausages to warm on the metal grating above the charcoal. "The lady is from the south, I think," he said, "but not Bavaria. Am I right?"

"Austria. We just arrived from Vienna."

"I should have known from the accent. And who is this charming little lady with you?"

Cathia ducked behind her mother's skirt. "That is Catherina. She is a shy little monkey today."

"I am not," she said, still hidden. "I'm a little squirrel. Papa says so."

The vendor leaned far to the side, trying to get a peek at Cathia. "And would the little squirrel want her sausage *mit Senf*? Do squirrels from the south like mustard?"

Cathia made a broad-jump out from behind her mother. "Yes, yes they do!"

Mary looked down at her. "Are you sure?"

"Yes, I'm sure."

"Okay, then, three, *drei Würstchen mit Senf*," Mary ordered.

"*Und sauerkraut?*"

"Of course."

"That will be two marks." He held out a square of newsprint holding the first of the bread rolls with its sausage and sauerkraut dripping with brown mustard.

"I only have gulden. I didn't think. We just came from Vienna."

The man put on a look of deep disappointment and shook his head slowly side-to-side. From the far side of the cart, a woman in a pale blue dress approached. Her silver-gray hair was pulled up tight under a broad-brimmed sun hat trimmed with a ribbon to match her dress. She came around to stand beside Mary, where she leaned in and whispered, sotto voce, "He's overcharging you."

"What should I do? I have no marks, only gulden."

"Wait, Mama." Cathia slipped off her rucksack and placed it on the ground. She undid the big button on the back and reached inside to pull out a small red cloth purse. She carefully opened the tucked-in flap. "Can we use any of this money?" She held up a fistful of notes.

"What is this? Where did you get this?"

"From Aunt Esterl. She gave it to me. She said we might need it when we traveled."

"Aunt Esterl? When did you ever see your aunt." Mary's eyebrows arched in surprise and confusion.

"Many times. She visits and talks with me. Is this good money?"

Mary looked at the wad of banknotes in Cathia's tiny hand: German marks, Austrian gulden with one side printed in German, the other in Hungarian, even some American dollars. "Oh, Esterl." She clapped her hands to her face and started to cry.

"Are you all right, Mama? Did I do something wrong?"

"No, little one, you did nothing wrong. I am so glad you and Aunt Esterl could talk. I didn't know. I only wish . . ."

The sausage vendor sighed. "Does the lady want her sausages or not."

"The lady does." It was the woman in blue. "And she'll pay no more than one mark. Fifty *pfennig* might be more the fairer. So, little girl, do you have any coins in that magic red purse of yours?"

"I think so." Cathia reached in and held out several coins.

"Can you find a coin with a big number one on it? Do you know your numbers yet?"

"Oh, yes. I can count. One, two, three, four, five, and, uh . . . Here, this has a one on it. Is this the right kind?"

"It is. You are a very bright little girl. Now, you can put the rest of your money away. Just give the coin to this man, and he will give you your sausage and the other two to your mother."

Mary turned to the woman. "Thank you, you are most kind, most helpful."

"There is no need to thank me. I remember what it was like traveling when Werner and Maxi were small. Are you on an excursion?"

"Not exactly, we are on our way to America. We have to get the train to Hamburg. There is a ship . . ."

"Ah, indeed. My husband and I have made the crossing twice. If the weather holds, it should be a fine sailing. Look, you will have to get to the *Hamburg Bahnhof*, and you have your child, and . . . well, in your, shall I say, condition. If you will permit me, I can have my carriage take you.

"Oh, yes, oh my, forgive me. I am such a scatter-wit this morning. Please permit me to introduce myself. I am Cecile Schiller, at your service." She held out her hand to Mary.

"Mary Samson, at yours. Catherina you have met. And that is my husband, Josef, who is trundling toward us with the towering handcart about to tumble its contents onto the pavement."

"Oh, my. Well, I shall get Gunther to come to his aid. Just wait here, please, and I shall return in but a moment."

⇒⇒ ⇐⇐

At Cecile's insistence, the ride in the Schiller's ample carriage became a tour of Berlin. "There is no hurry for you to meet your train, and how could you leave Berlin without seeing something of our great city. You know, since it became the capital of the Empire with so much built anew, it is now said to be the most American city in all of Europe."

With its broad avenues, open plazas, many-storied new buildings, and countless bridges, the effect was one of great pretentions that Mary found overwhelming. At the grand tree-trimmed plaza of the *Königsplatz*, Gunther stopped the carriage for everyone to stretch their legs. Cathia ran ahead to chase a red squirrel up a tree while the grownups took their time taking the air around the vast oval.

Mary shaded her eyes from the high sun as she looked around. "This one plaza seems larger than all of Frauenkirchen. If this is what America is like, I don't know how we shall cope."

"Quite well, I am sure. You have already shown yourselves to be most resourceful. But, whatever the writers say, I believe even the best of America's cities have nothing on our Berlin. And now, everyone back to the carriage and on to the *Hamburg Bahnhof.*"

By the time they finally approached the train station, Cathia was overtired and fussy. "I don't want to see another house for trains. I want to go home."

Cecile took her into her lap and nuzzled her nose. "You are a squirrel, are you not? Didn't your father call you his little squirrel?" Cathia nodded. "Well, there are squirrels everywhere. For squirrels, everywhere is home."

"Everywhere? Even in America?"

"Even in America."

"How do you know? Have you been to America?"

"I have. I have been to America twice. And there are squirrels in America, I can tell you that. There are squirrels in New York City, in Central Park, and in Boston. Squirrels belong everywhere. You know, sometimes I think I am a bit of a squirrel, too, like you. I was born in France, in the Alsace, and now I live in Germany, and I have visited America and

England and Spain. Squirrels are everywhere. Also little girls."

"I have cousins in America. I don't know if they are girls. Are my cousins girls, Mama?"

"Yes, one, and boys."

Cecile tapped Catherina's nose. "There you have it. You are off to see your American cousins and American squirrels, and you will have a splendid time. And one more thing."

"What is that?"

"You will have your mother write to me and tell me all about you and your squirrel adventures. I will give her my address, and you will make certain she posts a letter to me. Will you do that?"

"I will." Cathia nodded gravely.

⇒» «⇐

At the *Hamburg Bahnhof*, Josef repeated what was becoming a ritual responsibility of setting forth to secure tickets and arrange for their baggage.

Cecile and Mary had hardly stopped talking during the entire carriage tour of Berlin, and now they stood holding each other's hands, taking their time at goodbyes.

"I don't know how to thank you," Mary said.

"Nor I. Sharing your daughter with me was a gift. She reminds me so of my Maxi at that age."

"And how old is your daughter now?"

"Six."

"Six? Forgive me, but I had somehow pictured you as having grown children. I am so embarrassed."

"Please don't be. My son is grown, an architect living in Frankfurt am Main, with three nearly grown children of his own. My daughter died when she was six, when the influenza struck in '51. She will always be six years old."

"I am so sorry."

Cecile struggled to maintain her composure. "What is ... what is so troublesome, is that it never stops hurting. Never." She turned to the side for a moment, then turned back with a smile, genuine and forced at the same time. "Treasure each moment, hold her close even as you let her go, and never take any moment of your time together for granted." She gave Mary's hand's a last squeeze. "You have my address. Do please write me from America."

Chapter 16
Crossing

Hamburg, Germany, S/S Allemannia, 1882

For Josef, the days had already begun to blur. Another interminable ride, another city, more people, Mary more tired and Cathia more whingy. The night at the emigration center, a warehouse for the departing, was worse than sleeping on the train, and by morning, Josef was exhausted, eager to board their ship and be on their way to New York.

The man next to him, whose worn tweed jacket smelled of rain and cigar smoke, was a talker who seemed determined to fill even the shortest pause in the steady din with yet more words. "'tis a new ship, you know, nearly new. That'll be good for us 'n' all. Built only last year in Glasgow, she was, and her maiden voyage to New York was just this time a year ago. She's the second ship by this name for the line, you know." He spoke German with a thick accent that made Josef wonder where he was from. "We Scots are the best shipbuilders in the world."

"You are from Scotland, then?"

"Aye, but I have lived here and in Bremen for years. Too many, I say. My brother says it is ever so much better in America: better work, better pay, better women. The Germans, especially the women, are, no offence to you or your good wife, mind you, somewhat on the stiff side. Present comp'ny excepted, I would say, I am sure." He nodded toward the sleeping form of Mary beside Josef on the bench.

"We're not German. We are Austrian."

"Same difference. And you and the missus are off to the New World, then, are you? Where might you be headed? My brothers are, like me, in shipbuilding. From New York, I'll be headed to Bath, that's in Maine, I'm told. The Germans, if you don't mind my saying, are fine engineers when it comes to trains and bridges and the like, but when it comes to shipbuilding, they just have not got the hang of it all."

In hopes the man would end his monologue, Josef nodded politely and looked away to where Mary and Cathia were still sleeping.

The man continued. "Now, over in Bremen, that is where you can get the faster, better passage to America, on Norddeutscher Lloyd. They run steamships that cut the time to New York by days. Here, Hamburg-Amerika Linie, they can't keep up. Some of their older ships have even been fitted with a second funnel to look like the faster ships, but it's a fake.

"So, I would imagine you be wondering why I am not sailing out of Bremen. And I would wonder myself, were it not that I have not the funds to get to Bremen and also pay the premium for a shorter crossing. Hamburg and Bremen are in the fiercest competition, you know, so it is cheaper to go from here. I imagine that is why you are sailing from here. What with a wife and child — and it looks like another in the oven — you would want to shorten the voyage, if you could, that is."

Josef was able to extricate himself from the talkative Scot only when the representative of the company entered the hall holding aloft a sign that read *Hamburg-Amerikanische-Packetfahrt-Actien-Gesellschaft*, the official name of the steamship line. He called for attention, starting a wave of shushing that spread through the hall like the tide on a sloping shore. It was a false alarm. Instructions they had already heard were repeated, and they were told to wait.

⇢≫ ≪⇠

Cathia, after two days already a seasoned traveler for whom trains and immense stations were no longer frightening, cowered behind her mother at the sight of the ship. The S/S Allemannia was nearly three-hundred feet long, rigged with tall masts fore and aft to carry sail and with a pair of funnels amidships spewing smoke from the coal-fired steam boiler into the calm morning air. Josef noted smoke coming from both funnels and smiled to himself.

"See that long bridge ahead?" He pointed. "It is called a gangway, and we are going to walk all the way from the dock here, all the way up to the ship." When the time came, Cathia insisted on taking both their hands, which meant Josef had to manage all their hand luggage with only one free hand. Reluctantly, he passed one trussed cloth bundle to Mary. The trek up the long gangway stretched on and on, marked by frequent pauses without explanation as some holdup or another ahead halted the procession of nearly four hundred third-class passengers.

At the temporary overnight quarters for emigrants, Josef had begun to appreciate the meaning of third-class accommodations and to learn just how it was that they had been able to afford passage all the way to New York plus onward travel by rail halfway across the American continent to the city of St. Paul. Other travelers who were better informed, whose relatives had led the way and shared more details of their journeys, had provided a quick education.

"The board will be plain but ample, God bless the Brits. They made it a law, forcing the German and Italian steamship lines to meet the competition, if you know what I mean.

I tell you," the pretty young woman had said to Mary, "when my sister made the crossing in steerage six years ago, you had to bring and cook your own food. It took her ship twenty-one days, on account of weather, and there were some very hungry people 'tween decks by the time they disembarked at New York Harbor."

Mary scowled. "Are you sure about the food? Maybe I should try to buy some before we board tomorrow. My Cathia is such a skinny little squirrel as it is. I wouldn't —"

"Naw, it'll be good. I got a letter from my sister just last month. Her neighbor made the crossing from Hamburg earlier this year and said there was no shortage of food, only a shortage of room to breathe. She told me to spend as much time on deck as the crew and the weather permit. That's my plan. Oh, and you might see if you can get some oranges on the dock. Apples and prunes is all you can expect in the way of fruit until landfall."

≫ ≪

At the top of the stairway leading down into the between decks accommodations for steerage passengers, Josef was hit by the smell. "Antiseptic soap. At least it will be clean," he said to Mary. The man behind him muttered, "For now, that is. Just you wait until we are at sea for a week without it being cleaned again."

The forewarning about room to breathe quickly proved itself. The steerage passengers, that is, those with third-class tickets, were herded into a windowless cavern divided into three sections. Single men were sent to one section, single women to another, and married couples and families were assigned to a third section that served as a buffer between the quarters for single passengers. The accommodations consisted of rows of narrow bunks on either side, stacked three high with barely two feet of head room and only a narrow aisle between the stacked beds. Each bedframe was topped with a thin straw-filled mattress. Down the middle of the space were long tables butted end-to-end and flanked by simple wooden benches.

"Where do we stow our things?" Josef said to a steward who was telling people to move along.

"Take a bunk. That's yours. That's it. Do with it as you like. Now move along."

Josef urged Mary and Cathia to follow him. He stopped at each empty stack of berths and turned his face upward. Finally he made a beeline for one. "Here, this one; the air will be better." He pointed to what appeared to be a vent overhead. "This is what we will do. You and Cathia will share the bottom bunk, easier for you to get in and out of, and I will sleep in the middle one. We'll stow our things up top, out of the way, maybe a few things underneath the bottom one, too. See? Plenty of room for everyone and everything."

A young steward with a pock-marked face and a crucifix dangling from a leather braid around his neck pushed through the milling passengers. "Hey, you there. Let me see your tickets."

Josef fished in his pocket for the tickets and handed them over. "I also have the letter from the agent that says that we paid, that we were guaranteed passage."

"Well, I don't know nothing about letters, Mister, so you keep it." He spoke with a Bavarian accent that reminded Josef of home. "If they let you board, that's good enough for me. But I wouldn't settle in just yet. I've sent for the ship's surgeon. When he gets here we'll see whether you're allowed to sail with us. Just stay right here."

Before Josef could ask what it was all about, the steward

left and wove his way back to the stairs. Soon, a portly man appeared at the top and struggled to negotiate the steep stairs, nearly tripping on the last step. As he approached with the steward, the smell of alcohol was evident, but when he came over to the Samsons it became clear that the odor originated with his hands, which must have been freshly rinsed with strong spirits for medical reasons.

"Ah, I see, this is the couple," he said. "Is this your wife?" he addressed Josef while looking at Mary.

"Yes, I'm Josef Samson, and this is my wife Mary. We are on our way —"

"May I just speak to your wife, please? Thank you. Madam, can you tell me when you were last with the curse?"

Mary was taken aback, but immediately figured out what the steward was concerned about and why he had been summoned. "March, no February," she lied, as she quickly counted in her head.

"So, you are in your sixth month, then. Is that right?"

"Yes, as I reckon. We are expecting in November. I think it is a boy from the way I am carrying."

"Hmmm. Very well then. We prefer not to take on passengers who will be giving birth even as we are setting out to sea, if you can understand. Try to take the air as often as you can and avoid eating pulses with your salt pork, if you can. It does not agree with mothers-to-be, in my experience." He turned to the steward. "Carry on, and try not to summon me for every little thing."

Cathia, who had been cowering at the back of the bottom bunk with her doll, finally peeked out with her thumb set firmly in her mouth. Mary sat down beside her on the edge of the bunk. "Everything is right, my little one, and soon we will be setting to sea, and then soon we will be in America."

It was taking a long time for the passengers to settle in, and there were some arguments over who might have which berth, especially when it came to the couples without children, all of whom seemed to expect to have a three-berth set to themselves. When the steam whistle sounded and the low grumbling of the big vertical steam engine increased in pitch and volume, there was a rush among the passengers to hurry back up to the deck to watch the departure back down the Elbe and into the North Sea. Josef carried Cathia up, but she quickly became bored and asked to return to her mother.

⋙ ⋘

On the third day under steam, the Allemannia put into port. Cathia was excited. "We're here. We made it to America."

Josef picked her up. "No, my silly squirrel, this is France not America. We stop here at Le Havre to take on more passengers."

"More passengers? But where will they sleep. There are no more beds."

"That is a very good question, and I don't know the answer."

The answer was that some of the tables were dismantled by crew and stowed below, making room for more bunks to be stacked at either end of each of the three sections. When the boarding French passengers arrived, they were told to find what place they could. In the end, there were more unaccompanied young women seeking to sail to America than the female section could hold, and several women were told to find space among the couples and families. This resulted in a fresh round of disputes that was settled only after one of the stewards intervened with a threat to call the captain and have a particularly vocal couple thrown off.

The disputes and arguments became a part of the rhythm of life aboard the Allemannia as it headed west across the Atlantic. There were arguments over the food, which the stewards left in bowls and kettles in the center of the long tables. This the passengers dished out themselves onto enamel plates that they were also expected to wash. There were disputes over territorial incursions and items that disappeared from one bunk or another. And there were reprimands for children who whined about the food or played too loudly or who chased each other along the benches when the tables were not in use for meals.

The astringent smell of freshly washed deck gave way to the stench of sweat and air made foul by uneaten food and by seasick passengers who failed to reach a bucket in time. Until the first storm, Josef took to spending much of his waking hours on deck. For three days, the hatches were sealed and steerage became a dark hellhole of sickened and frustrated passengers with nothing to do and nowhere to go. Meals became irregular, with children crying that they were hungry as their parents moaned with nausea and prayed for the rains to end. Then the weather cleared. By comparison to the bad weather days, life between decks was good again, or at least bearable.

⇒ ⇐

The fever struck without warning. One day, everyone who was not seasick was fine, the next it seemed as if a quarter of the passengers in steerage were lying listless and feverish. On his daily check, the ship's surgeon ordered that all those with what he called "shipboard fever" be isolated from the rest of the passengers. There was not enough room in the ship's hospital for all the sick, so the stewards organized for the single women to vacate their section and move in with the families, converting the vacated section into a temporary isolation ward.

An older man who had been traveling with his daughter and grandchildren was the first to die. As the blanket-wrapped body was carried out, people covered their mouths and turned away. While the crew members hoisted the body up the steep stairs, the room filled with a quiet cacophony of mumbled prayers in a blur of languages and disparate traditions.

The following morning, as the ship's surgeon made his way down the row of bunks on his regular rounds, Mary quickly removed the damp cloth from Cathia's forehead, which she wiped dry with the sleeve of her dress. She tucked the rag behind her.

"And you, Missus . . ."

"Samson, Mary Samson."

"Yes. Any fever, palpitations, abdominal distress?"

"No, I'm well, thank you. My husband also. He's taking the air on deck."

"And the little girl?"

"Tired from playing hard up on deck yesterday. I thought I'd let her sleep."

"Mmmm." He put the back of his hand to Cathia's forehead for a second, then shrugged. "No, no fever." He moved on to the next bunks, and Mary stopped holding her breath.

For the rest of the day, Mary tried to get Cathia to eat and drink to keep up her strength. She squeezed juice from the last of the oranges into her daughters mouth, but it dribbled out when Cathia's head dropped to the side. Mary did her best to hide her actions from the others, but eventually, a delegation of mothers, one of them nursing her baby, confronted her.

"Your kid is sick. She has to be quarantined. You're putting us all at risk."

"She's only three. She needs me. And she'll be better soon, I know."

"If you don't take her, we'll tell the stewards and they'll take her. That's the rules."

"No, I'll do it. I'll go with her. Someone has to take care of her." Mary slid awkwardly out of the bed and lifted her sleeping daughter.

The women shook their heads in unison. "How many months? When are you expecting?"

"September. We want the baby to be born in America."

The nursing mother looked toward the ad hoc isolation ward. "You can't go in there, you'll be risking your baby, too."

"And what am I to do? Cathia is also my baby. Would any of you take care of her in the quarantine section? No? And would any of you just leave your child alone there? No, of course not. Now, please make way so I can take her to quarantine. I'll be back for her things."

"No, that's all right. Let me help."

The next morning, just after breakfast, a cry of anguish broke the quiet in the quarantine section. It was a woman's voice, crying out in Yiddish, a language that only a few of the passengers recognized.

⇛ ⇚

The ship had slowed against the winds now coming off the starboard bow. Sparks flashed amidst the smoke pouring from the twin funnels as the boilers were fed extra coal to maintain headway. Gentle swells had given way to rising seas and the fore and aft masts, sails furled, whistled and whimpered like bare trees in winter.

Mary was facing away. She would not allow herself to look

at what rested on the three planks lined up at the leeward rail, each flanked by deck hands. On the recommendation of the ship's surgeon, the captain had ordered that the bodies of all victims of the outbreak would not be stored and carried to port, but would have to be buried at sea. Of the three sailcloth bundles stitched shut, one seemed impossibly small. Josef stood at the head of that plank, stoically staring out to sea.

From amidships, a man dressed in simple black vestments approached the small group gathered on deck. His round face was accented by round spectacles and was set with a determined expression, perhaps meant to convey sympathy but grim in its effect. He came first to Josef and held out both hands. "I am so sorry for your loss. I'm Reverend Constantine, Trico Constantine. The Captain has asked me to preside and to say a few words."

"You're not a priest, then?"

"No, there does not seem to be a priest aboard, neither Catholic nor Anglican. I am, however, a man of God, an ordained Methodist Episcopal minister."

He turned to the other mourners, a young woman who had lost her husband and an older man whose wife had died only hours before. He introduced himself and took their hands, then stepped back to speak to the group. "My deepest sympathies go out to all of you, but the captain has asked us to be brief, on account of the weather taking another turn for the worse."

True to his word, he began immediately, "I am the resurrection and the life, saith the Lord. Whosoever believeth in Me, though he were dead, yet shall he live, and whosoever liveth and believeth in Me shall not die, but shall have life eternal.

"Let us pray. Our father, who art in heaven, hallowed be thy name. Thy kingdom come . . ."

As the minister continued, Josef whispered the words, but then stopped when he realized they were reciting slightly different versions of the same prayer. Why, he wondered, did we all have to make so much of such small differences? Were we not, as Miriam had once said, all children of the same God? Children. His eyes dropped to the shroud on the wooden board in front of him. A slight bulge betrayed where, on Mary's insistence, the doll Hannah had been placed in Cathia's arms. Josef gritted his teeth and tightened his fists at his side, fighting back tears.

Reverend Constantine had moved on, turning to the Psalms. "The Lord is my shepherd, I shall not want," he began. Josef turned to where Mary stood, still facing away, her body rocking rhythmically in that way she had once explained that Jews moved when they prayed. He closed his eyes and listened to the Psalm, recited in a preacher's voice that rose above the sounds of wind, of waves, and the grinding of the engines below deck. "And I shall dwell in the house of the Lord forever."

The man stepped over beside Josef and put his hand on Josef's back before praying once more, this time in a lowered voice. "As we commit the earthly remains of our sister Catherina Maria Samson to the deep, grant her peace until that day when all who believe in You shall be raised in glory to a new life. We ask this in the name of Jesus Christ our Lord and Savior. Amen."

Josef watched as the sailors loosened the lashings holding the body to the plank, tilted it, and let the tiny white bundle slide over the side. Above the wind and rush of water, no splash could be heard. Josef gulped. Behind him, Mary fell to the deck and wailed. He knelt down beside her and held her as the same brief ritual was repeated twice more. Then it was over, and the boson was directing his men to return to their duties, then telling the few passengers assembled that they should get below.

Before leaving for his cabin, the reverend made the rounds of the mourners, saying a few words of consolation to each. Josef thanked him and asked how it was that he was aboard.

"I'm returning from Bulgaria where I was arranging to do missionary work starting next year. I'm heading home now, to my wife and my young son, in Minnesota."

"Minnesota? We are bound for Minnesota also, for St. Paul."

"Ah. And you and your wife are Catholic?"

"Yes, we . . . we are."

"I am sure you will find a parish in St. Paul that will welcome you. There are many Germans there."

"We are not German, but my brother-in-law tells me there are also many Austrians among his neighbors, so I am sure we will be welcome. You speak German very well. How is that?"

"I am a missionary. I need to speak the languages of the people I hope to reach. I was raised on Bulgarian and Greek and have studied German, French, and Italian — whatever it takes to carry God's message."

Mary dabbed her eyes with a handkerchief. "And what is that message? Is it that God punishes innocent children with pestilence and early death?"

Josef gasped. "Mary, please."

Reverend Constantine placed his hand on Josef's arm. "No, it is all right and understandable in her grief. But God has his plan for each of us. Your daughter was baptized, right? Well, then, even now, she is already with God in his Heaven. That you must believe."

Mary looked up at the man. "Must I? Heaven is a Christian invention to comfort the bereaved and to entice the misbehaving. My daughter is with the fishes and the Leviathan, in the salty cold of the sea. My daughter is not even consigned to the earth, as we are commanded in Deuteronomy."

"I see you know your Bible. You are a woman of faith, then."

"Faiths. I believe, help thou mine unbelief."

"For all of us, death tests our faith, demands of us to reach for perspective on our all-too-brief earthly journey, but —"

"Enough, Father. Or Reverend. Or Rabbi. It is God who has abandoned me. I have sworn before God and man and kept my vows to both. Josef, please help me below deck. The air up here is becoming bitter, too laced with brine." She looked straight into the reverend's eyes before turning away.

Chapter 17
Arrival

New York, New York, 1882

Mary went into labor just four days out of New York. As the Allemannia steamed on toward port, shuddering from the force of the engines as the captain sought to make up time, Mary was moved to the birthing room of the ship's hospital. Despite the earnest screening of some of the stewards, already two babies had been born during the crossing: a boy and a girl, not enough to compensate for the eighteen souls lost in route, including a boy of sixteen who had been swept overboard after he had hidden from the deck crew when the seas had roughened unexpectedly.

Whether for the stress of the voyage or the ceaseless motion of the ship, Mary's labor was long and difficult. Josef was not permitted to see her and had to rely on word conveyed by the stewards. The news, when it finally reached him, was simple and direct.

"How goes it with my wife, Mary Samson?"

"The baby didn't make it, sir." And that was that. Within the hour, Mary was helped back down to steerage. The birthing room was needed for what would prove to be the fourth and final newborn of the voyage, another girl. The three women who had been so unsympathetic with Mary when Cathia had taken sick were now doubly solicitous. In her exhaustion and grief, Mary wordlessly accepted their kindness. She spent the last two days of the crossing lying in the bottom bunk, eating soup fed to her by Josef, but saying nothing.

Her silence continued as she and Josef waited to depart the ship. They were in the last group of steerage passengers to be escorted onto a barge, then taken to the reception depot at Castle Garden at the tip of Manhattan. As the barge edged up to the landing, the sight of the circular building, once a venue for concerts and events and before that a fort, brought shouts and cheers from the passengers. Josef looked to Mary for his cue, but she was staring at her hands, white from clutching the rail. They walked in silence from the barge, jostled by others more eager and less somber.

The cavernous interior of Castle Garden, with its high dome atop slender pillars, echoed with the chaos of voices from the milling humanity. Josef and Mary sleepwalked through the hours of queueing for questions, the indignity of a medical check that proved perfunctory, and then the wait for the delayed arrival of baggage.

With most of the day gone, they finally exited the facility with their luggage but short the large trunk, which either had never been loaded aboard the Allemannia or had been retrieved by another passenger. Mary cried when Josef told her it was nowhere to be found, but it was not so much for the contents as for the accumulation of loss that had finally become too much for her to bear.

On the street, they were assaulted by an army of hustlers and self-proclaimed helpers ready to assist or to relieve them of their cash and belongings. "Hotel? Transportation to the trains? Day work?" Josef turned around to be sure Mary was still with him. Over her shoulder he spotted a sign in German: *Arbeiter Bureau*. "Look, it is a Labor Office. They will speak German and maybe can help us.

The first man Josef spoke with did not understand him, but he called over a colleague, a short man wearing a bowtie and leather suspenders who spoke German with a Prussian accent. "You're looking for work?"

"No, I am looking for help. We just arrived, and —"

"You and a thousand others. I can help you find work here, day labor, while you and the wife settle in. That's what I do. Do you have any special skills?"

"I'm a wainwright. I can do carpentry, some smithing. I'm good with my hands, but I only —"

"I've got work at a brickyard. You can start in the morning. Can you read?"

"Yes, in German, of course, but —"

"Here, I'll write down the address and also a hotel you can stay at for now, by the day or week. No rats. Board is extra but reasonable. You ask for Fritz. At the brickyards, you want to talk with the frog, Maurice, but he's from the Alsace and speaks German, too."

"Thank you so much, but I already have work in St. Paul."

"Then why did you come in here?"

"Because I thought you would speak German and could help us find a place to stay and to get to the trains."

"Why didn't you say so. Just go to this hotel, tell Fritz that Gerhard sent you and he'll treat you fair. He'll tell you how to get the train you want. Now, I got work to do."

Outside, the squad of shills and shysters descended once more on the couple. Josef knew he could not get to the hotel on foot with all their baggage, but he was determined to try. He stacked the heaviest pieces. From his rucksack he fished out a length of rope, which he used to lash the stack together leaving a rope handle at one end. The two lightest bundles he handed to Mary and slung the straps of the remaining two cases over his shoulder. His first attempt to slide the tied assemblage along led to the entire lot tumbling to one side. He was redoing his rope work when a boy who looked to be ten or twelve came up to him and stood, feet planted wide, with his hands on his hips.

"That will never work. Where are you going? I can get you there."

"You speak German."

"*Natürlich.* I'm Bobby Metzger. What do you expect? So, which hotel? Let me guess. Broadmore, right?"

"Yes, that's right. How did you know?"

"You talked to Gerhard, at the Labor Exchange, right? See, I'm smart. And I'm strong."

"Not strong enough to carry all these, you're not."

"No, but smart enough to get my kid brother and his wagon to help." He put two fingers into his mouth and made a piercing whistle. From across the way, a boy started pulling a wooden wagon toward them.

"This here is my little brother, Mark. It's his wagon, but I'm the brains. It'll cost you ten cents. A nickel for each of us."

Josef was not sure what a nickel was, and he had no idea whether he was being overcharged or not, but he needed to get Mary, himself, and the luggage to someplace to stay the night. "Good," he said. "Let's go."

Chapter 18
Divergence

It was only many years later that I came to understand ambivalence and its role, its pervasive presence in human affairs. It was so much easier for me to see it in you than to acknowledge it in myself. After all, I was a man — or nearly one — and I knew full well what I wanted and what I did not. I wanted you, and I wanted to spend my life with you, although in retrospect I barely knew you at that point and barely knew myself, to be truthful. I was, nevertheless, ready to marry you. Such is the certainty of youth, which is based as much on denial as on conviction. You, on the other hand, seemed to know your heart, which was deeply conflicted. You wanted that baby, as you wanted me, and you wanted a way forward that was not predicated on either of these things and that would find you at the end both credentialed and teaching. For you, moreover, the longing for redemption was far more salient, while for me it barely registered.

We passed the summer interlocked, bound by love but sundered by our separate realities. Of the two of us, you were far more in touch with the contradictions of your psyche. You knew you wanted me and wanted us to be together, or so I was convinced, yet you were also keenly aware that you wanted to run and hide — from me, from impending motherhood, from the unforgiving re-

alities of a time and a world without room for unwed mothers. No wedge was needed to drive between us. We provided our own, along with the mallet with which to strike it.

The Minnesota summers could be the bookend to match its bitter-cold winters. August had opened with a brutal heat-wave that kept temperatures in the Twin Cities around ninety or above for a full week. The Osters had taken to re-treating for the evening to the screened-in gazebo in their small backyard where they would sip lemonade and read until the light faded.

Morrie closed and set down his newspaper. "I do miss *The Globe*. What has it been, four, five years since they folded?"

"Four, dear."

"Why do things have to change? You would think that something like a newspaper would last, wouldn't you."

"Everything changes, Morris, everything. Have you noticed our Maggie lately?"

"I have not, which is one of the things that endears her to me. Except on rare occasion, she now goes about her duties with unobtrusive diligence."

"I did not mean that. And I will point out that you were the one with the reservations about her at the outset."

"Really? I don't think so. I've always liked the girl."

"Your memory is as short as your eyesight these days, Morris. So, I don't suppose you have noticed."

"Noticed what? What is there to notice? Do enlighten me, Sadie."

"Well, I mean her weight, of course. She does seem to be becoming somewhat more rotund."

"Then good for the girl, I say. She was rather too skinny."

"You are impossible, Morris. I meant . . . well, never mind." She reached for the little brass bell on the side table and gave it a shake, then two more before setting it back down and looking toward the house. "Ah, there you are, Maggie. Please refill my glass, if you will."

"Yes, ma'am." She entered the gazebo and retrieved Sadie's empty glass. "And for you, sir, more lemonade?"

"I think not, thank you. Any more and I might start floating away."

"Very well. I'll take your glass in. And I'll be back with more for you, ma'am."

As soon as the back screen door closed behind Maggie, Sadie leaned toward Morrie and spoke behind her hand. "Now do you see what I mean?"

"About what?"

"About Maggie. She has definitely put on some inches, and her face has rounded."

"Oh, I suppose. It's really no concern of ours. At least she is getting enough to eat. We shouldn't worry ourselves."

"You are impossible at times, Morris."

Maggie returned with the lemonade and set it on the side table. "I've finished with the silver, ma'am. I'll be leaving for home, if that's all right with you."

"Yes, of course. You wouldn't know where Jakob is, would you."

"Yes, he is out front. Would you like me to fetch him?"

"No, no, that won't be necessary. I just wondered what he might be up to."

≫ ≪

Maggie sat down on the front steps beside Jakob. "I think your mother suspects. The way she looks at me and makes a point of eyeing my waist when she does . . ."

"Perhaps. Then perhaps it is time that we make some decisions about our future."

"Our future? Your future and mine may not be one and the same."

"Marry me, my Lena. Make me a happy man and let me make you an honest woman."

"So you are to be made happy, but I am only to be rendered honest? Does that strike you as a fair exchange?"

"Why do you always have to be so . . . so contrary?"

"Honest, not contrary. So, you see, I am already an honest woman without any help from you."

"I hate it when you get this way, when we argue over the choice of words or the meaning of a phrase."

"Once you seemed to like that in me, when we would argue theology or debate politics."

"This is neither. This is life. Why can't we just enjoy it, take pleasure in each other's company and make the best of an evening that is still too hot but beginning to cool." He gave a quick look around to be sure none of the neighbors were watching, then kissed her. To his surprise, she returned the kiss with ardor.

"I had begun to wonder whether you still felt anything for me."

"I love you, Jakob. That hasn't changed. And there are nights when I lie awake wishing you were beside me, holding me. But those are wishes, and I see no way they might become true."

"I do."

"You do? And what magic lamp will you rub to grant them?"

"You have a right to a vacation, a week off from your work, and I still have an invitation to join my friends out at Lake

Minnetonka. There are extra bedrooms, and my friends will leave us to ourselves when we want. Run away with me, let's leave our families and our obligations behind, at least for a while."

"Your magic lamp has it all worked out except for the Hoffmanns. How is it that I could ever explain a week away from them? No, I'm afraid your dreams will have to remain just that, mere dreams."

"But, if I could devise a way, you would do that, you would go with me?"

"If there were a way, I would. Yes, I would." This time it was she who took his face in her hands and kissed him.

"My Lena, my mysterious Lena. Sometimes I simply cannot make sense out of you."

"Sometimes? You sound as if it were a rarity rather than a common occurrence."

"And there you go again, turning a sweet moment into another fencing match."

"There I go? I see. Perhaps I should just go, then. I am finished with my work. I should head back to the Hoffmann's before the light is gone."

"I'll walk you home. We can keep talking."

"No, I've told you why you can't do that. I'll manage just fine on my own."

He patted her abdomen. "There will come a point in the not-distant future when walking that mile will become too much for you."

"Then I shall have to find some other work or some other way."

"Is it always so easy for you? To find another way?"

"It is certainly not always easy, but there is always another way. This I believe with all my heart. Now" — she kissed him again, with even more passion — "perhaps you and your magic lamp can light the way." She returned to the house to get her purse, then left Jakob sitting on the front steps, more confused than ever.

Chapter 19
Wishes

St. Paul, Minnesota, 1909

Despite my persistence, we never managed to orches-
trate a honeymoon on Lake Minnetonka. With the end
of summer and the resumption of classes at the univer-
sity, free time became a precious commodity. We ar-
gued less, in part because we talked less, but also be-
cause, I think, I was growing weary of the tension over
our uncertain future in the face of the swiftly ap-
proaching certainty. It was becoming ever more diffi-
cult for you to hide your condition, although you grew
clever in your attire and perhaps delayed the inevitable
confrontation by a few extra weeks.

When we did talk, we omitted talk of the future, as if
we had come to an agreement, as if we had already
committed to a life together, even though neither of us
could yet see how that might actually come about, and
no real plans had been laid. True to form, it was my
mother who brought the issue to the fore.

Jakob was at the university, Morrie was still at work, and the
cook had yet to arrive. Sadie chose the pause in the household rhythm to approach Maggie, who was dusting the
bookshelves in the front parlor. "Maggie, could I have a
word with you?"

"Of course, ma'am." She tucked the feather duster into the
pocket of her apron.

"I'll get right to the point, then. No reason to beat around the bush on such matters, is there. Are you pregnant, Maggie?"

Taken aback, not so much by the question as by its bluntness, Maggie considered denial but could see nothing to be gained by it. "Yes, ma'am, I am."

"And when is the baby due?"

"In February."

"Is the father going to marry you?"

"I don't think so."

"Then you are going to give up the baby?"

"I don't think so."

Sadie cocked her head as if she were not sure she had heard correctly. "This is a very serious matter, Maggie. You can hardly raise a child on your own, now, can you."

"Perhaps. In any case, I will continue to work for you as long as I can and as long as you'll have me."

"Well, we'll have to see about that. I think it depends in part on what you decide to do. I can put you in touch with a very reputable adoption agency, and I can probably help you find placement with a home for unwed mothers for your confinement. You are not the first young girl to find herself in this situation. There are resources."

"I appreciate that, ma'am, but it won't be necessary. If you wish to be of help, though, I would ask that you not say anything to my aunt and uncle."

"Well, I would think they will figure out matters on their own, if they haven't already taken note of your condition, that is."

"I don't think they take much note of me these days. Between working for you, church, and studying at the library, I am not at the house all that much."

"Be that as it may, sooner or later they will know."

"Later would be better. Perhaps by then I will know just what to do."

⇒ ⇐

Jakob, who had been with friends at a University of Minnesota football game, came home fired up with excitement. In the den, his father looked up from his book. "And how was the game?" he asked.

"Brilliant. They sang the new song, you know, the one that won the *Tribune* contest. It was truly a 'Minnesota Rouser' that warmed everyone and brought them to their feet with their hats off. Very appropriate to the chorus."

"Bully for that. So, I would imagine we soundly defeated Michigan then."

"No, we lost despite the cheers."

"Pity. Oh, by the way, your mother wishes to speak with you. She said you'll find her in the sewing room."

Jakob knew better than to ask his father what it was about, and he knew better than to keep his mother waiting. He went straight upstairs to the sewing room, which had originally been a bedroom intended for the younger brother or sister who had never arrived.

Jakob could not remember when he had last seen his mother sewing. There was an image in his mind, but it had become sepia-toned and faded, an undated childhood memory from the years before the two had become locked in the struggle over her expectations of him.

"You wanted to speak with me, Mama?"

"I did. Have a seat and I'll be with you as soon as I finish basting this hem."

He knew she could just as well have set her sewing aside when he entered, but the ploy asserted control, making him responsive to her rather than the other way around. He sat on the upholstered bench by the door and waited for her to decide when enough time had passed for the proper effect.

"There. It is so hard to keep up with fashion. Tova Goldfarb just returned from her autumn in Paris, for which I confess to uncharacteristic envy. She said the women there are no longer dragging the hems of their morning attire on the ground but making to clear it by a precise five centimeters. What is a woman to do. I cannot go to Paris, and I cannot purchase an entire new wardrobe for the sake of a few centimeters. And so, here I am and that is that. Men have it ever so much easier."

She set the dress aside. "But I am sure none of this is of the slightest interest to you as a young man and future attorney-at-law. I imagine you want to know why I asked that we talk."

"Yes, Mama. Please go on."

"Well, there is something rather delicate that I feel compelled to ask you about."

Jakob braced himself but nodded and cocked his head in a pose calculated to imply polite but measured interest.

"Did you know about Maggie?"

"Know about Maggie?"

"Yes, that is what I am asking. Did you know?"

He scratched at his ear while he sorted through possible responses. "There is something about Maggie, then? Some news? I guess that I would have to say I really don't know."

Sadie's patience was reaching its limit. "Well, it is becoming rather hard not to notice. But then, you are a man, and men, especially younger men, do tend to be somewhat oblivious to the obvious. Our girl, it seems, has gotten herself in a family way."

Jakob raised his eyebrows ever so slightly. "Really now. Are you quite sure?"

"Of course I am, or we would not be having this conversation. Your mother is hardly the one to gossip, now is she?"

"No, Mama."

"Exactly. And you didn't know? I mean, the girl does seem to engage in conversation with you — rather more than I think is appropriate, considering her station — but I have chosen not to interfere. I assume that as young people you have some things in common, though what they might be escapes me. I just thought she might have said something or dropped some hint or another. Perhaps you know something about how this calamity befell her."

Jakob was looking at his mother at the same time he was straining to keep a straight face at what was, for him, a ludicrous conversation loaded with irony and comedic potential. "No, I am sure you realize it is hardly the sort of thing the two of us would discuss."

"As I suspected, but I thought I should ask, in case she had said something, maybe dropped some hints at who the father might be. I would hope that the young man would do the right and responsible thing and marry the girl, but it seems the cad has abandoned her."

"Uh, perhaps there is more to the story."

"What more could there be? If young people misbehave and get caught for it, they should shoulder the consequences properly. It is as simple as that. The young man, whoever he is, is a cad and a coward."

"But, Mama, perhaps he is a student at university or comes from a very different family or . . ."

"Nonsense. I am sure the young man is much the same as our Maggie, the poorly tutored child of immigrants."

Jakob tried not to let show how much fun he was having with the exchange. "And what am I? I am hardly the pure-blood descendant of the early Pilgrims."

"That, Jakob, is not at all the same. You would never take advantage of a young girl. The very thought of it is rather worthy of ridicule. At any rate, I thought you should know of the matter and might shed some light on it. Obviously, we shall have to let her go."

"Let her go? But she needs the work, now more than ever. If anything, we should do whatever we can to assist her."

"I have tried, believe me I've tried. But she will have none of it."

"But why do we have to let her go?"

"I would think it would be obvious, even to a young man. It just would not do, having a single woman, a mere girl, who is working for us and so blatantly with child. The neighbors will begin talking, if they have not begun to already. No, I'll keep her on until the end of the month, but then I will have to let her go.

"No! How can you do that? And just before Christmas."

"You have been spending much too much time with your gentile friends at the university, I'm afraid. Christmas is hardly a holiday within our observance."

"But it is within hers. She's a devout Catholic."

"Hardly devout, I would say, given the evidence of her current condition."

"Mother, that is quite enough. This is Maggie you are talking about."

"I do not like your tone, Jakob. That will be quite enough. She is our servant, not a family friend. If anything, this demonstrates the folly of permitting too much familiarity with those in our employ. I can assure you, that will not be allowed to happen again. But, out of deference for her beliefs, I will delay her dismissal until the end of December. I hope that satisfies you. And now, I have sewing to finish."

→» «←

November had closed with unseasonable weather; over Thanksgiving weekend, the temperature reached the sixties. Inspired by the sparkling warm day, Morrie and Sadie were off on a rare Saturday excursion, visiting distant relatives across town after morning services at the temple. Jakob had begged off under the pretext, not entirely fabricated, of extra studying for an upcoming exam.

Maggie was busy in the kitchen, finishing the cleanup from the night before. Jakob came up behind her and put his arms around her waist. "My, but we are getting rather round." He massaged her belly as he kissed her neck. "It has been such a long time. I wish . . ."

"Keep rubbing the lamp, Aladdin, and you just might get your wish. Perhaps a bit lower might awaken the jinn."

Jakob let his hands slip down the curve of her belly. "Really? It would be all right?"

"My second cousin, who married young and has been secretly supportive, told me the baby is safe. And, oh yes indeed, the magic of the lamp is awakening." She turned into him, and with the pressure of her against him, he was instantly aroused.

They did not climb the stairs to his bedroom, but decided to anoint the divan in the front parlor, where its curves and mounded padding along with Maggie's shape, inspired them to experiment with new positions. Afterwards, they drifted into sleep until the intrusive pressure of Maggie's bladder reminded her that there were other demands. "I must go, Jakob, and finish my work before your parents return. And before I make a mess of the divan that will be difficult to clean up."

"I love you, my Lena."

"And I love you, my Jakob. Remember that."

⇒》 《⇐

December was another story. By the first night of Hanukkah in the second week, the Twin Cities had plunged into a bitter cold snap, with nighttime temperatures below zero and another half-foot or more of new snow falling every day. The coal furnace in the cellar required extra attention to keep it stoked.

Tuesdays were Jakob's long day at the university, and the first candle was already flickering in the menorah in the front parlor window when he arrived home. He removed his overshoes, hung his heavy wool coat and scarf on a peg, and rubbed his hands to warm them as he entered the parlor. His parents were sitting on the divan.

"*Chag semeach*, Mama, Papa."

"Thank you." His father smiled. "And happy holiday to you, son, although not everything or everyone is entirely happy at the moment."

"What's wrong?"

"Your mother —"

"I'm sitting beside you, Morris. I'm quite capable of speaking for myself."

"Of course, you are, and I'm sure you will." Morrie folded his hands in his lap in exaggerated deference, a gesture Sadie noted but did not remark upon.

"Maggie did not show up today," she said to Jakob, "which is most irregular and uncharacteristic. Whatever else might be said of the girl, one could set one's watch by her punctuality."

148

Jakob sat down in the side chair across from them. "Did you try to ring the Hoffmanns? Perhaps she has taken ill. There is a nasty sort of cold going around, what with the ups and downs of the weather."

"I tried to ring, of course, but they have no telephone, so I sent the neighbor boy to go up there with a message and wait for a reply, but he returned empty-handed."

"Well, I am sure there is some simple explanation. As you say, it is not like Lena . . . uh, like Maggie to miss work." Behind his nonchalant words, his thoughts raced. What might have happened? Had the baby arrived early? He did some mental arithmetic. Six months. Too early. Premature. A tragedy. Perhaps a blessing. Suddenly he became aware that his mother was speaking.

"I asked whether you might have any idea where she could be or what might have transpired?"

"Ah, no, Mama. I'm sorry, I have no idea and no guesses."

"Well, I thought she might have said something to you."

"No, nothing of note. I have been rather distracted by extra assignments, what with the holidays approaching and all and now my work on the *Minnesota Daily*. I really had no idea how demanding of one's time a school newspaper could be. Maggie and I have hardly exchanged a dozen words since Thanksgiving." He immediately regretted his phrasing, which implied they might otherwise have had more regular conversations. His mother's expression altered just enough to let him know that his wording had been noted. He resisted smiling, which would be misread, but his thoughts were skipping back to the Saturday after Thanksgiving.

"Well," — Sadie stood — "there is nothing to be done at this hour and with the snow still falling as well. Perhaps we shall be enlightened in the morning. In any case, I have instructed our new cook in the preparation of latkes, by personal example, I must say. They are not quite your grandmother's lacy version, but I think you will find them acceptable."

Morrie stood and took her hand. "Then I say we should retire to the dining room and celebrate the first night of the holiday with potato latkes."

⋙ ⋘

Jakob arose early the next day. After penning a note for his parents, he set off in the half light of the predawn for the hike to the Hoffmann house up on Van Buren. In the bitter cold, he trudged as fast as he could through fresh snow that squeaked and complained with each step. When he arrived, there was no answer to his knock, and when he peered in the front windows, no lights were visible. Perhaps it was too early. He was already down the front steps and to the sidewalk when he heard the door open behind him. "Yes, can I help you?" Mary Hoffmann was dressed in a house dress topped by a thick cardigan that she held closed with one hand.

"I was looking for Maggie, Maggie Samson."

"Well, she is not here. And who are you?"

"Jakob Oster. The Osters, you know. Maggie works for . . . for my parents. We . . . they are wondering if she is quite all right."

"You certainly have the nerve. She is gone, far away and won't be back until . . . Well, you won't find her. And don't you ever come back. We want nothing to do with you or any of you people." She stepped back in and slammed the door behind her.

Chapter 20
Pursuit

St. Paul, Minnesota, 1910

Sometimes it is the smallest things by which we assert our independence. Sometimes we are granted our liberty in error. When you failed to show for work, I was proud of you even as I was furious with you for having said nothing to me before leaving. My fury was no match for my mother's. You had trumped her bid to dismiss you. No one was going to let you go; you would choose your own moment. By that one unexpected development, my mother lost a sizable piece of her sense of control. If she could not command a servant, what and who could she direct?

Of course, in the final analysis, we control little or nothing save our own actions, and perhaps not all of those. I made my own bid for mastery over my life with my next precipitous and unanticipated move, yet even that was in response to yours, which was a hand forced by my mother's play, which was in turn . . .

We can no more unwind cause than we can turn back the clock. In looking back, we choose evidence and select a stopping point which we then call the beginning, the ultimate cause. For want of a nail . . . And always something came before.

The telephone call from the university asking after Jakob was the first sign to the Osters that the sudden and unexplained disappearance of Maggie was not the only radical development.

Sadie answered the call. "No, I don't understand. He has not withdrawn and he is not ill. He is not here at the moment, but I expect him to return from classes within the hour. I am sure there has been some mistake, and I am equally sure that my son can set everything straight. If you will give me your number, I will have him ring back straightaway on his return home."

➤➤➤ ⫷⫷⫷

Sadie greeted Jakob as soon as he entered. "One of your instructors, a Professor Slagle, rang this afternoon inquiring about why you have not been in his class since the first of the year. I told him that he must be confused, since you have not missed a day so far this year. I took his number and left it by the telephone in the hall."

Jakob said nothing for several seconds as he weighed his options. "Thank you, Mama. I'll be seeing him tomorrow and can straighten out the matter then. Don't worry. Right now I need to get right to studying. I have no less than three exams coming up this week."

"Very well. Would you like to have the new girl bring you some coffee and something to sustain you until supper?"

"New girl?"

"Well, yes. We can hardly function without a domestic, can we. Olga is Swedish and barely manages in English, which does somewhat complicate the training but also ensures she will not become distracted by idle chit-chat on the job. I think she will work out, as she is not nearly as immature nor as delicate as our last domestic."

"Our last domestic had a name. Do we no longer refer to her as Maggie though she has been gone but a month?"

"In view of how irresponsible she was — first in her personal habits and then in vanishing without giving proper notice — I hardly see a need for the familiarity of first names. And nipping in the bud any future familiarity, you may refer to the new girl as Mrs. Gustafson."

"So, the new 'girl' is a married woman?"

"That she is, and well familiar with hard work, having been a laundress until recently."

"Indeed. Then, Mama, would you be so kind as to instruct the former laundry woman in how I take my coffee and have her bring a cup and carafe to my room at her earliest convenience. And a plate of tea biscuits, too, if she can manage. Now, I am off to my studies, if you will excuse me."

⫸ ⫷

The woman who delivered the coffee and biscuits looked to be in her forties with a waistline of similar measure.

Jakob had to give his mother credit for her savvy recruiting. "Thank you, Mrs. Gustafson. That will be all." In response, the woman offered a dozen words so rapid and heavily accented that Jakob was not exactly sure what had been said. Before he could ask her to repeat herself, she was already out in the hallway and closing the door.

Jakob addressed the door. "Well, I do not think there will be much fraternizing with the help for my mother to contend with."

He poured himself coffee, dropped in two lumps of sugar, and stirred it. From his briefcase, he pulled the interim results of his sleuthing: a sheaf of papers, a legal pad, and two local newspapers. Since the New Year, he had been dividing his days between looking for work and looking for Maggie, taking on the latter as his self-imposed first assignment as an investigative reporter.

His attempts to learn anything from the Hoffmanns had, on multiple occasions, gotten nowhere, but the effort had given him some ideas. His mother had spoken of offering to help get Maggie into a shelter for unwed mothers, an institution that was new to him. He had subsequently made the rounds of homes for wayward girls in both Minneapolis and St. Paul. When his inquiries were rebuffed by the staff at the first of these, he devised a ploy, claiming to be a courier with a letter to deliver to one Magdalena "Maggie" Samson. Some of those he spoke with responded from personal knowledge, others first checked a register. In every case, the letter was politely handed back, and he was told there was no such person there. Correctly or not, he was now convinced that Maggie was nowhere in the Twin Cities, at least not in one of the designated homes.

He wondered if he next would have to inquire with possible relatives. The daunting prospect of calling on every Samson and Hoffmann to be found in the Polk Street Directory for the Twin Cities led him to set that tactic aside.

As he again scanned his notes, he started replaying in his head the last words of Mrs. Hoffmann when she had closed the door on him. Maggie was far way, he would never find her, and she would not be back until . . . Until what? He assumed not until the baby was born. That last point led him to check homes for unwed mothers, but perhaps he was looking too close to home. What other cities in Minnesota were big enough to have such institutions? The reference librarian at the public library might be able to help. That would be his plan for the next day.

⇛ ⇚

The telephone rang as Jakob was preparing to leave for the day. His mother stepped from the front parlor just as he was about to slip out the door. "Jakob, please answer the telephone when you are the one nearest to it."

"But I have to go, Mama. I don't want to be late for class."

"Certainly another thirty seconds will not make you tardy. But, very well." She picked up the receiver. "Hello, Oster residence. Yes, in fact, he is right here. Just a moment, please." She held out the telephone to Jakob. "It's your professor again."

"Please tell him I'll see him in class. I really must go."

"I am not your office assistant, Jakob. You are right here and can very well tell him yourself."

Jakob realized he was trapped. He took the phone from her and stepped as far away as the cord would permit. "Hello, this is Jakob speaking." He wanted to turn away from his mother, who stood in the doorway, arms folded, but thought better of it. Best to end the call as rapidly and ambiguously as possible. "Yes, Professor. No, Professor. Yes, I will see you in your office. Thank you. I must go. Goodbye."

Knowing that he would need to talk with Prof. Slagle in any case, Jakob headed to the university campus, stopping first at the main library. There he confirmed that, after Minneapolis and then St. Paul, the third largest city in Minnesota was, by a substantial margin, Duluth, largely owing to its rapid growth in recent decades as a major port for iron ore. Duluth fit the bill of being far away, about as far as one could get without crossing into Canada. The towns farther north at the border were barely more than villages.

A check of a medical directory confirmed that Duluth was indeed blessed with a number of hospitals and a single home for unwed mothers, the Bethel Home for Women and Children, located at 430-432 Sixth Avenue East. A search of directories did not produce a telephone number for the place, so he decided to exploit the U.S. mail by addressing a first class letter to Maggie in care of the Bethel Home. The mails could take time, but if he sent the letter right away, he could get his reply — or a letter returned as undeliverable — within a week or so. There was no guarantee Maggie would write back, but if he got neither a reply nor a returned envelope in a couple of weeks, he could assume she was there in Duluth. Using a blank sheet of notebook paper from his briefcase, he wrote a quick note. He could get an envelope and postage at the University branch of the Post Office.

It was not until he had sealed and stamped the envelope at the Post Office that he realized he had a problem. What could he use as a return address? If he used his own, Maggie might refuse to take delivery should she prefer not to be in contact with him. Then he would wrongly conclude she was not there when she actually was. He would need an address she would not even associate with him. Who did he know. He could not be sure about any of his extended family. His cousin Naomi would be the obvious choice, but if her parents intercepted the return envelope and opened it out of curiosity, it would be a disaster for him. Rachel Baumgarten, from the university! She lived in Minneapolis, and he had even once been to her house for a study group.

He opened his pocket address book to the *B*s and copied the address onto the back flap of the envelope. He would make a point of talking with her on campus, if only he could find her. If not, he would call on her at her house.

He still needed to visit Prof. Slagle to stave off more telephone calls. He was hoping he could keep his parents in the dark until after his birthday in three weeks. The fireworks would be just as loud, but he would have the advantage of being twenty-one and legally able to make his own decisions. If he had actual employment by then, it would be all the better.

His father would be the unknown quantity in the question of whether he was to be kicked out of the house. He had always been told that he would have his parents' full support as long as he was in school, and the assumption had always been he would continue until he graduated and would begin the practice of law the moment he passed the bar exams. Nothing had ever been said of what might ensue if he dropped out of college; that possibility had been unthinkable. Now, the unthinkable was already fait accompli.

For the moment, Jakob would need to bluff his way through a meeting with Prof. Slagle, then look for Rachel in her usual haunts before heading downtown to resume his job search. He kissed the envelope in his hand before dropping it in the mail slot. One way or another, in a few weeks he would know.

Chapter 21
Renewal

Everything was small. The rented house, though it often felt cavernous, was small. The bed was small. Even time felt small and pinched to Mary. She turned her face to the wall. "No, Josef, not tonight, not now."

"Not now, always not now. Then when? You are always saying that, that Hebrew saying: if not now, when." He propped himself up on an elbow. "We have not . . . we have not been together since we left Austria. You are my wife. It is your duty to please me, and it is our duty to bring children into the world."

"It is your duty to honor me, husband, and to please me also. We brought children into this world, and they were taken from us. I will not bear another child only for it to die."

"We do not know that it will die."

"We do. All children die. We all come into this world to die. There is no other plan but that. But it is wrong for mere babes to die when their parents live on."

"You have become so dark, Mary. Once you were so bright and full of life. And now . . ."

"Now I am an old woman who has seen too much and come too far. I have lost too much on the journey. With every mile on the train from New York, with every hour farther from the ocean that is the only grave of my child and my baby, another piece of me was snuffed out. Now we are here, and we toil, and that is our life, nothing more."

"We are building a life. We have a roof over our heads. I have work, and soon, in some years, we will have a house that is truly ours. I love you, Miriam. Come to me."

"Why is it that you speak to Miriam at times like this? There is no Miriam. She was dying on the steamship, and the last ember of her died on the train. As Mary I will cook for you and keep house for you and dutifully accompany you to your church, but Miriam is gone. Now sleep. Your work starts early and you will need your rest." She edged toward the wall.

Josef tugged at her shoulder, firm and persistent. "Not yet."

≫ ≪

The ember within Mary flared into life once more when their son was born, then was extinguished when he died only weeks later. Josef took comfort in the fact the boy had been baptized, but for Mary there was no comfort, only another loss, another reason to turn from the world.

Her only friend was Hilda Gunderson from around the corner. The Gundersons, an older couple who had not moved on when their grown children had left, were one of the very few families in the neighborhood who were not German or Austrian and who were not Catholic. It was the lack of a common language that had first connected the two women. Hilda spoke only a few words of German, and Mary had only the rudiments of English. With nothing to fall back on, Hilda became Mary's language tutor.

≫ ≪

Hilda raised her finger to interrupt. "If I had known, not 'if I had knew it.' With have or had or was or is, you use the word 'known'."

"Why is that?"

159

"How should I know, I am only a housewife. I am not myself a teacher, but I have been speaking English since I was six and my family brought us all here. I graduated from high school with good grades, and I read. *If I had known* you would be asking why, I might have paid more attention when sentences were being diagrammed." She grinned, showing the gap in her front teeth. It was the beauty mark in a handsome face that seemed ageless. Hilda always sat up ramrod straight and kept her silver-stained blond hair long but pulled back. Mary had recently learned the word "stately" and had filed it with her mental image of Hilda.

"I also read," Mary said, "but it is not always a help. Who can tell how a word in English is said? In German, there is only one way to say each letter, each sound. Pronunciation, that is the word, right? In English, how does one ever know? In the newspaper I read that some plans of the city had gone awry. I had not seen the word, so I asked the woman at the library what it meant. I thought it was something like 'awful' and said it like that, 'AWE-ree.' She had no idea what I was talking about until I showed her the article. 'She told me to say 'uh-RYE' and then told me it meant wrong. Who can figure it out. In German, words are put together whole to make new words, and it always makes sense, and you know how to pronounce them."

Hilda laughed, which set Mary to laughing with her. Only with Hilda did smiles and laughter easily reach Mary's lips. Within both women lurked someone, someone else. The two soon discovered they shared a sense of being at sea in a world that was often confusing and many times intriguing. Mary had arrived in an alien culture by moving from one side of the world to another; Hilda had found herself there by staying put as the world around her moved on.

"It is not just language, you know," Hilda said. "These people, the Germans, the Catholics, they think differently. Of course, not you, it seems. I hope I can say that."

"You can say that. And you did." Mary smiled.

Hilda smiled back. "That was a very American sort of thing you just said, a game with the words. But perhaps you can tell me more about Germans and the German language and the Catholics. I have lived beside them many years, but we do not talk of these things. We cannot. In America, everybody accepts every religion and knows nothing of any but their own. In Sweden we were all Lutheran and what we knew of the Catholics was only what we were told that Martin Luther had rejected. The Catholics were wrong and had failed to see their errors when the reformation was laid before them. They rejected Luther as the Jews rejected Christ. But in the eyes of Martin Luther, the Jews were ever so much worse than the Catholics."

Mary's eyes narrowed in provocation. "And in your eyes, what am I?"

"A friend, a confident, and an interesting young woman. That you are Catholic makes you all the more interesting because we can talk and learn from each other. That is something important to me." She reached over and took Mary's hand. "May I ask you something? Why do you not have more children. You are young."

"I am old. I have not turned thirty and already I am old, too old to bear children."

"Nonsense. You should try."

"That I have done, and God has told me to stop."

"God speaks to you? Is that because you are Catholic?"

For the first time in her life, Mary truly wanted to confess, not to a priest but to a friend. She wanted to blurt out the truth, the full story of who she was and why she was being punished. "God speaks to me by His actions. Four times I have been with child. Twice they have died at birth. My daughter lived for three years and my son for three weeks. God's message is plain. I will not be forgiven."

"What, my child, could you possibly have done to believe God is punishing you?"

Mary's resolve to confess faltered, and she only shook her head in silence.

"You needn't tell me. We are all only human, limited. God's grace and compassion know no limits. I think you should keep trying. Children are truly a blessing. When they are not a curse, that is, which is also God's truth."

"You believe, Hilda, that much is clear. Nothing is clear for me other than that there might be sins, betrayals, that go beyond those limits that you do not believe God has."

Hilda shook her head. "I know not what limit you think you have crossed, but I know you as a loving young woman, and I hope God grants you the joy of children."

⇛ ⇚

Within the small house and the demands of daily life, it took time. Josef was surprised when Mary finally turned once more to him with willingness and even sometimes with passion. Both were surprised when months passed, and then years, with no new life beginning in her womb. Only after they were becoming resigned to their life as a childless couple, did Mary finally become pregnant again.

When another daughter was born in August of 1886, Mary did not want to name her and would look away as the baby nursed. She was christened Maria Josephine and she thrived. Ever vigilant against more heartache, Mary remained aloof from her daughter. It was not until the end of the following year, when Jonathan Michael was born, that smiles would again flash across Mary's face. They now had a girl and a boy, Mary was thirty-one, and the Samsons settled in to enjoy their two children and continue to build a life in the growing city of St. Paul.

Chapter 22
Surprises

Baby Joseph was not expected. At thirty-five, Mary assumed her childbearing years were behind her. Jonathan, their youngest, was nearly four when she found herself once again caring for an infant, another boy, whom her American neighbors called a bonus baby and Hilda called reassurance of God's generosity. Joseph Martin was named for his father, but the New World spelling was chosen as a further declaration of allegiance to their new home. Then, at a time in life when most of the women in the neighborhood were happily finished having children, Mary became pregnant yet again.

With three young children to manage, the heat of August in the city added to the challenge of being pregnant at her age. Joseph Martin was an exuberant toddler who seemed to have gone from crawling to running without ever having learned to walk. To Mary's relief, Maria, a precocious five-year-old, had taken on the role of surrogate mother to her younger brothers. Jonathan accepted her protective control with his customary indifference, but Joseph Martin rebelled, running from his big sister and resisting her ministrations at every opportunity.

On a warm morning that buzzed with cicadas, the midwife, a plump gnome of a woman named Klara, arrived with her daughter soon after she had been summoned by Mrs. Hoffmann, who had stopped by on her way to the greengrocer to ask if there might be anything her sister-in-law needed. "You can bring me the midwife," Mary said, "and two ripe capsicum."

Klara arrived before the peppers. "Hello again, my dear." She gave Mary's shoulder a friendly squeeze. "Not through having babies, are we?" She set her bag on a chair by the bed. "This is my daughter Frances, who is learning midwifery from me. How far along are we?"

"I was not sure if you would arrive in time."

"Well then, let's set up some chairs and be on with it. Please don't deliver until we are ready, or you will conclude you had no need of my services and therefore no need to pay me." It was indeed almost too late. By the time everything was in place, the baby was crowning.

"Oh, yes, I can see the top of the head. And now nearly the whole head. And, there. Slow down, girl. Ease off for a moment while I turn the baby. Okay, bear down a bit. Enough. Slow down. Now. Easy. One shoulder. The other. And there. It's a girl!"

"So soon. Almost before I could complain."

"It is not your first, that much is clear. You seem to be well practiced." She handed the baby to her daughter, who cradled it while the afterbirth was delivered. The midwife clamped and cut the cord before her daughter started to clean the baby gently in an enameled basin. "How many?"

"Seven. I guess the body learns even when the mind does not."

"I have had eight. I lost one to the grip, but the others have fared well. My oldest is a motorman on the street railway, my youngest is still in school but promises to quit next year to help support his widowed mother. And Frances you have met."

"You lost your husband, then. I didn't know."

"Yes. Not two years after my last was born. My husband worked at the railyards. A load of lumber tumbled from a wagon. It had not been properly tied. The railyards are a dangerous workplace. He died on the way to the hospital."

Mary said nothing as they helped her back into bed and placed the baby at her breast. Her thoughts were on Josef, who by this hour would already have reached the railyards and be starting his work. She pushed away black thoughts of what it might be like to be a widow with four children to raise.

"What are you going to name her? Do you know?"

"My husband said if it was a girl, she would be Magdalena. So, now we have two boys and two girls: Jonathan and Joseph and Maria and Magdalena."

"Magdalena. A pretty name for a pretty baby. Considering how easily she entered the world, she should be an easy child. But then, girls are always easier than boys, let me tell you."

"I had always thought it was the other way around. But it is good to have both. At least girls help around the house, and it is the daughters that are the caretakers when their parents turn old."

"I hope you are right about that one. I only have the two sons, the firstborn and the last. My oldest, the motorman, never visits, and the youngest has dreams of putting to sea. Well, Frances and I better be off. I'll check in on you tomorrow, but you seem to be doing fine, not bleeding too much, and I'm sure you already know how to take care of yourself." She retrieved the bag with the tools of her trade neatly repacked by her daughter. "Oh, it looks like you have a caller."

Hilda ducked to clear the doorway as she entered the bedroom. "I see, Mary, that God still favors you. Who is it that He sends to grace your house and our neighborhood?"

"This is Magdalena."

"Two of each, a balance restored."

"Is that how it works, a divine balance?"

"If not God's, then Nature's plan. Two-by-two they were created, and two-by-two they entered the Ark."

"What do you think, Hilda? Are God and Nature one and the same? Are faith and science one dominion or two?"

"My, but you are of a philosophical bent this morning."

"Perhaps it is bringing new life into the world that inspires, perhaps it is just the release of old impulses long buried. Josef and I once talked of such things, but now he has his work and I have my children and a home to manage. There is little time and, on his part, no inclination to talk of deeper things. You are now the only one who listens with interest and responds with something other than dogma."

"That is a common complaint, true. Men show interest in what we say and engage with us, and then, after the engagement, the interest wanes. It was that way with my Ivar, but since the children are now off and busy with families of their own, he is sometimes prone to talk again, although sports and politics seem more to his taste than religion and philosophy." Hilda bent close to get a better look at the baby. "Ah, the dear is drifting off already. May I hold her."

"Of course."

Hilda lifted Magdalena in her big hands, then cradled and rocked her. "As a girl, I wanted to be a barrister, you know. Ivar and I met at university, both of us so full of ideas and ambitions, but then we left Sweden and the work was hard and there were so many babies. Neither of us returned to school. Perhaps one of my girls . . ."

"It is harder for girls," Mary said. "My father was a tailor and wanted his son to follow in the trade. For me he wanted a husband, though I was the one more skilled with needle and thread."

"And what did you want?"

"More. I wanted more. More ideas, more arguments, more knowledge, more languages. Well, I did get that last one. With your help I have learned English, and even a little Swedish, to add to German and Yiddish and —"

"Yiddish?" Hilda pulled back in surprise. "You know the language of the Jews? How is that?"

Was this the moment, Mary wondered, the moment to bare her secret, or was that moment already long past? Or never to come. "I, well, . . . Frauenkirchen, the town where I was born, had a Jewish quarter, a ghetto, really. Nearly a third of the village were Jews. One picks up things if one is open to learning."

"So you know about the Jews. I have always wondered what they are like."

"Not that different. Like me."

"But they keep apart, to themselves."

"And you, we, do not? Everyone around us is German or Austrian. When our neighbors speak English — if they speak English — they speak it with a German accent. They are all Catholic, or nearly all."

"You overlook me in your civics lesson."

"I am sorry. We are both exceptions, perhaps. But if one were to go only a few blocks west or north, everyone is Scandinavian and the churches are all Lutheran. Cross the river to the West Side Flats, and you will be surrounded by Russian Jews. Do you hear Russian here or German in the northern suburbs?"

"Is this a bad thing, that each and all stick to their own kind?"

"I don't know. Good and bad, I think. It is comforting to be within the bosom of the familiar, but we learn nothing new when everything around us is already known."

"I would learn more, then, of Frauenkirchen and the Jews you knew as a girl, but I also see that you are tired from your labor. We will save this talk for another day."

"We will. You are a good and dear friend, Hilda."

"And you as well, my Mary. Now rest with your baby while you can. The days ahead will be demanding, as well you know."

≫ ≪

December snow clogged the streets, and horse-drawn wagons had trouble making their deliveries and completing their rounds. Josef and several friends from the railyards had found and taken over a ramshackle barn abandoned at the edge of the yards. On weekends, they met to repair and refit wagons with skis. They were rather pleased with themselves for the extra money they pocketed and looked forward to spring when they could play the same game in reverse.

With Maria in her first year of school and Josef at work nearly every day, Mary felt taxed to her limit. Unlike his older sister, Jonathan resented looking after his little brother. "Joey is a bad boy. He runs away and throws mud balls and won't listen. Why do I have to take care of him?"

"Because I am taking care of the baby and your big sister is at school and you are nearly five years old, that's why. And, I should add, Christmas is nearly here. You want a visit from Saint Nicholas, don't you? Didn't your father warn you about the goat-demon Krampus who torments children who misbehave?" Mary had little enthusiasm for the Austrian folklore she had inherited from Josef's clan along with his religion, but she was not above reciting the myths at moments like this when Christmas approached. In her own mind, she had already become a worshipper of idols when she converted; invoking witches and demons could hardly make her sin much worse.

Jonathan's eyes widened. "Is there really a half-goat half-demon who travels with Saint Nicholas?"

"I don't know. You will have to ask your father, but that is the story." *That is the story.* It was her way of answering many of her children's questions about faith and folklore.

"All right, I will play with him. Can we play in the snow?"

"If you bundle up and help Joey with his boots and jacket, yes, you can."

⇉ ⇇

Mary had just finished nursing Maggie and tucked her into the crib for a nap when Jonathan came through the front door. "Mama, Mama, come quick."

"Don't leave the door open. We do not have enough coal to heat the whole city."

"But Mama, come quick. It's Joey."

Mary ran out without even putting on a coat. The ragman with his cart was stopped in the street, his swayback horse angled to one side.

"There was nothing I could do," he said, "nothing. He ran right up to Ingrid and tried to grab her leg. She . . . there was nothing I could do."

Beside the horse lay the still form of a small boy, his face covered in mud, his chest caved in and smeared with blood. Mary closed her eyes, then turned away. She walked slowly into the house and returned with a blanket. She wrapped her son in the blanket and carried him in silence into the house as the ragman and neighbors from both sides of the street looked on.

The funeral was on Sunday. On the next night, the fifth of December, *Krampusnacht* in Austrian tradition, Jonathan cowered under his bed, hiding from the goat-demon he was sure would come to torture him.

THREE: Direction

The past is never dead. It's not even past.
— William Faulkner

Chapter 23
Commitment

Duluth, Minnesota, 1910

Sometimes we act on knowledge, sometimes on faith. We may call the latter intuition or impulse or instinct, but to then take action on it is still an act of faith. Weeks had gone by with neither a reply nor the letter I had posted to Duluth returned undelivered. It was possible that the mails were slower than I had surmised; it was possible that the letter had been mishandled by staff at the Bethel Home. Many things were possible, but only one made sense to me. You had been exiled, banished to the far north, to the Ultima Thule of the Zenith City, as Duluth was known.

On faith, I purchased a train ticket to Duluth. In the dead of a cold and miserable winter, I was heading north, true testimony to my commitment — or to my folly. Looking back, I see it as the birth of those instincts that have enabled me to pursue stories, to chase down informants, and to find my way to discoveries that oth-

ers walk by unheeded. But at the time I was only a young man in love, trying to locate again the love of his life. Was it also an aside to my mother, whose reaction to my withdrawal from college exceeded even the hyperboles of my imagination? She had tried to legislate my future, but I had betrayed hers.

Knowing now what was to follow, I have more sympathy, and I have long since forgiven her and my father alike. They were doing their best dealing with a son and a circumstance that were beyond what nature and experience had equipped them to surmount. Their only son had stepped off the path, not only the Path of the Righteous, but the path of the reasonable. I was giving up college and career to pursue a fantasy, one whose details they were beginning to see but had not yet fully translated into words — or accusations.

The wind outside the railway depot in Duluth struck Jakob like an icy glove to the face. The Chicago, St. Paul, Minneapolis & Omaha Passenger Station was a dreary brick building smaller than some of the grander houses in St. Paul. From it, a simple canopy extended alongside the single track. Jakob knew that no one would be waiting to greet him even as a part of him wanted for someone to run up to throw arms around him and welcome him. He was in unknown territory, and the circumscribed world of university life in St. Paul might as well have been on another continent.

He had arrived with intent but no plan. Making it up on the spot, he decided the first objective would be to find shelter from the arctic conditions, the second to obtain something to eat. A decent hotel would meet both criteria. He walked into town, toward the waterfront, where he figured he might find cheaper lodging. There, a four-story brick hotel advertised rooms he could just afford. A saloon across the street offered free sandwiches. Free, of course, meant for the price of a pint of beer or a shot of whiskey followed by at least another of the same. If he nursed his drinks and ate his fill, he could stretch his savings for a few weeks.

The steely overcast was slowly giving way to threatening smears of charcoal-shaded clouds. Against the darkening sky, the skyline at the waterfront was dominated by the city's famed aerial bridge across the shipping canal, its grand gondola suspended by spindly steel legs from the trestle span high overhead. He watched, mesmerized, as passengers and cars were loaded onto the platform of the gondola and slowly ferried across above the ice-spotted waters of the channel.

The saloon was warm and noisy, filled with laborers and sailors whose work left room for a pint in late afternoon. As Jakob edged up to the bar, he could tell from the attire and facial stubble of some of the clients that they probably had the time because they did not have the work. A bartender in a drink-stained apron made a half-hearted swipe with a towel at the surface in front of him. "What'll it be?"

"A beer. And how do I get one of those free sandwiches?"

"You come in before two, you do. We don't feed people all day, you know."

"Well, my train just got in from the Twin Cities. I was hoping to get a bite . . ."

"Cook'll be back for the dinner crowd in another hour, but it'll cost you."

"Yeah, well . . ."

"What brings you up here, son? If you're looking for work, it's not the best time of year. Not a lot are hiring."

"Not looking for work, just looking for something to eat. I already have a job." He wished it were true.

"Oh, really? What do you do, kid?"

What do I do, he thought. He knew what he wanted to do, what he had always wanted to do. Why not start now? "I'm a writer. For the newspapers. With the *Pioneer Press*." The truth, safely stashed hundreds of miles to the south, did not seem likely to catch up with him.

"Oh, yeah?" The bartender polished a glass with a towel that seemed to leave behind more than it wiped away. "You one of those cub reporters you hear about?"

"I guess you could say that. A hungry cub at the moment."

"Hey, look, kid." The man reached under the bar and pulled out a plate of sandwiches: thin circles of salami between thick slices of rye bread. "Saved these from the lunch crowd. More'n I'll eat. Help yourself. There's mustard in the pot there. And here's your beer. Pay me before you leave or my brother will find you, and that would not be a good way to start your week."

"Thanks." He picked up one of the bulky triangles of bread and meat. "Thanks for the sandwich. You sure you have enough?"

"Yeah, I'm sure. You know, you're the first reporter I ever talked with. What are you reporting on?"

"Uh, well," — think fast — "the Bethel Home."

"Which one? The Lake Avenue mission or the one for wayward women?"

"Uh, really both, you know, the whole story for a Sunday supplement feature."

"Well, really now, ain't that something. You come all the way up here to write about drunks and ladies of the night, eh?"

"Well, I don't think they're all, well . . . That's what I'm here to learn about. That's how it works with reporters; we try to find out the real story."

"Real story, eh? You know, when you walked in I almost took you for a student, maybe looking for your dad or something."

The unintended irony was not lost on Jakob. "I know, I get that all the time. I look younger than I am."

"Hmmm. Well, good luck with them do-good preachy types that run the missions." He held out his hand for a shake. "People call me Ole. That's because they think it goes with my last name, Pignoli, and they think everybody up here's gotta be a Swede. Ole Pignoli. See? And if you ever want to do a story on how an Italian from the warm and sunny tip of Italy's boot ended up in this frigid hole, you come back here, and I'll give you one hell of a tale."

"Thanks, Ole. You can call me Jake. I'll keep your story in mind."

→» «←

Jakob figured his impulsive lie about being a newspaper writer working on a story about the Bethel missions would be good cover, but he regretted not having done more research in advance. He knew of the Bethel Rescue Home but nothing about the Lake Avenue mission. He started early the next day by locating the mission for men, in hopes he could get some sense of the organization and pick up some names to drop before heading over to the shelter for women.

The four-story clapboard building on Lake Avenue in the canal district was a utilitarian pastiche that looked as if the architect and builders had been recruited from among the drifters the Bethel mission had been chartered to serve. When he remarked on the construction, the clerk who greeted him inside explained that the building had twice been raised to add another floor, first in 1893 and then again in 1899.

The clerk was a big man whose beard was inexpertly trimmed and whose gray shirt was clean but had not benefited from an iron. When he smiled, which he did to punctuate every other sentence, he flashed the gap of a missing front tooth. "We do our utmost," the man said. "The need is so great and it only grows with the passing years. But we're here to serve and to save souls. To our thinking, no man is too low, too lost, to be unworthy of Christian charity. But, as we say among ourselves, the spirit is willing, but the building is small." He laughed, a high-pitched snort. "Seriously, it breaks my heart when we have to turn someone away because all our beds are filled.

"But, and I say this with gratitude and humility, the Lord provides for those who labor in His name. Next year we will be moving into a fine new facility, a fireproof brick structure up on Mesaba Avenue. I've seen the drawings of it, a vee-shaped building with the open arms of its two wings spread wide to welcome one and all."

The clerk seemed eager to talk, even to boast a little, though always with an apology or qualifier. "Of course, I am not one to speak. I greet the guests and keep the registry, but, as God is my witness, I would not be alive today were it not for the Reverend Doctor Salter and the work he started here."

"Is the Reverend available? I would like very much to speak with him."

"I am afraid not. The good Reverend, God rest his soul, passed away more than a dozen years ago. Dr. Moody, a most able successor, now leads the mission. But I regret to say he's not available this week. He's out raising funds for the furnishment of our new building."

Jakob spent the entire morning with the clerk, a semi-permanent resident of the mission who turned out to be an able informant and encyclopedic source on everything about the Bethel Society and its work. In the course of the day, Jakob was introduced to various of the "guests" and volunteers and was led on a tour of nearly every square foot of the building, including the boiler room and the very crowded kitchen. Before leaving, he was cajoled into taking part in a midday prayer meeting in which he was introduced to all in attendance, who then laid their hands on him and prayed for the Lord to aid him in spreading word of the mission's good works.

Lunch back at the saloon, a beer and two sandwiches followed by a beer to wash it down, was spent poring over his pages of notes from the morning and committing to memory the names and positions of people who had been mentioned or introduced to him. He set off in good spirits for the Rescue Home on Sixth Avenue.

⇛ ⇚

The young woman who greeted him was formal and uninformative. She looked to be about the same age as Maggie and in a similar state. Her blond hair was done in a prim bun at the back, and she spoke with an accent that made him think of Swedish but not any dialect he had ever heard. He told her he was a reporter and produced a steno notebook for effect.

"I'm sorry," she said, "you'll have to speak with our superintendent. I really can't answer any questions. I'm afraid it's not allowed."

"Very well, may I speak with the superintendent?"

"Miss Mauck has not yet returned from lunch. She is speaking to a group of Baptist women about the work here. Well, actually about keeping young girls from sin."

"Could I wait."

"No, we have strict rules about men in the building, and there's really no place for you to wait. You could come back at half-past two if you wish. Perhaps Miss Mauck will see you then."

"It's rather brisk outdoors today. I could sit over there, out of the way. I promise to be quiet and not to intrude." He stepped toward a ladder-back chair standing against the opposite wall.

"I really must ask you to leave. If you wish to return later, that would be fine, but I can't let you stay."

Recognizing her resolve, Jakob accepted defeat. With few alternatives, he headed back to the saloon across from his hotel. Ole was not around, and the bartender on duty said he would have to buy something or leave, so Jakob ordered his third beer of the day. The semblance of a warm glow spread through him, and he passed the time thinking about the article which he was not actually writing but which was taking shape in his mind.

⇒》 《⇐

The sign on the door read Jessie E. Mauck, Superintendent. The woman at the small desk did not look up when he was ushered in by the same young woman who had first greeted him earlier in the day. The superintendent finished the entry she was writing in a large ledger, capped her fountain pen, and set it down before standing behind the desk. "I'm Jessie Mauck, and you are . . . ?"

He was about to give his name when he realized it might be a liability, since he did not know what Maggie might have said about him or if she might hear of his visit. "Jake, Jake Isaacs, at your service, Mrs. Mauck."

"*Miss* Mauck. One of my girls says you are a reporter."

"Yes, that's right, working on a story about the work of the Bethel Society."

"Well, then, Mr. Isaacs, let me remind you that our work involves helping the unfortunate and the fallen as well as fighting against sin in all its guises. That, Mr. Isaacs, includes the Devil's own brew. We do not continence intemperance anywhere, and certainly not in the presence of our girls. If you had said you were a sailor off one of the tugs or a logger taking a break from the north woods, I might make more sense of your weakness, though I still would not approve. But you claim to be a reporter, a literate person charged with the task of writing to keep the public informed. It is incomprehensible that only hours past midday you would arrive in this state." She sat down again.

"The story of our work deserves to be told and told widely, Mr. Isaacs. Moreover, that telling might well help advance our cause. It is only for those reasons that I will agree to meet with you at all, but only after you have sobered up."

"I . . . I don't understand. I am sober."

"Adding untruth to your trespasses will not aid your case. Even with a desk between us, I can smell the alcohol on your breath. Now, please go, and do not return until your sobriety is restored." She picked up her pen, removed the cap, and began to write another entry in the ledger lying open on her desk.

Chastened and embarrassed, Jakob left. As he approached the reception desk by the door, he noticed the receptionist talking with a girl whose back was to him. From the sound of her voice and the shape of her gestures, there was no doubt in his mind who it was. It was Maggie. He suppressed the urge to call her name.

It did not look like he would be able to casually slip past her on his way out. He looked around for someplace to duck into until Maggie and the girl were through talking, but there was only the closed door of the Superintendent's office. He rapped lightly on the glass, pushed the door open, and stepped in.

"My deepest apologies, Miss Mauck. You are so right, and I should not have indulged myself with beer at lunch. It is not my habit, at any rate, but perhaps you could find time in your busy schedule to talk with me sometime tomorrow morning."

She capped her pen and placed it in the crease of the ledger. "Sincere apologies to those we have hurt or offended are a step on the road to recovery and redemption. I accept your apology and will see you — sober, I trust — at nine sharp tomorrow morning. In light of your state today, I suggest you take the side entrance to exit without further risk of corruption for any of our girls. To the right down the hall, then on your right." She looked down at the papers on her desk and continued her work.

Jakob scurried down the hallway and out the side entrance without even a glance back. His heart pounded, not only from his narrow escape but also with the thrill of knowing that he had found his Lena.

⋙ ⋘

The trek from the hotel to the Rescue Home was becoming familiar but, with fresh snow from an overnight storm, no easier. He was breathing hard by the time he arrived. A different girl, with a pretty face and sad eyes, was at the reception desk. "You must be the reporter."

"Yes, Jake Isaacs at your service, Miss . . ."

"Tina. We don't use last names here. I'm Tina because there was already a Christina staying here when I arrived. Miss Mauck told me to show you to her office as soon as you arrived." The girl rocked herself awkwardly up out of the chair, and Jakob could guess that it would not be long until she would be delivering.

He wanted to ask her when she was due and about her stay at the Rescue Home, but the whole situation felt awkward. "I imagine new arrivals must be quite frequent. I mean babies, of course, not new . . . er, new girls."

"Yes, quite frequent, I would say. Just last night Maggie delivered a boy." She put her small fist in front of her mouth. "I'm sorry, we're not supposed to talk about the girls with strangers."

Jakob's heart sped up. "I'm not a stranger. I'm Jake. I'm a reporter, and I'm here to learn your stories and tell them. This girl, Maggie —"

"Oh, please forget I said anything. Frankly, I'm not sure many of us would want our stories told. I know I wouldn't. Oh, there I go, still talking. You'd think after nearly three months I would be accustomed to the rules and routine. My mother always said I was not good at staying on the path." She placed both hands on her midsection. "I'm the walking proof that she was right. And here I am still talking with you. Let me take you to Miss Mauck before I talk myself into more trouble. Please say nothing to her."

"Don't worry, I won't."

The superintendent was at her desk, wearing a dress that Jakob thought matched in all but its slightly darker gray the one she had worn the day before, and she was occupied with the same ledger book. She closed it before standing without extending her hand except to gesture for him to sit. "Please, let us begin. We have half an hour before my regular morning meeting with the girls. Let me start with the history of the Bethel Rescue Home for Women and Children." Without pause, the woman launched into a well-rehearsed chronology. Jakob extracted his notebook from his briefcase and began writing in earnest.

Nearly a quarter hour passed before she paused. "Any questions?"

"Yes, would it be possible to speak with any of the girls, to learn their stories?"

"No, out of the question, against policy. But I can tell you whatever you want to know."

"Well, let's see. Are all your girls from the Duluth area?"

"Most are, but not all. Some, of course, came from other towns for many reasons but fell into a sordid life once here. I remember a girl from down in Rochester, lured here under the belief she was to marry a local businessman only to be abandoned and left to walk the streets. A very sad case."

"I write for the city papers. Keeping in mind our readers, I'm wondering if any girls from the Twin Cities find their way up here."

"Not a great many, of course, as the metropolitan area has its own resources. But, yes. In fact we have one girl with us right now — we'll call her Martha, since you mustn't use any real names. She came to us after being taken advantage of by a college student. She was brought here by her uncle, under some duress if I must say. He did not want to risk the shame of her predicament becoming common knowledge in his rather tight-knit community. He was fully aware that we are not a Catholic charity — a Christian institution, yes, but not Roman Catholic — and he was quite comfortable with this despite his own adherence to the Roman faith."

"This girl, Martha, how has she fared?"

"Well, I would say quite well, considering. In fact, she delivered a healthy baby boy just last night. She named him Frank. But remember, you can't use that in your story."

Jakob asked her to tell him more stories about the girls and their babies, and she obliged. While she regaled him with vignettes laden with testimony to the power of faith and Christian love, he was thinking that he had only a week to come up with a plan for his infant son.

On his way out, he smiled at the girl still at the reception desk. "I don't suppose you would know anything about the Jewish community in town. It's for another story I'm working on."

"No, I'm new to Duluth, but I do remember Judith mentioning something about the Third Street shoal or school or something like that. She is of the Hebrew faith, but our evangelist thinks we can yet bring her to Christ. Oh, there I go again, using names and all."

"Don't worry, I'll not say anything." He winked at her and left.

Chapter 24
Covenant

Who is a Jew, and what makes him Jewish? How is this question different from asking who is Catholic, who evangelical? The answers vary with time and place, even with the asker. In the bible, Ruth becomes one of the Chosen People with the simplest of declarations. Your people will become my people, your God will be my God. No council of rabbis ruled on her fitness for what she was taking on, no onlooker challenged her assumption of the yoke of the Law. You and I spoke of this more than once and without resolution. We debated old matters anew, not because we believed we could outdo the rabbis and scholars with their learned arguments and calculated counterpoints; it was because the question was so personal, as it had been for so many of our forbearers, because it weighed so heavily in our futures.

Some are born into identity, some have to choose. Some struggle to break free, others to remain. As a young man, I was already well on the path of the wanderer, walking away from the Goodly Tents to roam the stark sands of disbelief, even as I was praying for you to enter the encampment and to declare yourself, as Ruth did, or at least to acknowledge that the blood of the Tribe ran in your veins. When it was but us two, the question hovered over us, a bee buzzing for attention. When we became three, it descended like the sirocco, scouring me with its gritty blast and driving me to new desperation.

Jakob now had a deadline. A little library research revealed the deep roots of the Jews of Duluth, who numbered some two thousand from a mix of Germanic and Slavic backgrounds. A couple of days of planning and reconnoitering took him to the large white Byzantine-inspired building of Adas Israel, known to the local community as the Third Street Shul. There, the full-bearded Rabbi Saperstein was less than enthusiastic about Jakob's request.

"This is not how we normally do things, you know, and offhand I do not see how it squares with *Halacha*. It will require some review of Jewish Law and some reflection before I could even consider it. You should know, there are three other synagogues in Duluth: Tifereth Israel, B'nei Israel, and Temple Emanuel. Come to think of it, you might fare better over at Emanuel. It was founded by German and Hungarian Jews of the Reform movement. They are much more, what shall we say, *flexible* in their interpretations and observance."

Yes, thought Jakob, those are my people.

Temple Emanuel on Duluth's East End stood out from its surroundings. It was smaller and older than Adas Israel, but with its Moorish entrance under an imposing central onion-dome and four smaller domed spires atop the façade, it was also more ornate. Rabbi Mendel Silber had just finished leading a minyan in their morning prayers when Jakob arrived. In a bid to build instant bridges, Jakob introduced himself and gave his Hebrew name, *Yacov ben Mordichai, haLevi*, explaining that he had become bar mitzvah under Rabbi Hess at a Reform temple in St. Paul: Mount Zion.

"Ah, my good colleague Emanuel Hess. It has been many years. How is he?"

"Rabbi Hess, may his memory be a blessing, died three years ago . . . no four."

"*Baruch Dayan haEmet.* Blessed be the True Judge. I am sorry to hear this news. He was a fine man. Welcome to the Zenith City, young man. What brings you, and what can I do for you?"

Jakob told him a condensed version of the story he had been constructing, elaborating it to suit his request.

The Rabbi stroked his beard. "So, let me see. You're here in Duluth with your wife, your son was born two days ago, your wife is bedridden but recovering, and you want to bring your son here in the middle of the night for a *bris*? That is rather strange, so late, you must admit."

"It is . . . a family custom, going back to my father's days in Austria where he was raised and where observance sometimes needed to be hidden in the night. It is my way to honor his memory, may it be a blessing." It was a fabrication of the moment, one Jakob hope would be believed.

"Well, I have never heard of that, though many of our members are also from Austria and Hungary. However, to honor your father, perhaps we can manage it. Let me check my calendar to see whether we can arrange everything for your son's eighth day."

⇥ ⇤

Jakob left the temple knowing that he had just completed the easy part. To set in motion the hard part, he made a return visit to the Bethel Rescue Home for a third meeting with Miss Mauck. She warmed after he apologized again for his inexcusable first encounter and thanked her profusely for all that she had shared with him. "If you have but a few minutes to spare," he said, "I have a few more questions about how your program works."

"Certainly, I can make the time to be sure the story is correctly told."

"Excellent. So, tell me, do the girls leave once their babies are born? What happens next?"

"Some do leave quite soon after giving birth, if they have someplace to which to return. Most stay on for some weeks or months to recover and get back on their feet until a suitable placement or a reconciliation with family can be arranged. And some are with us much longer."

"So, for example, this girl" — he made clear he was checking his notes — "the one we called Martha. She is still here? Headed back to the Twin Cities? What?"

"Well, I really can't speak of her plans, but for now she is here and recovering from a somewhat difficult delivery."

"And the baby? Do I understand the babies are kept in a nursery? Is that right?"

"Yes, and they are brought to the mothers for nursing or other reasons. Newborns have their own section separate from the older ones, as they can sometimes start crying in consort and it is quite stressful for all, as you can imagine."

"I don't suppose I could see the nursery. It would help me to write the story in a way that can make it come more alive for the reader."

"No, that would not be possible, but I can show you a photograph taken last year, if that will help."

"Oh, most definitely."

She rose to riffle through a stack of documents atop a cabinet. "Ah, here it is."

Jakob studied the picture. "And this nursery, it's on this floor" — he pivoted — "just where?"

"No, it's down the hall from the mothers' dormitory, at the back."

"I see." He asked a few more questions for the hypothetical feature story that was now growing quite long. "Oh, yes, I was wondering about security. Given the babies and the mothers, and the sort of people who pass through Duluth, I imagine you have a night watchman."

"We hardly have the budget for that, but the caretaker sleeps in his quarters in the basement adjacent the boiler. He does make rounds at midnight, to make sure the radiators are working and the windows and doors are secure. And, of course, some of my staff also overnight. Babies do not arrive or become hungry by the clock, you know."

After the interview, Jakob once again exited by the side entrance, stopping at the water closet on his way. There he wedged a piece of pasteboard in the sash of the high window after jimmying the latch so it just barely held. He tested his work to be sure it would stand up to a quick inspection in the dark. Next, a shopping spree in the afternoon and he would be ready.

⇛ ⇚

Recent days had delivered a warming trend, but overnight temperatures still fell well below zero. A gibbous moon shown through scattered clouds as Jakob set out from the hotel. He was beginning to have real doubts about whether his plan was at all feasible. He had dressed all in black and with a dark wool scarf, purchased that afternoon, wrapped around his face. The basket he carried was stuffed with a feather pillow, borrowed from his hotel room and flattened into a comforter, and a wool blanket folded triple. He knew little or nothing of infants and could only hope it would be enough to keep the baby warm.

Timing was everything. At the Rescue Home, he would have to wait for the caretaker to complete his rounds before entering, and then be out and running to reach the Rabbi's residence before he and the *mohel* gave up waiting. Across the street from the Rescue Home, Jakob watched for the light in the basement window, then held his breath until it went out again. The caretaker had finished his rounds for the night.

Jakob walked around the building until he located the correct small window. He used the upended basket as an unsteady stepstool while he levered the window with the large screwdriver he had slipped from his belt. The sash did not open until he rattled it up and down several times. He looked about to see if the noise had drawn attention, but the street was quiet.

Hoisting himself up and through the window took all his strength and agility. He tugged at the cord tied to his belt at one end and tethered to the basket at the other. When the cord jammed, he panicked, thinking that the basket might be too big to come through the window. A quick peek out confirmed that the basket only needed to be turned endwise to fit through.

He was in.

The floorboards creaked underfoot as he headed toward where he remembered the nursery to be. Every few steps, he would stop to listen. Overhead, he could hear gentle footfalls back and forth, as if someone were pacing. He reached the end of the hall without having located the nursery, even though he had boldly opened every door for a glimpse.

The sign and arrow ahead were nearly invisible in the dark, but they pointed up a stairwell. He had misunderstood Miss Mauck, or she had misled him. He had no choice but to climb the stairs. His feet hugged the wall at each step in an attempt to avoid any creaking. The trick worked until a step near the top groaned loudly when he shifted his weight onto it. He lifted his foot, then stretched to skip the step, but in the process succeeded in banging the basket against the handrail. He froze. In some room ahead, the regular soft thuds of the pacing paused, then continued.

The first door on his left was ajar. He looked in to see a row of cribs, each with a tightly swaddled baby asleep within. In the corner, a small lamp with a dark shade left the room in dim light and deep shadows. At the foot of each crib hung a chart. He checked each until he found one marked "Frank (Maggie's)." This was it. He looked down at his sleeping son. So beautiful, he thought, and so tiny. As a boy, Jakob had twice held a newborn cousin for a few seconds before being relieved of the duty. Now he would have to pick up his son without awakening him, tuck him into the basket, and make his exit back down the stairs and out without getting caught.

He opened the basket and placed it strategically close to the crib. Slipping one hand under the baby's head and the other under his back, he gently lifted the bundle up and over the side of the crib. The sleeping Frank let out a slight whimper as he was tucked into the basket and the blanket and comforter were pulled around him. Jakob ever so gently closed the lid and redid the toggle holding it. He waited. Not a sound.

He tiptoed toward the door and slowly pulled it fully open. The hinges squeaked, and behind him was a sharp cry, then another, then a high wailing that rippled along the row of cribs. Just as he stepped into the hall, there was a scream, very loud and very high — and very near. Before him stood a young woman in a nightshirt and robe holding a baby who was now crying a soprano descant to her screams. Before he could move, a nurse in a white cap was running toward him, heavy swift footsteps were coming up the stairs behind him, and the hall was rapidly filling with young women.

To a chorus of shouts, the lights in the hallway were suddenly switched on.

"What are you doing?"

"He's stealing one of the babies."

"Kidnapper!"

"Call the police!"

Behind him, a man's voice, calm and commanding, told him to put down the basket.

"I ... it's not what you think. Don't call the police. I'm only taking him to ... I can explain. Not the police." Jakob set down the basket and undid the long cord from its handle.

"What are you doing here, Jakob?" Maggie walked toward him through the knot of young women.

"You know this man?" the nurse asked.

"Yes, Nurse Macintyre, I know him."

"And what is he doing here?"

Maggie came over and looked up at Jakob. She leaned close and spoke in a near whisper. "Are you crazy? What do you think you are doing here?"

"I wanted ... our son ... I wanted him to be circumcised. To become a —"

"What did he say?" The nurse was now beside Maggie. "Did he say something about circumcision?"

"I did, I ..."

Maggie smiled indulgently up at Jakob and shook her head. "You'd go to jail, you know. It's kidnapping."

One of the girls had opened the basket and now handed a still-sleeping Frank to Maggie.

Jakob hung his head. "I was only trying to . . ."

The nurse was indignant. "This is twentieth-century America, and we follow modern medical practice. All male babies are circumcised unless there is medical reason otherwise or at the mother's request. But I do not see why that would concern you."

A young woman with long black hair stepped forward. "I think I know, Nurse Macintyre."

"And how is that, Judith?"

The girl named Judith started to explain what a *bris* was. With everyone turned toward the nurse and Judith, Jakob saw his chance. He whirled and leaped for the stairs, taking them two at a time before the caretaker could react. He ran straight toward the front entrance, undid the latch, and hurried out into the night, still trailing the cord by which he had hoisted the basket.

As he ran, he was thinking of his son, *Ephraim ben Yacov, ha-Levi*, the infant son he had just abandoned.

Chapter 25
Mass

Mary Samson stared at the floor of the bedroom and shrugged her shoulders. "I'm just not hungry."

Josef pleaded to the doctor. "But can't you see? She's wasting away, she's as skinny as one of the light poles in the street. I tell her to eat, and she just says she's not hungry."

"But, I keep telling him, eating makes me feel sick. Why should I eat if I'm not hungry and food makes me ill?"

"All right." The doctor stopped tapping his knee and stood up from the chair beside the bed. "Mr. Samson, would you please wait in the other room while I examine your wife."

"I can pay, you understand. I'm not asking for charity."

"Of course, Mr. Samson. Now just please wait in the other room while I examine your wife and see what the problem might be."

Josef looked anxious. He squeezed Mary's hand and let go of it with some reluctance. "I'll be in the living room."

⇢⇢ ⇠⇠

Dr. Bergen open his bag and started with the usual procedures, taking her pulse, listening to her heart, and testing her reflexes. He took note of her distended abdomen, and when he pressed in on the right side, she winced.

"You know, doctor, I have been so bloated at times lately that I was beginning to wonder if I was pregnant again. But that's ridiculous."

The doctor said nothing and continued his examination.

195

The whites of her eyes were stained, and her skin had taken on a sallow tinge. When he asked about itching, she expressed surprise. "That is funny you should ask, doctor. I seem to feel itchy all the time. It must be some form of pollen attack or something. I mean, with the spring and the summer-like weather and all. Right?"

Dr. Bergen was already narrowing in on a diagnosis. "How is your shoulder? Any pain up here?"

"Yes, how did you know? I think I must have strained it somehow, but I don't remember when or how."

"I don't think you injured it, Mrs. Samson. Let me check your abdomen again." On the right, he palpated a large, firm mass and on the left found her spleen to be enlarged. He told Mrs. Samson to get dressed again while he left to fetch her husband.

"Well, I am sure you both want to know what is going on, why Mary has become so thin and sickly." He leaned forward in the chair. "I am sorry to tell you that the news is not very good. I believe it's cancer, cancer of the liver."

"What does that mean?"

"If it's true, and I am quite sure it is, it means there is not very much that we can do. At the University they have started using x-rays to treat some cancers with a certain measure of success, but liver cancer is not among those. I am so sorry. The cancer is already very advanced, which is often the case with liver cancer when it is finally diagnosed, and it appears to have spread."

Josef was getting quite agitated. "But what are you saying, doctor? What does this mean?"

Mary took his hand. "My dear Josef, it simply means that I am dying, that I am soon to meet whoever was my maker. That is what the doctor is saying."

"No, that can't be, you're not even fifty yet. You can't be dying, you can't have cancer. How did she get it, doctor? How did she catch it?"

"We really know little about what causes cancer, but we do know you don't catch it. It just happens. Part of the body goes wild and starts growing and damaging everything around it. Some few cancers we can treat or remove surgically, but not liver cancer, not yet, anyway. I'm sorry, very sorry."

�➤➤ ⫷⫷

The weeks ahead were a strange duet for Mary and Josef and a confusion for their three children. As Mary weakened, Josef leaned on her all the more for emotional support. It was Mary who had to buoy his spirts, Mary who still had to care for the children, Mary who had to have breakfast waiting before work and sandwiches packed into lunch pails before school. The pain increased and became her constant companion until the doctor prescribed morphine. And then May arrived, and Mary could not rise from bed. On the third of May she did not wake up.

Maggie found her in the morning and knew right away what had happened. She kissed her mother's forehead, then knelt by the bed and prayed for her mother's soul before rising to tell the rest of the family and to summon the priest.

The St. Agnes community closed ranks and came to the aid of the Samsons, ladling out sympathy and dropping off packages of food at their doorstep. Mary was buried beside their son, Joseph Martin, who had loved horses too much. After the graveside service, Josef took two river-rounded pebbles from his pocket and placed one on the marker for their son and one on the ground at the head of his wife's still open grave.

Maggie looked up at him. "Why did you do that, Papa?"

"I don't know, exactly, my little Lena. It is something I promised your mother, something her people do at the grave of a loved one." As he stood holding Maggie's hand he whispered, "Goodbye, goodbye my Miriam."

He did not cry then, but Josef was devastated and spent the rest of the day sitting on the porch, staring into the street. His two younger children were lost but quickly immersed themselves again in schoolwork and the distractions of friends. Only Maria seemed to fully grasp what was happening to the family and rose to the role that was demanded of her. At sixteen, she became the lady of the house. With the same quiet stoicism her mother had always manifest, she took on household duties and comforted her father, who threw himself into work but became ever more despondent at home.

➸➺ ⋘

Josef was now the one sitting on the side of the bed. "I don't know what it is, doctor. I am sorry to be calling you back so soon after ... after Mary, you know ... well, I was feeling down. I guess that is to be expected, but now I seem to have no strength. I had this cough, back in June, like a summer cold that wouldn't go away. And then, even the least exertion would leave me out of breath, and by the end of the day at work I'm exhausted, wheezing. I come home and go to bed. And see, look at me." He lifted his shirt. "I'm losing weight. But that's not why I called for you."

"Tell me."

"The cough. I'm coughing up blood. First a few spots, then more. Now, if I have a coughing fit, the handkerchief is soaked in bloody clots."

"We need to get you into the hospital."

"No, doctor, no hospital. We can't afford that. Besides, you go to the hospital, and then you die."

"It's not really like that. In a hospital we can keep an eye on you, do some tests, try medicines — "

"No, no hospital."

"All right, we'll see. Let me examine you."

-»» «««-

The children were in the kitchen and rose in unison when Dr. Bergen came in from the bedroom. As the oldest, Maria took the initiative. "What is it? What's wrong with him?"

"Your father, I am sorry to say, is very ill. He needs rest, but he refuses to go to the hospital. He is becoming too weak to take care of himself. If it is consumption, as I suspect, there are not many options. Minnesota does not yet have a sanitarium for the care of those with this affliction, but there is talk of starting such an institution in the near future. I fear it's going to fall to you to nurse him back to health. If that's possible. It could take a very long time."

Maria straightened her posture. "I can do that, just tell me what to do."

"And I'll help," Maggie added.

The girls established a routine, dividing the day and the duties. As the oldest, Maria took on the night shift, with Maggie relieving her in the morning. Their father insisted that there was no need for anyone to keep a vigil, but Maria had taken to sleeping on a folding cot outside the bedroom door.

The following Sunday, Maggie rose early to bake sweet biscuits, working quietly so as not to awaken Maria. She balanced the plate of biscuits and jam in one hand as she slipped gingerly past her sleeping sister and slowly opened the door.

Her father was turned away, facing the wall. The pillow was stiff with dried blood and the thin sheet spread over his shoulders was not moving. Maggie set the plate on the floor and dropped to her knees, for the second time that year praying for the soul of a parent. It was three months, nearly to the day, after his wife had died, and Josef, who had many times told Mary that he could not live without her, had surrendered to his own prophesy.

Dr. Bergen argued that an autopsy was in order. He had diagnosed tuberculosis but admitted it might have been cancer. As the oldest, Maria vetoed the autopsy. "Pulmonary tuberculosis" was recorded as the cause on the death certificate, but cancer was whispered at the funeral and became enshrined in family folklore.

At the funeral service, the three children sat with their uncle and aunt and the Hoffmann children through the long and somber Mass. Instead of returning to their own home, they followed the Hoffmanns in silent parade to the house on Van Buren. That night they slept on cots set up on the screen porch, whispering in the darkness late into the night, talking about what they would do, how they would cope with a new life.

They were orphans.

Chapter 26
Surrender

St. Paul, Minnesota, 1910

Acceptance can be difficult for the young, yet you always seemed to excel at it beyond your years. It had taken much time before you would talk with me about what had happened, how you had lost your parents, and to begin to show me the hidden scars from that summer of loss. Slowly, I began to see how needy you were, how desperate you were to have a family, to belong, and how deeply you had been let down by the Hoffmanns, who had sheltered and fed you but failed to nurture and protect you. I wanted to say more to you about my growing understanding, but I had closed all doors with my one act of midnight idiocy in Duluth. I wanted to embrace you and tell you that we could work things out together, but I could not risk even approaching the Rescue Home for fear that I would be arrested and ushered off to prison.

I had come to Duluth, buoyed by the belief that soon our son would truly become a Jew. I had failed.

Am I no longer a Jew if I eat the flesh of a pig or sprinkle cheese over my pasta and meat sauce as the Italians do? Or am I still a Jew, but one who has broken a commandment? Am I less a man because long ago, a piece of skin was cut from my manhood? Is our son less a Jew because I was unable to steal him away and take him to the rabbi?

In truth, I am not sure whether I was more concerned for the wellbeing of you and the baby or for myself. In any case, after a week of hiding out in my hotel room during which I pretended to be writing a newspaper article, I purchased a return ticket to St. Paul, girding myself for an uncertain future.

Jakob rang the doorbell and waited, hands politely folded behind his back. The door opened only after some minutes; his father stood in the doorway, mouth agape. "Hello, Papa. I've come to pick up some of my things. I won't bother you for long."

"I don't know what to say, son."

"You could say, 'Come in, come in out of the cold, Jakob.'"

"Well, yes, of course. You know, your mother and I have been at wit's end not knowing where you were or what might have happened to you. Let me get your mother." He turned. "Oh, here she is. Dearest, it's Jakob," he said, turning. "He says he's here for some of his things."

Sadie's lips quivered for the briefest moment. "I can see that, Morris. I do have eyes, you know. Well, don't just stand there, you two, keeping the door open to the March winds. Have some common sense."

Jakob stepped in and set his empty valise to one side. "Thank you for the warm welcome, Mama. I see you haven't changed in my absence." The moment the words escaped his lips, Jakob regretted them. "I am sorry for causing you distress. There was something I simply had to do and very limited time in which to do it. I did miss you both, and I do apologize."

Sadie stepped forward beside her husband and took his arm. "I can't imagine what was so pressing, Jakob, that you had to leave without notice and without so much as a departing explanation."

"I left you a note."

"Nineteen words, Jakob, nineteen. 'Dearest Mama and Papa, I must travel away for a time. Please do not fret. Your loving son, Jakob.' I have received longer notes from the milkman."

Jakob tried unsuccessfully to suppress a grin. His mother had committed the note to memory, along with the word count. "Again, I apologize. I really don't want to cause you any more distress. I'm only here to collect some of my things, and then I'll be on my way."

"And what way is that?" she asked.

"Yes, where will you go?" his father added. "Where will you stay?"

"I have a couple of friends from the university who have a small apartment over in the Grodnik, what's also called Little Town, a neighborhood near campus. They have an empty bedroom. They have allowed me to stay there until I find work and a place of my own."

Morrie cleared his throat. "We have an empty bedroom here. You could — "

"Morris!"

"I just . . ."

Sadie shook her head. "Well, yes Morris, you just this and just that, starting and then leaving us once more in suspense over the remainder of your thought."

Jakob reached for his valise. "Perhaps I should come back at another, more convenient time."

"Perhaps inconvenience is unavoidable, Jakob. At any rate, your father in his unfinished sentences is true to the facts. We have not rented out your room. I can confirm that it remains available for your use under appropriate conditions."

"And what might those conditions be?"

"That you resume your studies at the university, that you apply yourself with the greatest diligence to making up for these lost weeks, and that you commit to completing your degree. And, of course, you will accept without protest a curfew that we impose."

"Of course."

"Then you agree?"

"I would consider it but for the fact that I have already withdrawn from the university under less than favorable circumstances. Whether I could be readmitted on application is in doubt, and certainly not for the current semester."

"Ah, but there you are mistaken. An inquiry at the administrative offices will confirm that you are still enrolled, although seriously behind in your classwork."

"I mean no disrespect, Mama, but in this it is you who is mistaken. I completed and filed the forms myself before I left for . . . well, before I left."

"That may be the case, but perhaps you might want to read this letter before reaching the wrong conclusion. I took the liberty of opening it, which seemed justified and prudent in light of your uncertain whereabouts when it arrived." She handed him an envelope bearing an official University of Minnesota return address.

Jakob slipped out the contents: a letter from the university and three pages of forms, his forms. Jakob laughed.

Morrie looked puzzled. "What is this letter? Will somebody please tell me what this is about?"

Jakob read aloud: "Dear Master Oster; As you failed to sign your petition of withdrawal, it cannot be accepted. If it is still your intent formally to withdraw from study at the University of Minnesota, please sign and return the accompanying forms to this office along with the $2.00 fee for special processing."

"Well?" His mother leaned forward expectantly.

"I surrender."

"Very well, then." Sadie smiled as she let go of Morrie's arm. "Dinner is at seven. The new girl, by the way, is showing her merit in all the domestic arts. I think you will find the brisket quite good. And I needn't remind you to dress for dinner. Unless you have lost track of the calendar in your wanderings, you already know it is the start of Shabbat. Do be on time."

In his room, which seemed to have shrunk during his weeks of absence, Jakob took out his journal from the desk drawer and began to write: "As I had underestimated my mother's fury when I jumped ship, so, too, I had underestimated her willingness to accept me back onboard, provided I paid the added fare. And so I am here, sailing on, my status downgraded from first to third-class. This I can endure. For now."

⇛ ⇚

Jakob pushed the stack of textbooks aside and stared at the wall until the pattern in the wallpaper shimmered with afterimages. The end of the semester was fast approaching, and it was looking like his best efforts to catch up with his studies were not enough. He was facing nothing better than a gentleman's *C* in every course but one.

He took out a sheet of stationery and started writing another letter to Maggie. After a couple of lines, he crumpled the sheet and tossed it into the wastebasket. What was the point? None of his letters sent to the Rescue Home or in care of the Hoffmans had been answered. He had tried without success to find out where she and their son were.

His work with the *Minnesota Daily*, the student newspaper, was the one bright spot in his life, that and the writing seminar in which he was doing *A* work. Over the semester he had seen his writing improve, and he was also learning that the best way to chase stories was not always straight down the road.

Realizing he was getting nowhere on any front, Jakob decided to take a break and get some fresh air. As he reached for his jacket on the peg at the bottom of the stairs, the flap on the mail slot in the front door popped open and a thin stack of letters dropped to the floor. He picked them up, riffled through them looking for a letter to him, then set them all on the hall table.

Suddenly inspired, he bounded out of the house and took off on a trot after the mailman. A few quick questions gave him the information about mail routes that he needed. He headed north.

It took some time crisscrossing streets and avenues in the area just south of the Church of St. Agnes before he caught up with the postman.

"Hey there, I'm looking for my cousins. They used to live with the Hoffmanns on Van Buren, but now it seems they moved out. I was thinking maybe if they lived somewhere around here, you of all people would know."

"Maybe. What's their names?"

"Samson, Jonathan and Maria Samson. Do you know where they . . . ?"

"Yeah, they didn't move very far. The blue-gray house across the street just down the block from the Hoffmanns. I delivered a letter there just yesterday."

"Thanks, thanks a lot."

⇛ ⇚

Jakob was still unsure of what his best tactic might be when he approached the front door of the small wood-frame house with its steep-pitched roof.

He knocked on the screen door. "Hello? Anybody home?"

A woman came to the door and Jakob's heart skipped. It was Maggie. Through the screen she said, "Yes? Can I help you?"

The face was right but the voice was not. "I'm a friend of Maggie Samson's. I've been away at school, and we lost touch. I don't know if I have the right address. I wonder if you know her."

"I know her. She's my younger sister. And I know you. You're the Oster boy. She wrote and said you might show up."

"She's not here? Do you know where she is?"

"I do, but she wrote that she doesn't want to see you and doesn't want me to tell you where she is."

"Then she's still in Duluth?"

"She's not here, that's all I can say, which is more than we told the census taker who came by in April. I know you tried to help, which is why I won't lie to you."

"Can you at least tell me whether she is well?"

"You really care about her, don't you?"

"Yes, I really care." He wanted to say more, to blurt out that he was in love with her, that he wanted to marry her, but he pushed the words back down. "I just want to know if she is all right."

"She is doing her best. We all are, trying to figure out what to do next. At the moment, I think that is hardest for Maggie. Jon and I don't have the responsibilities she has. Not yet, anyway. Jon has a girl he is sweet on, though, so who knows what lies ahead."

"Can you tell Maggie that I came by? I mean when you write."

The woman was silent.

"I guess I better go. I won't bother you again."

"Sometimes ... sometimes we just have to accept what happens even when we don't understand. Everything happens for a reason."

Jakob nodded. He turned and walked away before the welling tears betrayed him.

Chapter 27
Journalism

St. Paul, Minnesota, 1911

I did not continue studying law at the University of Minnesota. By the age of twenty-two I was already a failure — or a success — depending on your perspective. If forced to confess after a beer or two, I might admit to a relentless sense of failure and futility; if asked in the course of my work, I would speak of nothing but striding from triumph to triumph.

At least I did not have to continue my academic struggles to the point of being expelled in disgrace. While still a student, I was offered my first full-time job, writing for the tiny St. Paul Weekly, *a community newspaper that printed mostly human-interest stories with a local connection. I accepted the offer without hesitance and without even asking about the salary. It would not have mattered in any case. The salary was barely enough for a bachelor to live on, a fitting beginning for a long career of being underpaid and generally undervalued. In that first position, I did it all: chasing stories, making them up, editing, rewrite, and even soliciting ads from local merchants. And I loved every minute of it.*

I was not on a trajectory for a Pulitzer, but I took my assignments seriously and gradually honed the skills I had forged at the University and in my after-hours hobby of pursuing you. Along the way, I developed

*sources and strategies that enabled me to keep a remote
eye on you and my distant son.*

Jakob wondered just how long a Catholic wedding could last.
The angle on which he had pitched the story to his editor
was that it would be the last wedding before the June rush,
but Jakob was there for personal reasons. It was the day he
had wished for since leaving Duluth over a year earlier.
Across the street from the main entrance to St. Agnes, he
paced, camera in hand, waiting. With his fedora shading his
eyes and with his newly grown mustache, he was hopeful
that no one would recognize him. The church doors finally
opened, and a rush of well-wishers came out to line the
steps. The wedding party emerged amidst a rainstorm of
rice from either side. Jakob recognized Jonathan from a
picture Maggie had once shown him. The bride, yet another
Mary, the former Mary Kindl, also looked familiar, but
Jakob could not think how he could possibly know her.

He waited for the rest of the wedding party to line up at
the top of the steps. The official wedding photographer with
his tripod set up at the foot of the church steps would be in
the shot, but Jakob decided this would make for a more distinctive newspaper photo. He focused and clicked the shut-
ter. Taking his eye from the viewfinder, he realized someone
was missing. He did not see Maggie. Where was she? Surly
she had to be there for her brother's wedding. There was her
sister, Maria, among the bridesmaids, but no Maggie.

He watched with growing impatience as the church slowly
cleared. Was it possible she was still inside with the baby? It
didn't make sense, but he couldn't leave without at least trying. He crossed the street and climbed the now empty steps.
At the top he hesitated, thinking back to his first time at St.

Agnes. Though it felt silly, before he entered, he muttered to himself, *"Shakets teshaktsenu, veta'ev teta'avenu ki kherem hu."*

The church was empty. If Maggie had been at the wedding — which certainly she must have — he had somehow missed her. Crestfallen, Jakob folded his camera and left for the office.

He followed up with the priest the next day to verify the spelling of the names of those in the wedding party. "And wasn't there also another Samson?" he asked. "A younger sister? Wasn't she there?"

"No, if you're referring to who I think you are, she is still . . . away."

⇛ ⇚

Jakob stepped off the train and shook his head. "I can't believe I am once again trekking to Duluth in the dead of winter."

The man who had gotten off just behind him laughed. "This is not the dead of winter, son. It's only November. You should be here in February. That's the dead of winter."

Jakob turned and smiled. "I do know what you are talking about. I've been here in February. At least it's not snowing now."

"Just wait, it will be. Look at that sky. Those are snow clouds if ever I've seen them. You here on business or pleasure?"

"Yes, both. I'm hoping to see a friend. And I'm working on a story for one of the Twin City papers." This time it was true. It had been a hard sell, but eventually he had persuaded his editor to do a story on a prominent St. Paul businessman who had pulled up stakes and relocated to Duluth.

"What paper?"

"One you probably never heard of, the *St. Paul Weekly.*"

"You're right, never heard of it. Good luck." He picked up the sample case at his side. "Ah, there's my wife. I'll see you around, maybe."

Although his paper was covering his expenses, it would only reimburse for his train ticket and a night's lodging. Jakob wavered for a moment but decided to stick with the cheap and familiar and check in at the one hotel he already knew. To his surprise, he found Ole still tending bar at the nearby saloon. That the man remembered him was an even bigger surprise.

"So, mister reporter, you back to get my story this time?"

"One of these days, for sure, but I'm only here for a couple of days this time. Quick in and out."

"Quick if you don't get stuck by a storm, that is. What can I get you?"

"A beer and one of those free sandwiches."

"Free sandwiches only before two o'clock. Or did you forget?"

"No, I remember. Then how about a beer and one of those sandwiches you got stashed under the bar."

"I only got sandwiches stashed for lost boys, and that ain't you anymore, that I can see."

Jakob grinned. "Fair enough. A beer and no sandwich, then."

→» «←

Although it was a different girl who staffed the reception desk at the Bethel Home, she was clearly kin to those he had seen before.

"Hello, I've got a letter I was asked to deliver to a Miss Maggie Samson."

"There's no Maggie here."

"Are you sure? Maggie or Magdalena?"

"Well, pretty sure. I only got here last week. We're not supposed to say if someone is here, but I guess we could say if someone wasn't here. I could check with the superintendent if you'd like."

"No, no, that won't be necessary. I wouldn't want to put you to the trouble."

"Oh, it isn't any trouble. She's right here." The girl leaned to one side and looked past Jakob. "Miss Mauck, this gentleman has a letter to deliver, for someone named Maggie Samson."

"This is no gentleman, and if he doesn't leave immediately, I will have to summon the police."

"That won't be necessary. I'm leaving."

"I cannot fathom why you would return, Mr. Isaacs. Or is it Mr. Oster? After what you attempted last year I would think you would be ashamed and too frightened to show your face anywhere in Duluth. The only reason you are not right now in prison, as you should be, is that the young woman pleaded your case so persuasively. Your timing is once again impeccable, as she came to her senses barely before you now reappear, and now she is gone, as so should you be."

"Indeed I should." He stepped away from the desk. "And the baby?"

"Taken care of and not your worry. Now, please leave before I use the telephone to call the police."

Jakob had learned to pay close attention to the words people chose. He had just missed Maggie, so she most likely had left the Home within the past week or so, maybe within days. She had come to her senses, and the baby was taken care of. It was easy to guess that she had given up the baby. And he had noted an adoption agency, the Children's Home

Society of Minnesota, only blocks away from the Rescue Home. How convenient.

The woman who greeted him there was young, but not as young as the girls at the Rescue Home, and she did not appear to be in a similar condition. "How can I help you?"

Knowing better than to plunge into direct questions, Jakob said he wanted to know more about the Children's Home Society because he was working on a story about the Bethel Society and expanding it to include closely related institutions. The woman gave him a printed brochure and began to explain how her agency worked.

Jakob nodded with interest and waited for her to finish. "So, how often do you get women coming over from the Bethel Rescue Home wishing to give up their children for adoption?"

"Quite often, I would say, not a steady stream, mind you, but it certainly happens with some regularity."

"I see. So, when was the last time?"

"Why, just last week, as I recall."

"I see. I understand you must hold names and other details in confidence, but can you tell me a little about this case? I mean, in the most general terms."

"Well, yes, I suppose I could tell you a little about this case. Let's see? She was a young girl, somewhat frail, with her son, who was not quite two. A very well-behaved child, I would say, considering that he barely cried when his mother left him in our care."

"What has he been like, this boy, since he came into your custody? Let's see, what shall we call him for the story? Oh, Frank or something."

The woman flinched but recovered her composure quickly. "I suggest we call him Toddler A."

"Certainly. And so, please continue."

"He seems to be adjusting, as do most of our charges, the poor little angels. Some are more stoic or easygoing than others, as was he. Does that answer your question?"

"Yes, thank you? And the mothers who give up their children for adoption? What happens to them? Do you know about the mother of this boy, Toddler A? In general terms, of course."

"No, we do not inquire into such matters. We also make very clear that this is not a decision to be entered lightly nor on which one can change one's mind at some later date. There can be no further contact of any kind at any time in the future. Naturally, all adoptions are also strictly confidential and the records are sealed."

"I see. Well, thank you for your time and for your help."

"Don't mention it. I'm happy to be of service."

Jakob walked out of the building weighed down with the knowledge that both Maggie and their son might now be lost to him. On the train back to the Twin Cities, he found himself noting every couple with a child, every mother with a babe in arms, even a young woman with a toddler beside her to whom she was reading from a picture book of nursery rhymes. The little boy kept squirming away from her to stand on the seat looking out the window as the snowy landscape whizzed past.

➤➤ ⫷⫷

Jakob didn't know how much of his persistence stemmed from his personal motives, how much from his growing professionalism as a reporter, but he could not let go of the need to follow up. After a month back in St. Paul making queries with everyone he knew, he headed for the Jean Martin Brown Home, a many-gabled three-story brick residence on Commonwealth used as a receiving home for children being put up for adoption through the Children's Home Society of Minnesota. Although the staff were polite, they could offer nothing to Jakob. "Certainly, you understand that all our placements are made under strictest rules of confidence. I cannot say anything about any of the children in our care nor about those who have already been placed or adopted."

"I do understand," he said, "but I have an interest in one particular case. I am working on this story about an unfortunate girl from St. Paul who traveled all the way to Duluth to have her baby and then gave it up for adoption in Duluth. Are children ever moved from one location to another?"

"We always try to find the best and most expeditious placement as possible, wherever we can find a suitable family in Minnesota. Does that answer your question?"

"Yes, I suppose. So, if a child did arrive from Duluth, how long might they stay with you here before they are adopted?"

"We have a good record. In many cases, they are placed within weeks, sometimes sooner, sometimes longer. To some extent it depends on the child, of course, but a healthy even-tempered child will likely find a new home in little time."

"If you had received a child from Duluth, say in the last month, he might already be placed or still be here?"

"I am afraid your inquiries are becoming overly specific. Here, I'll give you this brief history of the Home and also our guide to adoption, but I really can't answer more specific questions. Should you ever be interested in adopting a lovely and deserving child yourself, you know we are here."

He took the booklets and left, both more despondent and more determined.

Seeking some sort of closure, however unsatisfying, he decided to write up an actual feature story on the Bethel Society, using as the hook the case of an anonymous local girl he called Martha. Slipping in thinly disguised detail that only he could know, he walked a fine line between storytelling and his nascent sense of journalistic integrity.

There was no resolution to the story, which bothered him, both as a writer and because he wanted an answer for himself. He had faith that he would find her, someday, that they would be reunited, but he wanted to know how, to know when, and he wanted to know these now. He finished the story with a platitude about difficult decisions made for the best.

His editor liked it. "This is good. You're really learning how to tell a story and pull the reader in. But it's way too long for us. And the local connection is a little strained. I read more Duluth in it than Twin Cities. Maybe you can sell it someplace else. Give it a try, you have my blessing.

"Oh, by the way, we're running the piece on that businessman. It was also too long, but I shortened it by three 'graphs and it'll be in the next edition. Oh, yeah, right now I need you to head over to interview this lady with all the cats. Get some pictures if you can. Here's the address."

Chapter 28
Vows

We never know what will lead us where. The story about Martha that I sent to the Tribune *was never printed, but it got me a job offer. My underpaid apprenticeship at the* Weekly *had taught me much and helped me establish good habits. It also ingrained a perspective that would serve me well over the years.*

I had learned that everyone has a story, that every life has an interesting narrative. Behind each face you pass on the street, each person you encounter at the grocers, is an interesting history. Many people deny that their own story might be at all of interest to anyone else, and some do not even recognize the drama in their own lives. That is the job of the reporter, to discover the story in every soul and situation and to draw it out, then tell it in a compelling way.

Among the habits I learned was to read as widely as possible. For me it was not literature or books that provided inspiration but pamphlets and fliers, broadsheets and parish newsletters. Combined with the confidence that stories were everywhere and in everyone, I was always digging up human-interest pieces that others had missed. More than anything else, that became my beat over the years, and I developed a reputation among colleagues for crafting personal profiles about ordinary people with extraordinary stories to tell.

More than once I was urged to edit them into a book of collected stories, but I always demurred. There was no common thread on which to hang such a collection other than my own byline. Each story was distinct and of itself.

The stack of neighborhood newsletters and church bulletins on his desk had grown in his absence. Everyone at the paper knew of his appetite for small news and his nose for an unlikely story, so they collected whatever they came across and passed it on to him. In return, if he spotted something in someone else's beat, he would flag it and pass it back. No one else was willing to spend so much time digging through what they thought of as the trite and trivial in order to unearth the gem that might lead to a fresh story.

Jakob made short work of the first two items in his pile, a mimeographed neighborhood newsletter calling itself the *Groveland Gazette*, and a neatly printed report from a women's group on the beautification of Como Park. The third item was a parish bulletin from the Church of St. Agnes.

Jakob picked up the stapled bulletin and stared at the engraving of the distinctive bell tower on the heavy paper cover. The memory of his first visit, when he was too shy to enter, returned, followed by a flood of forgotten images and conversations. And then she was there, her face replacing the domed spire. "Lena," he whispered. He shook his head to clear it. "Well, my Lena, let's see what is happening at your old haunt."

On the third page he found a small item headlined "Following a Family Tradition."

Our community is especially proud to announce that our own Maria Samson has followed her younger sib-

*ling into the life of a Religious, entering the Order of the
Teaching Sisters of the Holy Virgin and taking on for
her religious name, Sister Mary Hermione. Sister Mary
Frances, known to us in her younger years as Magdalena Samson, entered the Order two years ago. The
nuns of this teaching order are well known to students
of our own parochial school, who benefit greatly from
the dedication and superior instruction of the Sisters.
Sister Mary Hermione joins her younger sister at the
Good Hope Convent of the Order in Winona, Minnesota.*

A nun in a teaching order. The thought rang in his head.
Maggie was now a nun, a teaching nun. She had found a way
to become what she had always sought to be and to do pen-
ance at the same time, but she was now truly lost to him.
Forever. He wanted to be proud of her and happy for what
she had accomplished, but the sense of loss that he had held
at arm's length for years descended on him like an ava-
lanche. He stood. The room spun and grayed. He sat back
down, shivering from the cold that welled up from within.

⇛ ⇚

If isolation were the objective, the Good Hope campus near
Winona, some hundred miles southeast of Minneapolis,
would be the destination of choice. That may have been part
of the original inspiration for a cadre of German nuns to locate their convent on the bluffs overlooking the Mississippi.
At the same time, the great water highway of the Mississippi
and the proximity of the thriving commerce of the town of
Winona connected the convent to the larger world the Sisters were committed to reaching as teachers.

After parking his borrowed car on the dirt road running
past the convent, Jakob walked up to the gate. He paused for

a moment, weighing the impulse to say *shakets teshaktsenu* before entering. "I am still tethered to my abandoned faith," he said under his breath, and left it at that.

The five buildings arrayed around a central quadrangle carried no signage, suggesting that visitors were infrequent and not necessarily welcomed with enthusiasm. Jakob had written ahead to announce his interest and intent to visit, but his car had overheated on the way and he was now hours past his stated arrival time. Only the chapel, with its cross-topped bell tower and slender stained-glass windows, announced its function. He reasoned that it was as good as any place to start.

Just as he approached, a group of women wearing the distinctive white-on-black habit of the Order, with its winged coif and wimple, exited the chapel and started on the footpath toward him. "Hello, excuse me. I'm here from Minneapolis and was looking for the visitor center. Or the administration building."

The four women kept their heads bowed slightly and their gaze fixed on the ground as they passed him in silence. "Well, good day, then. I'll just continue on my way and check in the chapel."

He was about to reach for the handle on the massive wooden door at the chapel entrance, when it opened out of its own accord. A priest emerged into the sunshine, smiling, then frowning, then smiling again. "You must be our visitor. Mother Superior told me we were having company all the way from the Twin Cities. I'm Father Manfred. Welcome to Good Hope Academy. Please, come with me. I'll show you to the school office."

He started his well-rehearsed introduction while he led the way across the quadrangle. "The Teaching Sisters of the

Holy Virgin are a small order of teaching nuns with convents in the United States and in Canada, where they had first arrived in the New World in 1856. In the ensuing decades, the Teaching Sisters have built ties to Catholic schools across the continent. The convent here, the Motherhouse, was established in 1871 as the headquarters for work throughout the Midwestern and Western states. Then, just three years ago, in 1912, we expanded our mission on this campus by starting Good Hope Academy, a residential high school for girls."

"And that's going well?"

"We are content with the progress. Our location here in the southeast corner of Minnesota is not only one of great beauty and quietude but also strategic. It enables us to draw students of the highest caliber from Wisconsin and Iowa as well as our home state. We even have a few girls from Illinois. We are very fortunate to welcome them all to our community of faith and learning."

"I see. And I would imagine the tuition of these students is also welcome."

Father Manfred cleared his throat. "Yes, well, our mission welcomes whatever beneficence advances our work. And here we are. This building houses the Academy; I'll show you to the office."

Sister Mary Angela, who had been assigned to be Jakob's guide, was waiting for them. A young woman with the rapid-fire delivery of an auctioneer, she had an animated face that almost seemed to struggle to escape her starched headgear. "The Academy is such a perfect endeavor, a veritable trinity of possibility. First, we attract some of the best and most dedicated girls from this entire region, girls who will become the bedrock of tomorrow's churches and communities. Second, the best and most dedicated of these we encourage to consider the religious life and, if they are called, to enter our order. And third, the Academy affords us our own, well managed training ground for the Sisters whom we send forth to teach in other schools.

"Let me show you our fully modern classrooms and facilities and introduce you to some of our teaching faculty. Let's start with Sister Mary Celine, Headmistress of the Academy. Her office is just down the hall."

"Is everyone here named Mary? How do you keep everyone straight?"

"Yes, well, we all take on for a first name the name of the Holy Mother as our namesake. And it is not that hard to keep everyone straight once we get to know each other. Sister Mary Bettina is even taller than Father Manfred, and Sister Mary Gertrude is short and quite plump. Sister Mary Renee speaks in a high voice and can be, shall we say, rather easily distracted. Sister Mary Frances is quite the opposite. She speaks with the same alto resonance in which she sings, and she is most resolute in her studies and all her work.

"We were made unique by our Creator, so it is easy. But," — at this she raised her index finger — "on the other hand, what does it matter whether it is Sister Mary Frances or her older sister, Mary Hermione, who is serving the potatoes or is teaching the catechism? We all are but servants of the Lord, equal in His eyes and serving with true humility."

Jakob nodded acknowledgement, but his mind was on one of the names mentioned in passing: Sister Mary Frances. It was Maggie, his Lena.

Perhaps with his questions in mind, Sister Mary Angela took care in introducing each of the teachers and administrators with which they spoke, repeating their names and supplying some biographical or personal tidbit by which he might anchor their identities. Throughout the tour and a long meeting with the Headmistress, Jakob took copious notes and asked his full quota of questions.

He was being escorted toward the gate when the priest approached. "Ah, before you go, one more thing. You made mention of the Church of St. Agnes in your letter of introduction, and I thought you might want to meet two of our novices who hail from your neighborhood. I asked them to meet us. Ah, here they come."

This was not how he had imagined seeing Maggie. All the well-rehearsed lines of his dreams and daydreams fled as the two nuns rounded the corner. They were nearly abreast of the priest before either recognized him. Maria was the first to react. Her mouth opened and her eyes widened; then, just as quickly she lowered her head, her stiff white wimple half hiding her face. Maggie, noting her sister's reaction, did not at first look at Jakob. When she did, there was a moment of puzzlement before panic spread on her face. By the time the two of them were even with Father Manfred, they had both regained their composure.

Father Manfred introduced them by their religious names. "This is Mary Hermione and her younger sister, Mary Frances, who have just this month entered the Novitiate."

"The Novitiate?"

"Yes, after spending time as Candidates, usually a year, those who remain on the path to a life of devoted service, become Novices. After another two years they take their first vows, a temporary commitment, though a serious one. The final vows, a commitment for a lifetime, indeed for all eternity, are taken only after another five years. These two are doing well. Both of them humble, diligent, and obedient, I am told by Mother Superior."

Jakob tried to keep his voice under control as he looked at the two women. "You must be proud and happy about the work, about all that you are doing here."

Mary Hermione smiled. "Pride is a sin, Mr. Oster, one we do our best to avoid, but we are happy, happy to be serving the Lord."

"Of course, and for that, I am sure you are blessed."

She turned to the priest. "Is there something particular, Father, that you wanted of us?"

"No, just to let a former neighbor of yours see that you are faring well. You may return to your duties."

"Very well, Father, and thank you." Mary Hermione nodded toward Jakob. "The Lord be with you, Mr. Oster."

Maggie licked her lips and nodded ever so slightly. "The Lord be with you."

"And with you." The name Lena was on his lips but he did not let the syllables escape. He held her gaze, once again drinking in her familiar face now outlined in an unfamiliar frame. All four of them froze as if time had been suspended.

Father Manfred looked at Jakob with a question in his eyes. "Yes, well," — he turned to the Sisters — "I am sure you have duties, Mary Frances, Mary Hermione. Thank you."

"Thank you, Father." They turned to leave, one smartly, the other with just a tinge of reluctance.

The priest watched them retreat across the quadrangle.

Jakob broke the awkward silence. "I feel badly for having taken the Sisters from their routine."

"That's quite all right. I am sure they will recover. Here, I'll show you to your car. I look forward to reading your article, Mr. Oster. Is it for the *Winona Ledger*?"

"No, it will be in the *Minneapolis Tribune*. Unless my editor changes his mind, you understand."

"You're not Catholic, are you?"

"No, I am not Catholic, but I grew up among Catholics and I have . . . I have good friends who are. I think I can write an empathetic story, one that will be true to the spirit of your new school."

"I trust you will, Mr. Oster. Do visit us again." He took Jakob's hand and gave it a quiet squeeze. "I believe you are here for a reason. I can see that. Then again, we are all here for a reason. We do not always know what those reasons may be, our own or others, but nevertheless they are with us, granting us direction." He glanced over his shoulder to where the Novices had retreated, then smiled at Jakob and walked away toward the chapel.

⇛ ⇚

Alternating between melancholy and confusion, Jakob had difficulty concentrating on the drive back to the Twin Cities. What had he hoped for? What had he expected to gain by the encounter? Was he waiting for some miracle? He replayed in his head the words of the priest explaining the Novitiate. The vows would not become final for years. Perhaps there was still some faint possibility that Lena was not truly lost to him, not yet.

And then, at the end, there were those minutes, those moments, those mere seconds when he and Maggie had looked at each other with sadness and something layered beneath. He knew what it was in himself. Underneath it all, he was still in love with her. There was no one else he wanted. Perhaps that was why he had to drive to the Convent, to know for certain his own heart. And her eyes had mirrored his. In them had lurked the same bittersweet amalgam of loss and love.

Chapter 29
Publishing

St. Paul, Minnesota, 1917

We are exhorted to hold fast to hope, and in our youth are told fairytales of dreams fulfilled. In life, though, to cling to baseless hope is madness. Yet, who is to judge what is truly beyond the possible? Around this question I danced in dizzying spirals that led to no comfort or conclusion. You were only a novice, not a nun, and even after the passing of the second anniversary of your entering the Novitiate, your vows were conditional, reversible. You could change your mind. But you had not. I cycled between irrational hope and irredeemable despair in fits of mania and depression that stretched into months and worried those around me.

Once more I had been reminded of my own talent for timing. Or is it those guiding Reasons of which the good Father spoke? All my life I have been a day or a month late, just short of just in time, as if the Fates and the faith I deny felt compelled to remind me ever of my own fallibility.

If I have learned nothing else, I have learned to expect the unexpected. If this is not a Great Law governing all of Life, it is certainly one ruling mine. Speeding toward the study of law, I veer — am steered — onto another road, a life of letters, not law. My profession may be regarded by some as barely qualifying, but I am a writer, and the letters I pen and the pages I type are literature of a sort. As with even literature of a higher kind, they sometimes languish in publishing limbo, awaiting sufficient space in some periodical or attention from the right editor.

"Hey, Jake, there's a guy on the telephone," — Adam held his hand over the mouthpiece — "wants to speak with you. Won't give his name. Wanna take it?"

"Sure."

Adam Dern was features editor and had a phone; Jakob was still a reporter and did not. He walked over to Adam's desk and accepted the handset held out to him. "Keep it short," he was told.

Jakob nodded. "Hello, this is Jakob Oster."

"Yes, hello, I just wanted to tell you I really enjoyed your piece about the school." Filtered by the telephone, the voice was almost familiar.

"Well, thank you. I appreciate hearing from readers. You could write a letter to the editor, which would be appreciated even more."

"Yeah, I just might do that, but I really called to ask if you might come over Friday for Shabbat dinner. We would love to see you, if you have the time."

"Who is this?"

"Has it been that long, that you don't recognize your own father's voice?"

"Oh, I am sorry. The connection is not that good."

"It's fine on my end. Do come. Your mother would really like it."

"She would?" In his chair, Adam was signaling his impatience by drawing circles in the air. "Ah, I really have to go, but yes, I'll be there."

"Six, then, Friday."

"Isn't that a little early? Sundown's not until — "

"We're Reform, son. Shabbat starts when we light the candles. See you Friday."

"Right. See you. Bye."

Adam took the handset from Jakob and set it back in the cradle. "Telephone service costs the paper, you know. It's not for personal business."

"It was a reader, telling me he liked one of my articles."

"Really? Well, isn't that something. And he telephones. Hey, everybody!" He waited until everyone in the department was looking up from their work. "Jake here has a fan, a reader who even telephones. What do you think of that?" There was a splash of laughs and quiet applause. "Now, back to work. We have a paper to put out."

⇉ ⇇

Jakob stood on the front steps holding a bouquet of flowers. As he reached to ring the doorbell, the door opened suddenly. Taken by surprise, he thrust the flowers toward his mother.

"My, you are the punctual one." She took the bouquet and slowly rotated it for inspection. "You needn't have brought flowers, you know. You're not a dinner guest; this is your home."

"Well, not exactly, not for a few years. I just thought, well, I remember you always liked fresh flowers on the table for Shabbat."

"I do, which is why I had Mrs. Gustafson cut some from the flower garden."

"Well, I see, mother, that you have not lost your way with words. For the flowers, you are welcome, no need to thank me. Aren't you going to invite me in?"

"Now what does that mean, 'way with words'? And now I am addressed as 'mother' rather than Mama? Is it that I am become too old?"

"No, mother, but I am the one who is too old. May I please come in?"

"Yes, of course. It is your home, after all."

Jakob held his tongue as he crossed the threshold. "Ah, there you are, father. You are looking fit. You are both looking fit."

Morrie stepped forward to shake Jakob's hand. "Welcome, welcome back. Give your mother a hug, and then join me in the gazebo for a drink before dinner while your mother supervises Mrs. Gustafson."

"She's still with you, then? Mrs. Gustafson, I mean."

"Very much with us, one might say."

Sadie's eyes narrowed. "Morris, what exactly are you saying?"

"That she is still here, that's all, my dear. Come, Jakob, let's have a drink and a chat."

⇒≫ ≪⇐

The gazebo had been repainted a forest green and now sported a matched set of wrought-iron chairs and a glass-top table. "Have a seat, son. What are you drinking these days? Your mother thinks only a sherry is suitable before dinner, but I prefer Scotch — on the rocks this time of year."

"I'll have the same, thanks."

"I could ring for Mrs. Gustafson, but I don't want to take her from her duties and risk the threat of a delayed dinner, if you know what I mean. So, I'll be right back."

While waiting for his father to return with the drinks, Jakob noted the strategically placed newspaper on the side table. It was open to his article in the Sunday edition.

"Here we go." Morrie balanced two glasses in one hand as he closed the screen door behind him. He handed one to Jakob and raised his own. "*L'chaim.*"

"*L'chaim.* I see you are now reading the *Trib*. I thought you were a *Pioneer Press* man."

"Both. I subscribed to the *Tribune* after I finally found out you were writing for them. My dental assistant told me she had seen your byline."

"I guess I'm not so good at some things, like keeping friends and family informed. I should have told you."

"Well, we don't talk a lot, do we? You and I have always been, well, somewhat distant."

"I'm sorry."

"Don't be sorry. I know you have always been closer to your mother."

"Closer is not the word that comes to my mind. Here I am a writer, and I am struggling to find the right word for my relationship with my own mother. Well, you heard how she welcomed me, if welcomed is the word."

"You have to understand about your mother. She is like someone who has a disorder of the inner ear, who struggles to remain upright, who must concentrate to maintain balance. Your mother struggles for control. It takes all she can muster to maintain some semblance of order in the chaos of a life that was not of her choosing and never will be."

"But . . ."

"Hear me out. You were the center that gave her stability. She orbited around you. Now you are gone and she has no center."

"What about you, you're her husband. You should be —"

"Should. Yes, perhaps I should be, but I'm not. Do you know the story of how we met, your mother and I?"

"Yes, she told me once. You met at a concert, in Vienna. She was visiting a city cousin and —"

"It was not a concert, more of a recital. A string quartet assembled from young musicians at the synagogue. But did she tell you who was there? Did she tell you about my brother? Did she mention that both Moritz and Wolfgang Austerlitz were in attendance? Did she tell you about the tall older brother, so handsome in his uniform, a medical officer in the army? No, I don't imagine. I, Moritz Austerlitz, was the consolation prize when Wolfgang did not return from 'the war'. Funny how it is always 'The War', as if there were only one, but there is always another, and another."

"I didn't know. I . . ."

"We are Levites, son. We are the second to be called to the Torah when it is read. You know that, right? Of course. And do you also know of the Levirate Law — a different root altogether, Latin, I think — that a man must marry his brother's widow?"

"You mean . . . ?"

"They were betrothed, not yet married, so she only became Mrs. Austerlitz once, but it was the same thing nevertheless. One can be married in every sense except for the ring and standing under the *chuppah*. One can be married in the soul. Do you understand?"

"I do."

"I imagine you do. At any rate, I was the second choice, never the soulmate, only the one who stepped in to console and distract a distraught young woman after her first choice was taken from her."

"I see."

"Don't get me wrong. I consider myself blessed. And things between your mother and me are not nearly as bad as it may seem to you listening to snaps and snippets extracted from a much more extended, more complicated dialogue. I do believe she has come to love me, and I know I love her. But I am, by my very presence, a living and unrelenting reminder that she does not control her life, that what she thinks is hers can be taken at any time."

There was a long thoughtful silence that the two men filled with downcast eyes and sips of Scotch. Morrie picked up the newspaper and laid it on the table. "I read your article. It's good."

"Thank you, but I would hardly single it out as an exemplar. Plus, it doesn't say, but Manny Hurwitz wrote a bunch to update it. My part, most of it, I actually wrote a couple years ago. It's been gathering dust until last week when they needed an extra few thousand words."

"Yes, well, modesty is admirable, but I was especially struck by the colorful description of the campus and the loving detail you devoted to one Novice in particular. It took some reflection, but I recognized her, even though you only used her religious name in the article. It's Maggie, isn't it, our Maggie. And I recognized something else. The affection comes through in the writing, even if it is underplayed."

Jakob almost choked on his drink. "It's just a newspaper article, father."

"I almost guessed what was going on when she was still here. I think I may have been choosing not to see what was right in front of me. At any rate, I wanted to tell you all this in person. You are a good writer, son, in what you say and what you do not. I . . ." He stood and turned away, toward the house. "Your mother will be having Mrs. Gustafson summon us for dinner at any moment. I have learned it never hurts to be just ahead of things with Sadie." He placed his hand on

Jakob's back as they walked toward the house, then dropped his arm before they reached it. Neither man could look at the other, and both surreptitiously wiped at their eyes before entering the dining room.

⇒≫ ≪⇐

The blessings said and the soup course served, Sadie assumed her regular role of conversation starter at the table. "You two seemed to be having quite the discussion out in the gazebo."

Jakob looked to his father but got no reaction. "Really? I mean we were just having a drink before dinner."

"Well, from the kitchen window it looked as if you were actually talking. That would be a precedent."

Morrie looked up from his soup. "Sadie."

"Morris."

Jakob ignored the rising tension. "The soup is good, Mama."

"So, now it's Mama again. Well, the soup is hardly my doing, now is it?"

"Well, then, good choice, good planning of the menu, good whatever."

"So what was so interesting to you two that kept you at it for maybe your longest conversation on record."

Jakob recognized that she was feeling left out and, therefore, out of control. "We were talking about journalism and an article I wrote."

"Oh, which one?"

"The piece on the convent school down in Winona."

"Not your best."

"Oh, really? Tell me, where did I fail?"

"I wouldn't say you failed, but I do think you are sometimes rather much too in love with words. Let's see. If memory serves, here are some egregious examples: 'a quadrangle alive with grassy iridescence', 'leaded-glass art, their polychrome plates casting saintly images across the floor'. Oh my. Please. And you spend paragraphs on things of only passing interest to readers. Why that one particular novice? Why waste valuable newsprint on just another young girl seduced into servitude to the Catholic church?"

Jakob looked to his father for help, but Morrie was busying himself extracting the last traces from his soup bowl. "Well, I guess different readers have differing preferences. I actually got a telephone call from a reader who raved about the piece." He sent a quick smile toward his father.

"It hardly counters my comments, nor does it speak highly of the readership of the once-esteemed *Tribune*."

Jakob shook his head out of a sense of hopelessness. "Well, I think we've settled the critique of that piece."

"Oh, please, Jakob, don't be so thin skinned. It was just an oversized filler anyway. They were short three or four thousand words so they tossed that one to the typesetters."

"Now you have nailed it, Mama. That is what actually happened, I swear to God."

"Jakob!" She did a convincing impression of genuine shock, but it too quickly shaded over into the look of triumphant disapproval.

"I'm sorry, Mama. At any rate, that's how it works in the newspaper business. Stories get cut, they get padded, they get buried, and some even get resurrected."

"Well, so you say. And when are they going to promote you? I think you would do even better as an editor."

"I disagree. Besides, I already turned down a promotion. I'm a writer, and I'm happy as a reporter. I've had two raises in the past two years, and I'm doing quite well, thank you.

Now I'm lobbying to be sent overseas. Editors sit at desks, reporters get to cover the action."

"Overseas? Where?" Morrie looked up with sudden interest. "You didn't say anything about going overseas."

"I want to be a European correspondent. Nothing's set, I'm still working on it."

Worry spread over Sadie's face. "Why on earth would you want to be assigned overseas? They are fighting a war over there."

"And that is why. Besides I should get some use out of the German I learned as a child and the French I studied in school."

His mother fanned her face with a napkin. "This really is too much, Jakob. I forbid it."

Morrie laughed and Jakob shook his head in disbelief. "Are you serious? I'm nearly thirty, mother."

"Well, I . . ." She seemed flustered and lost.

Jakob leaned her way and placed a hand on her arm. "I didn't mean to upset you, Mama. I understand — at least I think I do. But I'm not talking about reporting from the trenches or doing interviews in the mine fields. I can and will take care of myself."

Sadie put down her napkin and sighed. "I worry too much, I am sure, but you are my only child, and I want nothing to happen to you."

"I want everything to happen to me." He was thinking of Maggie.

"You know what I mean," she said.

"I do. And I suspect you know what I mean. So, now let's settle into the peace of Shabbat and see whether Mrs. Gustafson has yet to master the art of cooking a brisket."

Chapter 30
Homecoming

St. Paul, Minnesota, 1922

The war years were exciting and boring. I finally wrangled an assignment as an overseas correspondent, but not with the Tribune. *I was posted to London and wrote dispatches based on the field reporting of others until the Armistice was signed only months after my arrival. I had little opportunity to use either my French or German, save with impressionable young women who thought my Yankee accent to be charming.*

The change in employment and venue marked the start of a career of rotating allegiances and a kaleidoscope of bachelor apartments, all but indistinguishable despite their locations in scattered cities. The exception was Paris after The War, where an apartment with a view toward the Eiffel Tower from a third-floor walk-up was perpetually too cold in one room and too hot in the other. If I had been able, I would have slept in the kitchen and cooked in the bedroom. At least the vin de pays was plentiful and cheap even if short on subtlety. That post-war party ended when my paper decided they no longer could afford an overseas correspondent.

After Paris came New York, where, within days of arrival, I landed a job with a tabloid that folded its tent seven weeks later. I was learning resilience. The Inquirer *was next, and from Philadelphia I skipped cross-country to Chicago. Each job found me with slightly more in my pockets, a few more things to pack and move to another small apartment, and a few hundred miles closer to you. When I realized the message that my work history was telegraphing, I took charge of my fate, applied for a position with my father's favorite newspaper, and moved back to the Twin Cities.*

It was Friday. Jakob was confident his parents would be home, and he wanted to surprise them. He hesitated on the stoop, uncertain about the reception he would receive. When he rang the bell, it was not his mother who answered the door.

"Hello, may I help you?"

"It's Jakob, don't you recognize me, Mrs. Gustafson?"

"I will tell Mr. Oster that you are here." She closed the door, leaving Jakob in the dark. The outside light quickly turned on, and the door was reopened by Morrie Oster.

"Jakob, Jakob, you're back. Come in, come in. It's been so long — too long."

Jakob shook his father's hand, holding it extra seconds as he noted dark lines under the eyes. "Yes, it has been long." He looked around. "Where's Mama? Is she no longer the gatekeeper? What else has changed while the world fought and ended a war."

"The war's been over nearly four years, and the last letter from you was with news of moving to Philadelphia."

"I'm sorry. I'm a writer of everything but letters. But I am back, living near the university, and working as a senior statehouse correspondent for the *Pioneer Press*. What do you think of that?"

"I think that sounds rather good."

"Where's Mama?"

Morrie ran his tongue over his teeth. "She's upstairs. She's not feeling well."

"Oh, I am sorry to hear that. Can I see her? She'll be down for dinner, I assume."

"For you, I think she will be down for dinner. Let me go up and tell her the news that you're here. That should lift her spirits." He turned toward the stairs.

"Before you go, Papa, tell me, what is it? Is it serious."

"It is."

"Should she be in the hospital?"

"That's what the doctor says, but she wants to die at home. She says she has had enough of hospitals."

Jakob was stunned. "You must tell me what is happening. Surely she can't be dying, she's still young. Medicine has advanced so much in recent years. There must be something to be done."

"Jakob, she had breast cancer and then surgery last year. It took her a long time to recover. And now it is back, everywhere. There is nothing they can do. Please don't tell her that I said anything. She is so proud and refuses to speak of it. And try not to say anything about . . . well, there are many things she cannot do. After the surgery, she could not raise her arms. It is embarrassing to her, so please say nothing."

⇢⇢ ⇠⇠

Mrs. Gustafson helped Sadie into her chair at the big table. Once settled, Sadie lifted her head. "You should have told us you were coming, Jakob."

"I should have, you're absolutely right. But I wanted to surprise you."

"Well, you have succeeded. Of course, we do follow your work. At the library, they get out-of-town newspapers." She winced and closed her eyes for a moment. "Don't mind me, the powder can take a while to work. So, Jakob, the Eddington Prize. That is impressive."

"I suppose it sounds impressive, but the prize is for stories under a thousand words in small-circulation newspapers east of the Mississippi, so there are not that many entrants, and even fewer who can write. The prize, such as it were, is $25 and a letter of congratulations. My submission was written between jobs and sold to a Newark community paper for $5. But, it does look good on my résumé, largely because nobody has ever heard of the Eddington Prize."

"Well, I have heard of it now. I had the reference librarian look it up for me." She clapped her hands together weakly. "All right, enough talk of work and commerce. It is Shabbat. Darling, if you will move the candles closer and light them for me, I will say the blessing over them."

The candles lit, she lifted her hands barely inches off the table and made small circles in the air as she whispered the blessing. When she finished, Morrie and Jakob added, "Amen."

"And now the wine. Please do the honors, Morris."

He filled the silver Kiddush cup almost to overflowing. "It's French, Jakob, a Bordeaux, not kosher but very good. I opened it especially for you. Of course, you've had the real thing in Paris, probably much better."

"Unlikely. On my salary and allowance, I was drinking whatever the cafés were pouring from a carafe."

"Well, this should be good, a 1916 that was given to me by the Dental Society when I retired from the Board. Rather in short supply as the war intervened. Then this idiotic Prohibition came along and . . . I've been saving it. Anyway," — he raised the cup slowly, trying not to spill any and starting the chant. He finished with ". . . *borei pri hagafen.*"

From Jakob and Sadie came the enthusiastic "Amen."

"And now the bread. Jakob," she said. "Will you bring the challah over here and hold it while I say *mohtzi*."

⫸ ⫷

The dinner was leisurely. Both Jakob and Morrie matched their pace to Sadie's slow eating. By the end, she had eaten little at the cost of much effort.

"If you gentleman do not mind, I think I shall forgo dessert. I am rather tired and should get Mrs. Gustafson to help me up to bed."

"I can help you, Mama."

"Thank you, but no. Mrs. Gustafson and I have an understanding. She has been rather a great help to me in these days, a friend really." She reached out toward Jakob, who rose from his chair to kneel beside her and take her hand. "You do know I'm dying, Jakob. I'm sure Morris has already told you the whole sordid saga, and that's quite to be expected. I just want to thank you for coming tonight.

"Now, be off, you two. Have a brandy in the den and talk of whatever it is you men talk about when you don't have to contend with old ladies. I would like it very much if you could stay the night, Jakob, and have breakfast with us in the morning. Mrs. Gustafson does Swedish pancakes better than anyone I have ever known."

"Yes, Mama, I'll stay over. Unless you have rented out my room, that is." He grinned up at her.

"Oh, we have considered it. But the room is rather small, and it would be hard to find a boarder who was as erudite as our son. So, yes, it is as you left it." She gave Jakob's hand a squeeze, the best that she could manage.

He rose and kissed her cheek, then the other. "Goodnight, Mama. Sleep well."

"Oh, I will. I promise."

⇛ ⇚

Morrie swirled his brandy and breathed in the nutty caramel vapors. "It's good to have you here, son. Sadie never took to brandy, and I hate to drink alone. This bottle I had stashed has lasted until now."

"It's good to be here. Not in every sense, but most definitely in this sense. The wine was, as you promised, special, maybe the best I've ever tasted. And a brandy is the perfect conclusion, particularly as I have agreed to stay over and do not have to make my way home tonight."

"We have missed, you, son. I've missed you."

"I've not been much of a son these years, rather a distant one."

"Well, that is the path you've chosen, and I'm sure it's been an adventurous one. Might not it be time to settle in, settle down? Is there someone?"

Jakob thought about how to answer. His father answered for him. "Still carrying a thing for her, aren't you."

"A thing. Yes. If I could, I would marry her in a minute."

"But you can't. Surely you realize that. You have to let go. If you don't, you'll end up doing what your mother did, just in a different way, living with second best and resenting it. She never embraced me as her real choice, not until these recent months. If only she had allowed herself to let go of Wolfgang. He was dead. Maggie is dead, dead to you. You need to accept it."

"I would if I could. Perhaps that's how it works. We do what we are capable of. By definition, we cannot do whatever we are incapable of."

"I only know, son, that I don't want you to suffer, to live a life of suffering. A part of me, though, also understands. I knew when I married her that Sadie wanted someone else. It was a bargain I was willing to strike because I wanted no one but her. What bargain are you willing to strike?"

"I don't know. I only know that I'm not ready to bargain."

"Fair enough." Morrie raised his snifter. "*L'chaim,* son."

"*L'chaim*, Papa."

⋙ ⋘

It was a pretext, something Jakob was good at. His editor had no interest in doing a follow-up story to a feature once published in a rival paper, so Jakob was on his own, once more spending a Saturday in pursuit of ghosts. His Lena was a ghost, or soon to be one. If his reckoning was right, she was only weeks short of her final vows. Once more, he was driving toward Winona and the Good Hope Academy equipped with little more than a desperate hope and an easily punctured excuse.

As he walked through the gate, he noted that the drought had taken its toll on the lawn in the quadrangle. The green was no longer iridescent. A muddied green. A charred green. He could not stop himself from editing and rewriting his own thoughts. Would the stained glass windows of the chapel still be polychrome plates casting saintly images across the floor? Or would the overcast day project a smeared pallet of dulled color over the pews? Would his one last unhinged bid to reach his one true love prove folly, or would she see the light that was the radiance of his devotion and purest passion?

"Ha ha, my boy," he said to the rearview mirror. "You do tend to overwrite when you are in heat. Remember, you are not writing a feature for the Sunday supplement, Jakob, oh Jakob. You are trying to alter once and forever the life course of two actual people, maybe more."

It took less than half an hour to learn that Sister Mary Frances was not at the Motherhouse. She had already taken her final vows and been sent to teach in a parochial school in Washington state. Having committed to the charade of updating an old story, Jakob was compelled to spend the rest of the morning pretending to listen as he mentally plotted a course to the Pacific Northwest and wrote the screenplay for an impossible romance.

Chapter 31
Lessons

Clarkston, Washington, 1929

Sometimes the dying trick the living. My mother made a remarkable recovery as her cancer, against all medical odds, seemed to go into remission. The doctors actually used the words medical miracle, which struck me as an oxymoron of the worst kind, particularly as they had done nothing but load her with ever-increasing doses of drugs descended from opium and intended to ease her passing. What is it with scientists who cannot simply confess ignorance but must fall back on a faith most of them have long ago eschewed? My father had a simpler explanation: stubbornness. Sadie refused to let go. Maintaining control or its illusory equivalent had been her life mission. Even she joked about it. Somebody has to be here to supervise Mrs. Gustafson, she would say.

When it seemed that nothing could defeat Sadie Oster, I left the Upper Midwest for the Pacific Northwest, accepting a job with the Chronicle *in Spokane, the independent afternoon second stringer to the more influential and better known morning* Spokesman-Review. *Both papers were under the same ownership, but the* Chronicle *enjoyed somewhat greater editorial freedom. Never one to sell my literary liberty for a penny less than it was worth, I accepted a cut in pay and a drop in circulation to pursue my hidden agenda. I jest.*

A month after arrival I got the letter from my father informing me that my mother had managed her final revenge by dying in my absence. My father was understanding of my circumstances and forgave me for not being home to sit shiva with him.

The Jewish community in Spokane had a long history but supported only two synagogues: Keneseth Israel, an Orthodox shul, and Congregation Emanu-El, a Reform temple and the first synagogue built in the state. It was there, under its onion-domed cupola, that I joined in a minyan, once more among my people, those flexible and well assimilated Jews of German and Austrian descent. Each morning we met, and, at the appointed moment, I recited the Mourners' Kaddish for my mother.

Had I already found you, you would have asked why I did this if I no longer believed, and I would have pleaded no contest, supplemented with appeals to custom and family loyalty. Was I guilty of hypocrisy? Or was I yielding to some inner ember of faith? We would have talked long into the night on this matter and reached no conclusion, but along the way I would have admitted that in Aramaic lay my salvation. Were the prayer we say in honor and memory of the dead intoned in English, my tongue would have tripped over its lavish praise and extravagant exaltation of a God I had long ago abandoned. Only the last section of the ancient prayer, in Hebrew, ever spoke to me. It is a simple plea to bring peace to us and to all of Israel, to which I always inserted a coda of my own: "v'al kol ha-olam," and to all the world.

And let us say, amen.

Lewis and Clark had left their footprints across the North-west with a special legacy in the southeast corner of Washington in the form of the names of two towns at the confluence of the Snake and Clearwater rivers. Lewiston, Idaho, and Clarkston, Washington, faced each other across the water and the state line.

The Holy Name School started in Clarkston in 1922 was not the only thing parochial about the tiny communities. Isolation coursed through the very waters of the rivers and the dry wind that kept summer temperatures oven-hot.

For the second time in his life, Jakob Oster was living in the Twin Cities and writing for the *Tribune*, this time the *Lewiston Tribune*. Referring to the tiny towns as cities struck him as self-aggrandizing, but boosterism was in the blood of the locals.

His stay in Spokane had netted Jakob his first advancement to editor but had never yielded any contact with Maggie. A visit to tiny Chewelah near the Canadian border in upstate Washington, where she was rumored to have been sent to teach, led only to the news that she had been moved by the Order to teach in Clarkston.

The *Lewiston Tribune* was a promotion to Associate Editor and a substantial cut in salary. The newspaper was delighted to have someone of his caliber aboard — winner of an Eddington Prize and former Features Editor at the *Spokane Chronicle* — but they kept looking the gift horse in the mouth until he convinced them that he loved the climate, the lower cost of living, and the political winds of the area. There was some shred of truth in all but the last.

This *Tribune*, in Idaho, was a far cry from its namesake in Minneapolis. It offered him fewer chances to write and no opportunity to invent the need for stories about Catholic schools and teaching nuns. He was on his own in his search for Maggie.

⤞ ⤝

Though every window was raised, it was sweltering inside the streetcar. The wooden planks of the decking on the Lewiston-Clarkston Bridge rattled beneath the rails as the car crossed the high steel arch over the Snake River. The heat wave had not relented with the start of school. The only relief was the parched wind that flowed up the valley, but the windows of the streetcar were too small to let in more than a whisper of a breeze.

Jakob was relieved to finally get out on the Clarkston side. He put on his hat and started walking toward the school. He had left the office early, making excuses that no one cared about. The staff was used to editors who bent rules and worked their own hours.

In the tree-shaded park across from Holy Name School, Jakob picked out a bench and unfolded and started reading his newspaper, the newspaper that he had, only the day before, helped put together. Halfway through the front page, he reached reflexively toward his pocket for the red-and-blue pencil that would normally be there. It was not. He had left it on his desk. No one is perfect, he told himself, but typos, spelling errors, and mistakes in grammar offended him, especially on the front page. A talk with the copy editors would be in order on Monday.

He looked up just as several boys in white shirts and dark blue trousers burst out of the door of the school building. Behind them, a gaggle of girls in white blouses and plaid skirts followed at a more dignified pace, and behind them came their teacher, a nun in the habit already familiar to Jakob. It was Maggie. She looked genuinely happy.

She was talking with two of the girls who danced around her as the three walked across the dusty schoolyard. The taller of the two stepped in front, forcing Maggie to pause as the girl made some point punctuated by a sweep of an arm. Maggie laughed. As she did, she looked straight across to the park and directly at Jakob before turning back to her students. There had been not even the slightest sign of recognition. Jakob was now just some man on a bench reading his newspaper.

What did he expect? It was a question he had asked himself before and never answered. He had reduced himself to a stalker, a peeping tom who spied on nuns, and in the process had slowly derailed his career.

"I am sitting here, sweating in a two-pony town. I write for a local newspaper of little consequence. My personal possessions barely fill three suitcases. I have no car, no wife, and no future."

"Did you say something, Mister?" It was one of the schoolboys taking a shortcut through the park.

"No, just reading aloud to myself."

"Oh."

"You go to that school?"

"Yeah."

"Who's your teacher?"

"Sister Mary Frances. And Sister Mary Petronia."

"Are they any good."

He shrugged. "I guess. Sister Mary Petronia sometimes uses the belt. But Chuck asks for it. He talks back."

"And you don't?"

"No. My father would box my ears if I did and word got back to him. Anyway, I gotta get home. Chores to do." He trotted away.

Jakob refolded his newspaper and stood. "And that's what I should do: get home. I'm lost, that's for sure. I need to figure out which way home is. It's not here, that much is clear."

≫≫ ≪≪

Jakob was all the way back on the Lewiston side of the bridge before he realized he had walked the entire way. With nothing but heat waiting for him in his room, he continued to walk, heading toward the edge of town. By dusk, he had figured out where home was. By the time it was dark, he had figured out how to get there.

Chapter 32
Destinies

That I was no longer chasing a dream did not stop you from entering my dreams, which you did with some regularity. Those nights when I drank heavily, which for a time was not infrequent, you could be counted on to make an appearance. Those dreams were not always erotic, but when they were, they could become bizarre in the blending of discordant memories. We would be once again up in my bedroom in St. Paul, but you would be a nun dressed in your many layers, which we would struggle to remove. Each layer shed would reveal another garment beneath, until you were surrounded by piles of clothes but still dressed. In some dreams, you would finally be standing before me in your underwear and then I would wake up. In others, we gave up the undressing and tried to have intercourse with you fully clothed. In daydreams, however, which can be most vivid, you are always as you were in our first encounters, standing before me, proud and shy in your nakedness.

It took nearly two years to work my way back to Minnesota. I had to do something that would improve my market value. I started a syndicated column, "River Reflections," that was picked up by nearly a hundred small-town papers like the one I was writing for. I wrote short stories under several pen names and picked up a couple more awards that no one had ever heard of

> *but that got me written up somewhere and looked good on the résumé. I pumped up circulation by reaching out into the countryside and got a Chamber of Commerce citation for coverage of local news.*
>
> *All of this was planned, only the timing was not.*

"How are you doing, Papa?" Jakob tried to keep his tone of voice casual as he looked at his father lying in the bed.

"How do you think? I've had a heart attack. I'm stuck in a hospital, too weak to feed myself. I have to use that infernal pan thing over there to relieve myself. How am I? Oh, I'm doing well. Isn't that obvious?"

"What is obvious is that something has changed in my absence. You've been fine honing your sarcasm. You kvetch like an Olympic champion."

"And you've transformed yourself into a loving son."

Jakob laughed and bent over to give his father a hug. "I missed you."

"You took your time getting back."

"I took the first train after I got your letter."

"I meant the years in between. And the years in between letters."

"Well, for what it's worth, I've taken a job in Minneapolis, with the *Daily Star*, so I'm moving back as soon as I can wrap things up at the paper and help pick my successor."

"The paper, you mean that four-pager? What's it called? The Lumberjack Journal? Do people out there know how to read?"

"I think the doctors are wrong. You're in fighting form and ready to go home now. You're probably faking the weakness to get more attention from the pretty nurses."

"Speaking of pretty nurses, is there one in your future?"

"No, none. And no nun either. I'm a middle-age confirmed bachelor."

"It's not too late. It's never too late. Look at me, your father even has been seeing someone."

"What? So soon after mother died."

"Fifteen years ago, she died. And Tova lost her husband four years ago."

"Tova? Not Tova Goldfarb."

"Yes, Tova Goldfarb."

"Mother is turning in her grave. She hated Tova."

"She was just like Tova. They were sisters under the skin. Probably why they were always bad-mouthing each other. Anyway, Tova and I have a grand time together."

"She's probably interested in your money. Goldfarb the Gold-digger."

"Son, she could buy me five times over. Daniel left her sitting pretty, sitting pretty. What I need to do is get out of this damn bed and take her dancing again. Poor dear. That's what she talks about when she visits, you know, how she misses dancing with me and can't wait for me to be back on my feet."

"Papa, you're eighty-seven, you've had a heart attack. Dancing would kill you."

"So? Something will. Why not dancing with a lovely lady?"

"You know, I don't even remember what she looks like. Last time I saw Tova Goldfarb was at Mount Zion. Last time I was there would have been for Yom Kippur a few years after my bar mitzvah."

"Well, she has changed, put on a couple of pounds and a wrinkle or two — haven't we all — but she's still lovely. And how that woman can dance!"

⇛ ⇚

Jakob realized he was still in high school the last time he had asked someone on a date. He was not out of practice, he had never mastered the basics. Lorie Fishman, a feature writer working the city desk, was the only woman he knew that he would even consider a candidate. She was a petite brunette, somewhere in her thirties, smart, and single. Why, he kept asking himself, had he ever agreed to invite her out? His father was proving to be every bit as persuasive as his mother had been. As he walked past Lorie's desk, Jakob's heart started pounding in his throat.

"Hey, Lorie, uh, how is that piece on the mayoral race shaping up?"

She looked up from the typewriter. "Shaping up? Puny, a real yawner, but it's a story we have to report on. You know how it is."

"That I do. Well, at least it's in your capable hands. I know you'll find an angle to make it more interesting."

"Thanks. A real scandal or two wouldn't hurt, though. I don't suppose you have an informant with a lead on something I could use."

"No, but I'll keep my ear to the ground." He started to walk away, then turned back. "Do you have any plans for Saturday night?"

"Now how is a girl supposed to answer that?"

"Ah, I didn't mean . . . I just was wondering . . ."

"Are you asking me out, Jake? 'Cause if you are, the answer is yes."

"Right, well, I don't suppose you like to dance."

"I don't suppose you're suggesting we go dancing."

He could feel the sweat dripping down his neck. "There's this jazz club that my father and his friend really like, and . . ."

"Your father? Wait, you're asking me on a double-date with your father?"

"Not exactly. It's actually kinda worse than that, more like chaperone."

"Now this is a first. With every sentence, things are taking on an ever stranger tone."

"Well, if you don't feel okay about it, you don't have to."

"I didn't say that, Jake, but you know me well enough by now to know that I dig for the whole story. So, what gives?"

"Okay," he perched himself on the corner of her desk. "Here's the poop. My father is recovering from a heart attack. He and this woman — she's younger, a spritely seventy-two — really like to dance, but somebody has to, well, keep an eye on them."

"Are you sure about that?"

"Yes, but that's not the point. I went with them to the club last week, and I was a wobbling third-wheel all evening — hours of thumb-twirling, drink sipping, and nodding off. My father suggested I bring somebody."

"Somebody. And you immediately thought of me after, what, a hundred words of conversation in the two years I've been here?"

"I'm sorry. I'm not very good at this . . . this stuff. It's okay. I'm really sorry to —"

"Stop it, Jake. I already said yes. Just tell me what time and I'll give you my address and we're set. Sounds like fun. I love jazz almost as much as I love to dance."

⇢⇢ ⇠⇠

Lorie, glass in hand, gestured toward the dance floor. "Look at those two go. You'd think they were a couple of teenagers. This must be their third dance in a row without a break."

"Yeah, I'm a little worried. I don't want them to overdo it."

She put her hand on his arm. "Let them have their fun." The ice in her glass tinkled when she tipped it up. "And speaking of fun, any chance of another drink?"

"A very good chance." He signaled for the waiter and ordered two more.

She looked out over the floor packed with couples writhing to the latest rhythms. "Do you ever feel, well, maybe selfish or spoiled that we can be playing like this? I mean while we dance, Europe is on the brink of war again."

"People still listen to jazz and drink whiskey in Germany."

"Only if they're not Jews. I'm thinking about what happened last November, what they called *Kristallnacht*, and all the stuff since. I would sure hate to be a Jew."

"What? I thought you were Jewish. Your name, Fishman ..."

"No, the family's German but not Jewish, from the north, Bremen. The family is Lutheran, like most of us Minnesotans. Or so it seems. You know, sometimes I wonder if the Jews ask for it."

"Ask for it? How? How do you ask for your windows to be smashed, your children to be barred from school, and your businesses seized."

"That's not what I mean. You know how they are. They keep to themselves, always apart. And they weasel their way to get ahead. Take Gabe Finkelstein, how do you think he got where he is?"

"I assume by hard work and a bit of good luck being in the right place at the right time, just like the rest of us."

"Not like the rest of us. They're not like us."

"Sure they are. Look at me."

"What about you?"

"I'm Jewish, that's what about me."

Lorie held her mouth open searching for words that didn't come. She was saved by the arrival of the drinks, followed shortly after by the return from the dance floor of two winded oldsters.

Morrie held the chair for Tova, then, panting for breath, collapsed beside her. "Whew, that was something, wasn't it, Tova?" She grinned.

Jakob studied Morrie's face, flushed and beaded with sweat. "Father, maybe we should call it a night. You both look tired."

Tova made a show of studying Morrie's face. "Both of us? And your father said you were a gentleman."

"No, sweety, I said he was a reporter, the very antithesis. In any case, it's still early. We just need a couple minutes and another drink to catch our second wind." He tapped his empty glass on the table to get the attention of the waitress. "So, what have you youngsters been talking about?"

"The war," Jakob said. "The war that's just starting and doesn't yet have a name. The last one was The Great War, the War to End War. It wasn't great and it didn't end war, but it sure taught us how to wage war on a grander scale. Oh, yeah, and we were talking about Jews."

Morrie sat up and leaned in, looking around the table in a conspiratorial way. "We are really in for it this time. That Adolf Hitler is trying to rid Germany of the Jews, Austria too, ship them to Madagascar, some say."

Lorie was studying her drink, trying to be even smaller than she was. Jakob stepped into the silence. "Father, I think Lorie's tired. I better get her home. I can do that and come back for you two, or we can all leave now."

"I don't think we're ready to call it quits yet. What about you, Tova?"

She shook her head forcefully. "Not me, I'm just getting started."

Jakob took another sip of his drink. "Fair enough. I'll run Lorie home and be back in half an hour."

"No need to hurry, son. We'll be fine."

In the car, Lorie sat in silence until they reached her apartment building. "I'm sorry for the things I said back there. Thank you for being a gentleman and not saying anything with your father and his girlfriend. I really didn't know. I assumed you were Swedish or something like that."

"And I assumed you were Jewish, so we both made assumptions. If we had been on assignment, we probably would have done better, but we're just two people out for drinks and a dance. Look, we all stereotype others who we think are not like us. You know what they say about Lutherans, don't you?"

"No, what?"

"They don't. Lutherans are so boring there's nothing to say about them. Ha ha." He grabbed the steering wheel tightly. "But this, what's happening in Germany, is not about stereotypes and tasteless humor. Something far darker and more insidious is being unleashed. I don't know how far it will go this time. We are different, we Jews, that I will grant, because the Lutherans were never expelled en masse from any country and the Catholics were never forced into mass conversions under pain of death and —"

"I've read the history books, Jake. You don't have to lecture me."

"No, I don't. You're right. I'll see you to the door."

"No need. You should get back to those two."

"I will, but I want to say one more thing. I'm worried about war in Europe and what's in store for the Jews there, but

I'm also worried about what's happened — what's happening — right here. Cuba just rejected a boat load of refugees, nearly all of them Jews, and America prevented them from landing on our shores. Now they're on their way back to Europe, to an unknown but likely dire fate. What ever happened to 'give me your huddled masses yearning to breathe free'? Oh, right, those were not huddled masses on the decks of the St. Louis, those were Jews. Jews are different."

"Jakob, I'm not the enemy."

"Then who is?" He got out and opened the car door for her. Neither said anything as she left. He was about to pull out from the curb when there was a rap on the passenger side window. It was Lorie.

"I've never known any Jews," she said.

"Sure you have. There's me, Gabe, Rachel in sales, Leah —"

"You know what I mean. How about you? Have you ever known any Lutherans?"

"I . . ."

"Right. Why don't we do something about that? Dancing next week?"

"I really . . ."

"Right. I'll take that as an affirmative. Same time, same place, second chance." She winked and turned away.

Chapter 33
Return

If I were writing this as a novel, I would have found a way to settle down with Lorie Fishman. We did become good friends, and one night, to our mutual chagrin, lovers. We laughed afterwards, but it was the laughter of the defeated. She asked me about you — not by name, of course, but by implication. I confessed that there had once been someone, but that I had moved on. She laughed again. She was as generous with her laughter as you were with your repartee.

There were many lovely evenings with Lorie until she found Sean. He was an Irish Catholic from Belfast who had left Ireland and the Holy Roman church and was ready to move on in every sense. By then, she had learned about Jews and taught me about Lutherans and was ready to stay in place. They were a good match, and she told me the night before their wedding that, if only I had been born female, she would have asked me to be one of her bridesmaids. I was moved by this, which says more about me than I am ready to admit.

I watched Lorie walk down the aisle on the arm of her father and thought of you. Does the priest walk the nun-to-be toward the chancel to give her away to become the bride of the Christ? Or is that too literal?

Yes, I know better, as you would decipher, but even here, alone with my thoughts, I have to argue, to debate with the spirit of you, to which I have never surrendered.

I took pride in the fact that, though I knew when you had been reassigned to teach at St. Agnes, I had made no attempt to see you, even to glimpse you from afar. Then you were gone again, once more sent to enlighten the heathens of the Pacific Northwest. What was it like for you, forever at the beck-and-call of the church hierarchy, sent here and wherever according to needs that someone else assessed?

How different that was from my life of skipping from job to job in pursuit of a phantasm, or hopping from assignment to assignment at the judgement of editors who often knew less than I did. How different we are. Did you know all this? Were you surreptitiously following me? Most likely not.

As a modest donor to Good Hope Academy and the Teaching Sisters, I received their bulletin by mail, so I knew when your sister succumbed to cancer in 1937. From the obituaries in the St. Paul papers, I knew when your brother died of cancer in 1949. It was almost biblical, a curse, a scourge marching through your family, felling everyone too early.

And then you were back, back at the Academy, the last of the Samsons, and the urge to see you again became an incessant alarm in my head.

Jakob rose early, put on coveralls and a wrinkled shirt, loaded the station wagon with gardening tools, and headed to Winona before the traffic could pick up. At Good Hope Academy, he drove around to the service gate, parked the wagon well to one side, and took out his tools.

The hedge did actually need trimming. With a steady click of his clippers he worked his way along, lopping off stray branches that poked up and subtly reshaping the sides. Outside the infirmary, he stopped to listen. At the side entrance, he tested the door. Unlocked.

Inside, he tiptoed down the hall until he found the room. Beneath a disturbingly realistic crucifix, Maggie was asleep, her sweet face exactly as he had remembered it but with pain written across her brow. He bent to kiss her forehead. Her eyes fluttered open, and she smiled faintly as his lips touched her forehead and then were on her lips. It was a gentle kiss but lingering, slowly becoming something less than chaste.

He jumped at the sound of footsteps, then a voice behind him. "What are you doing?" He straightened up and turned.

And opened his eyes, his heart pounding as he sat up in bed and reached to turn off the alarm.

⇒》 《⇐

It was early. Jakob showered, put on a clean shirt and tie, and headed south on a road that was familiar though it had changed greatly over the years. At Good Hope Academy, he parked in the newly paved visitors' lot and headed to the chapel. He paused before entering but did not say *shakets teshaktsenu*. He sat in the back row and thought of Maggie.

The priest entered from the side. "Good morning. Can I help you?"

"I read about Sister Mary Frances and drove down from Minneapolis."

"I am sorry to have to tell you that you're too late. The funeral was yesterday. Are you family?"

Am I family? "Yes. I'm a . . . a cousin." Jakob fought valiantly against the welling tears, but lost to the assault.

"Sister Mary Frances." The priest bowed his head momentarily. "She was an amazing person, as I am certain you knew: devoted, diligent, and generous of spirit. She traveled the land to teach our children. What a tragedy, the cancer was so sudden and swift, but at least she made it back here, to the Motherhouse, when she was called from this life." The priest folded his hands as if in a two-second prayer. "I am sorry you missed the service. It was very moving."

"I'm sorry too. But I knew, well . . . I wanted at least to visit the grave, her grave. To pay my respects."

"Of course. Do you know where the cemetery is?"

"I do."

"Then I'll leave you to your thoughts. You should have no trouble locating the grave."

"Thank you, Father."

⇛ ⇚

Although it lacked a headstone, there was no doubt that the only fresh grave in the small cemetery was Maggie's. He placed a small round stone on the mound of red-brown earth.

"I've come to tell you again that I love you, Lena, that I never stopped loving you. I still do not understand what you did, though I have tried. Perhaps I never will. And here I stand, beside a grave, your grave, speaking to the wind that has no ears. And even though no one hears, no God bends an ear, I will say it, for as long as I live. I love you."

The words flowed from him unbidden. "*Yitgadal v'yit-kadash sh'mei raba. B'alma di v'ra chirutei . . .*"

Jakob finished the Mourner's Kaddish, wiped his eyes, and walked back to his car.

Chapter 34
Repairs

Minneapolis, Minnesota, 1953

All choices are two-edged. Every unopened door is an opportunity in wait, every crossed threshold an alternative left behind. How might both our lives have been different had you gone to work for some other family? Would we have fallen in love had I not pursued you while my parents were in Chicago? These are ultimately unanswerable, maybe meaningless questions, though they dog the mind. We opened the doors we did and lived the lives we lived. And we had a son. However distant he has been, he is ours. And I have seen him.

It was one of those encounters that shakes the faith of even so deep an unbeliever as me, a moment so unlikely yet so fitting that it seems, even as it is happening, as if it were arranged. My car, bought used and ever since neglected amidst the peripatetic life I lead, was beginning to complain on cold mornings and grumble with fatigue on late-night returns. When two days in a row I had to call a taxi to make it to the office in time — how I miss the old trolley lines now that the last have been stopped — I decided it was time to get my venerable Packard serviced — or to junk it and start anew with another hand-me-down.

I respect technicians but tend to distrust them, so I took the car to an official factory-authorized service facility in hopes that a somewhat higher fee might garner

more honest answers and a better outcome. I dropped
the car off at Packard Minneapolis in the morning and
was told to return at the end of the day. When I arrived
to pick it up — and to empty my wallet, I assumed — I
was told it was not ready, and that I should talk to Phil.
"You'll find him out back."

As Jakob rounded the corner into the service bay, he spotted a slight-of-build middle-aged man in blue overalls with "Packard Motors" embroidered over the breast pocket. The man was busy scrubbing his grease-stained hands at a sink against the wall, scouring with all the vigor and obsessiveness of a surgeon preparing for an operation. He dried his hands with equal care on the towel roll slung beneath the chromed dispenser on the wall to the right of the sink. Jakob waited for him to finish before speaking. "I'm looking for Phil."

"Well, you've found him." He turned to greet Jakob with a toothy smile and his right hand already extended. "What can I do you for?"

Jakob froze before taking the man's hand. The hand was cold, but his handshake firm and warm. "Hello, I'm Jakob."

"I'm Phil, at your service." To Jakob, he was unmistakably an Austerlitz. It was so clearly written in the bones and tissue of his face that he could have passed as a close cousin of the most renowned Austerlitz of the day, the dancer of cinematic fame. Before him, he was certain, stood Frank Samson, *Ephraim ben Yacov*, now a grown man. And Jakob was thinking also of all else that is written in one's gene plasm — more than we know, perhaps more than we would hope. He thought of his mother, Sadie Oster, and Maggie's parents, and wondered what inheritance he and Maggie had be-

265

queathed to their son, what pain, what early death or late reprieve might await him.

"That's my station wagon, up on the hoist over there. They said I should see you."

"Ah, the cream puff with the blown engine. The good news is the body is in great shape for a '41 Packard Station Wagon. The blue paint isn't even oxidized. You know how it almost always ends up that foggy purple. The bad news is your engine is shot."

"How bad is that news?"

"You need a complete engine overhaul. A car that old, it'll probably cost you more than it's worth. Time to think about putting the old mare out to pasture." He laughed, a nervous laugh that was slightly too big for the moment or the remark.

"Can I . . . can I still drive it?"

"Maybe, for a while, but you don't want to be on the wrong side of the tracks when you throw a piston rod or blow the head gasket."

"Just what's wrong with it?"

"More than you want to know."

The mechanic's conversation seemed rife with clichés and composed from strings of catch phrases yet always to the point. Wanting to keep him talking, Jakob dug down into his reporter's bag of tricks to draw out the man, who seemed affable and genuine, willing to share. Jakob offered him a cigarette, a classic opening gambit. He accepted it and pulled out a monogrammed lighter engraved in stylish initials: PFC. He lit Jakob's cigarette first, then puffed his own into glowing life.

"What's the middle initial for?" Jakob asked, nodding toward the lighter as it was snapped shut.

"Francis, Philip Francis. Never use it though. Just Phil to everyone."

Jakob took a deep drag on his cigarette and shook his head in dismay. "Not sure what I'm going to do. I need a car to get to work over in Bloomington. Let me tell you, editing a local newspaper is no way to get rich."

"Tell me about it. Same with being a mechanic."

Jakob smiled, picturing Maggie's brother. "An admirable profession."

"Well, I actually started out at the U. of M. to be an engineer, automotive engineering, would you believe? But I dropped out when I got married. So here I am, keeping them running instead of designing them."

"Yeah, I'm a college dropout, too." Jakob said, building the connection. "Any kids?"

"Three, a girl and two boys. Wanna see a picture?" He pulled out his wallet even before Jakob could say yes. He ticked off the names and described them with obvious pride, especially the older boy, whom he said was big on science and in love with words. "Takes after his mother, she works for a local newspaper, the *Anoka County Union*. Sorta like you, I suppose." He flipped to the next picture. "That's her, my better half. She's got the German in her, if you know what I mean. And you? Are you married? Any kids?"

"No, never married." Subject closed. But Jakob was thinking of his son, the son who might well be standing in front of him. "I really don't know what to do about the car. What do you think? You're the expert."

Phil laughed again, that warm but awkward laugh as if he were not completely comfortable in his own being. "You know what they say about experts. I'm just a mechanic — a good one, mind you — but I can't tell you what to do. Maybe I can help you, though, take your car off your hands. I'll buy it for more than you'd get for it at a junkyard."

"Now wait a minute. Are you trying something on me?"

Phil looked both surprised and genuinely offended. "No, I'd never do that. You want me to drop it off the hoist and let you try to drive it away, I'm more than happy to do that. I already earned my daily bread today, whatever you decide. You'll have to settle with the garage for the hours I put in, but that's not my doing. You don't believe me about the car, then ask somebody else. Hey, Smitty, my friend," he called over to a colored man putting tools away in the shallow drawers of a tall metal cabinet. "Got a minute? Come over here and tell this man about the engine on that woody."

Smitty was a big man who towered over Phil and looked massive beside Phil's slight frame, but the smile was the same — expansive and genuine yet slightly awkward. His handshake was tentative at first but bore down when Jakob responded firmly.

"That one's in bad shape, a goner. Head gasket, valve lifters, piston slap, maybe crankshaft ... Once you open her up, I bet my shirt you gonna find some or all them just waiting to go."

"How do you know this if you haven't, er, opened her up?"

"I got ears, mister. And my friend Phil here, he's got even better ears. He listens to an engine for a few minutes and then tells you what's wrong. Nine times out of ten, he's on the money. And tune up? Man, there's nobody can get an engine to purr like he can, just by listening. If he says something about a car, you can trust it." He walked back to his station and continued to sort and straighten his tools, carefully wiping each one with a red rag before setting it in place.

Jakob smiled. "Well, I must say, that's quite an endorsement."

"Yeah, I'll slip him a ten-spot at the end of the week." The big, lopsided grin returned.

"But why would you buy my car if it's only good for junk?"

"Because it's a cream puff. The body is in great shape: no rust, no dents, no scratches, and it's a classic woody. People go for that station wagon look. It needs an engine overhaul that would cost more than it's worth. That's what I do on my own time. I buy cars that are dying, spend a few months of nights and weekends doing major engine surgery to bring them back to life, drive them for a while, and then sell them at a pretty good markup. It's all kosher. My boss here knows. I can only do it so many times a year or I'd need to get a dealer's license, but it's legit. And I love doing it. Except like this time o' year — hard on the old hands because my garage at home is an unheated shack."

"You live around here?"

"No, we moved out to Anoka a few years ago — better for the kids than the city. And we're duplexing this old house we bought to turn it around in a few more years."

"Sounds like you're a hard worker. May I ask how old you are? What year were you born?" It was another ploy, the one-two question, a reach for the heart of a story.

"1910. My birthday's next week: February 23."

Jakob almost choked. "Really. Well, I got a couple of decades on you. Should be thinking of retirement soon." His mind was racing, and he was fighting back tears. He took off his glasses to wipe at his eyes with the back of a hand. "The fumes in here kind of get to you." He struggled against the impulse to blurt it all out and embrace his son, so close in front of him and so distant.

"Yeah, you get used to it over the years. Anyway, what do you want to do about your car?"

"Can I think about it a few days?"

"Naw, I gotta write up the paperwork before I leave tonight. And I don't wanna miss the bus for Anoka. My wife will be at the bus stop. Don't want to keep the little woman waiting. She may be petite but she can pack a punch. Know what I mean?"

"Yeah, I think I do." Jakob smiled at the thought of Maggie standing on tiptoe, telling him what he ought to have already known. "Okay, I'll sell you the car. How do we handle this? Do I settle with the garage first?"

"No, I'll take care of that, part of the deal with my boss. Here" — he took out his wallet and started counting out hundred dollar bills — "just sign the title over to me." He noticed Jakob's look of surprise. "Today's my lucky day. I sold my '46 Plymouth for cash this morning. Rear end went out of it. I thought about pouring some oatmeal in the differential—that can cover a lot of sins but not for long. Couldn't do it, so I took my licks. Now I can cross my fingers on the Packard and limp out to Anoka. I'll start work on it over the weekend." He reached out his hand to shake on the deal. "I thank you, good sir, you are a gentleman and a scholar."

And that was that. Jakob walked away with the cash down payment on a used car that he would shop for on the weekend while his son would start to tear down and rebuild the engine on a classic Packard station wagon.

For a few months, Jakob thought about finding an excuse to drop in at the garage and say hello again, especially after he bought his next and last car, a Nash Rambler that proved to be a lemon from the moment it was a block away from the used-car dealer.

But then Jakob took sick, and when the diagnosis finally arrived, it was deadly: leukemia, acute myelogenous.

Chapter 35
Reprise

Now it is my turn to face the void, and I am alone, bereft of faith, and, in my own mind, a widower. It was less than two years ago that I said goodbye to you, and now I am doing it again: saying goodbye to you and to everyone, except there is no everyone, only you. And even as I say my second goodbyes, I am finally forced to face, to allow myself to face for the first time, how angry I have been with you. No, angry is a weasel word. The editor in me strikes it out and writes "enraged." How could you have chosen a mumbling exile in a make-believe world of religious ritual rather than a vital life together with me in the real world? But, of course, it was not that to you. Yours was the real world, the real life, a life devoted to God, who for you was as real as I was. And you did go forth into that world that I find genuine, becoming the teacher you always dreamed of being, finding a way to make it happen, laboring to bring learning and joy to a new generation.

And yes, I too pursued my dream — and caught it. I became the writer I wanted to be, and in some small ways have been recognized for it. No Pulitzer, but at least I was read, and at least some backwoods juries of self-appointed literary arbiters saw fit to applaud my efforts. Would I have left my studies had your disappearance not forced my hand? Would I have instead completed my law degree and spent my years in what for me would have been drudgery, the dreary though financially rewarding practice of law, while you stayed home to raise a brood of good little Catholics or — if you had come around to my thinking — good Jewish children?

And so, I am compelled. First, I must forgive myself for my own choices. No one dictated my defiant loyalty, my unswerving devotion to a long-lost you. I have lived, I have lived to see our son, and I feel blessed. But, as Hillel the Elder said so perfectly, if I am for myself alone, what am I? I forgave myself, and now I forgive you. I do this now, in the middle of the month of Elul on the Hebrew calendar, because I do not expect to live to the High Holy Days.

I wonder, did you ever forgive me? For that matter, had you ever forgiven yourself? God, if he works as you believed He does, as you hoped He would, surely must have long ago forgiven you in full. And surely you must have confessed your love for me, if not once, then on many occasions. What else was there to confess? How many sins can a nun, a celibate and pious member of the Order of the Teaching Sisters of the Holy Virgin, have to confess?

For years, I dwelled on our differences, our contrasting choices, our diverging paths. Now, with the hindsight granted the dying, I see the parallels, convergent lines, and equivalent meanings, fresh truth emerging from the free association of a mind set free, no longer anchored to the demands of quotidian life.

We did both marry. You became, in your mind, a Bride of Christ, even as I was, in mine, always married to you. Neither of us graduated college, yet each of us led a life of the mind devoted to words and to sharing those words with others. Each of us traveled the broad land, made lasting friendships, touched strangers, and learned from them and from the stopping places along our journeys.

Did you miss me? Did you think of me, as I did you? Did you then turn to your confessor and seek forgiveness for this sin of the mind, the sin of memory?

Even now, you come to me with greater clarity than the images of my failing eyes. You are coming up the back stairs of the old house, or you are walking beside me at Cozy Lake. Or you are beneath me, in that warm embrace by which we created new life — and changed ours forever.

Propped up in the hospital bed, Jakob Oster drifted in and out of consciousness in the late August heat. A gray-green chapbook, splayed open, rested on his lap, the cover labeled in Hebrew dates: 5710-5713. The Cross pen that had been a gift from Morrie Oster shortly before his death at the age of ninety-two now lay on the bed where it had rolled from Jakob's hand.

He opened his eyes and smiled up at the face of Herb Rosenblatt, his boss at the newspaper.

"You never quit, do you, Jakob? Writing and rewriting to the last. Can I get you anything?"

"Five or six more years would be nice. *A sho'o in gan eden.* Ten minutes without pain. Any of the above. But I'll take a glass of ice water if you can't manage any of that."

"I'll get it from the nurse. Oh, Patty and Donna said they'd drop by later. And Lorie Fishman-Kelly. You're missed at the office, you know." He rested his hand on Jakob's shoulder for several seconds before turning to fetch the water.

Jakob fished around for the pen on the bed and turned the chapbook over. He watched the pen painting its squiggles onto the page as if it were powered by some alien agent. The words still came to him in rushing waves like a brook after an early spring melt. His fingers worked the pen with the kind of inbuilt energy and motor learning that the hands of an aging pianist might play a remembered recital piece. The rest of him was still, unmoving save for his right hand into which the last of his life force was focused.

When Herb returned with the ice water in a plastic glass with a bent straw, even the pen was still. He set the glass down on the bedside table, gently retrieved the chapbook, and folded it closed.

Epilogue
Beginnings

Twin Cities, Minnesota, last year

"I have something of yours." A suspect subject line on an email that arrived nearly two years ago — terse, cryptic, with a gmail.com return address and all the hallmarks of some sort of scam. "I found your old post in the Burgenland thread on JewishGen," it read. "I have something that belongs to you. Send me a postal address." It was signed "Your cousin Elsie." Elsie? I had no cousin Elsie, not that I knew of.

I might have simply deleted the email, but the sleuth in me, that part of me that conspires to craft the contemporary thrillers for which I am known as an author, was already pumping me with adrenaline-fueled anticipation and sending my brain spinning off into spirals of conjecture. I had, much earlier, spent almost two decades of detective work trying to track down my roots. Alex Haley had it easy by comparison. My family had no elaborate oral tradition to trace, and I was left with only a single piece of paper, my father's adoption decree, as my starting point. My genealogical journey had not ended with the chanting of a griot in Africa but with an archivist at an adoption agency in Minnesota who showed me a single-line ledger entry with blanks in key places. Even an appeal to the courts for a copy of a birth certificate was not enough to get past the redacted records that offered tantalizing clues but no real information. I knew my father had been born Frank Samson, that both his parents were identified as of Austrian origins. I had well-founded guesses about my grandmother and her family roots among the Seven Villages of Burgenland, but I knew nothing regarding my grandfather who was no more than a blank on forms and ledgers. Then Elsie Neuman wrote that she had something of mine.

We exchanged email over several months. Elsie, an eighty-six-year-old former teacher with time on her hands and an unfinished quest on her bucket list, lived in a Jewish retirement community in Minnesota. She had tracked me down through reading and research and a final flurry of Internet espionage much like the Google-powered tactics by which I had then so quickly confirmed that she was indeed who she claimed to be. The following January, I flew to the Twin Cities to meet her and to retrieve the material she held for me.

In light snow that could not decide whether to intensify or peter out, I drove directly from the Minneapolis-Saint Paul International Airport to the stretched out campus of the Chai Residence Community in Saint Louis Park to the west. There, inside a modern red-brick building that made me think of a hospital mimicking an apartment complex, Elsie Neuman was waiting in the Commons area when I arrived.

She might have topped five feet in her youth, but now, when she stood to greet me, the crown of her carefully teased silver-blue hair barely reached my chin. She said nothing at first, but looked up at me, her head bobbing with a slight tremor as her grin broadened. I chided myself at the thought that she had once been pretty. Was that fair? Once?

"Welcome, cousin!" she announced at last. She put a hand to my cheek, and I bent to kiss hers, but she surprised me and kissed me on the mouth. "You do look a little like my Ed." She muttered something that I recognized as Hebrew, but it was too fast for me to catch. I assumed it was *zichro livrachat*, of blessed memory. "But that's impossible," she continued. "You are *my* cousin, not his. Distant. Perhaps it's your eyes, like his: intense, intelligent, the color of A&W root beer." She giggled, and I laughed, and we were friends.

I was antsy with curiosity about what she had for me, things that her emails had described as "family history," but she insisted on first giving me a tour of the place. The tour included enthusiastic introductions to all her friends, among them a handsome, white-haired gentleman who towered over her and shuffled as if balancing on stilts while she introduced him with a wink: "My Marcus." I assumed they were an item among the residents. His is the only name I still remember from the many people I was introduced to that day. Elsie, on the other hand, appeared to be on a first-name basis with everyone and appended some biographical tidbit to each introduction. This one was a cantor, that one has eleven grandchildren, and over there, she published her first book when she was just seventeen.

"You are good with names," I said.

"Years of classroom drill, learning the names of twenty-five new kids at the start of every class." She backtracked, then turned a corner into a corridor that might have been one we had been through before, but I was by then thoroughly lost. I have never gotten the hang of navigating inside buildings. Outside, I have an unerring sense of direction, an inner compass and innate mastery of topography that keeps me oriented even without maps, GPS, or advance directions. Once indoors, though, confusion sets in after the second turn. "Here we are," she said, opening a door.

We entered her quarters, a small suite with a sitting area, a bedroom, and a bath, all finished with wallpaper featuring tiny flowers in muted colors. "These are store bought," she said, pointing to a plate of cookies on the glass-top coffee table. "They don't let us cook, except to volunteer in the kitchen, but" — her voice dropped to a near whisper — "I have a microwave in my closet." She giggled again in her infectious way, then flapped her hand in the direction of an armchair. "Sit down, sit. Please help yourself to the cookies. Oh, yes, and please open your present."

Between a bowl of varicolored polished agates and recent copies of *The Atlantic* and *Harper's* was a package wrapped in brown butcher paper and tied with sisal string in a classic postal style I hadn't seen in years. "I was going to mail it to you," she said, picking it up, a tiny hand on each side as she extended it toward me. "But then you said you would collect it in person."

I took the package from her and hefted it. "Wow, it's almost like Christmas again."

Her eyebrows arched.

"Well, Hanukkah, maybe."

She winked. "We're pretty eclectic here. We had a tree in one corridor, but they already took it down. Did you know," she said, shifting into what I immediately recognized as her classroom voice, "that nearly a third of Jewish homes in America put up a tree over Christmas? In any case, I'm not offended and certainly not surprised. My children played Santa to each other when they were school-age. They knew they were Jewish, but that didn't stop them from getting into the generous spirit of the season."

She was in full swing in her lecture mode. "Nearly all holidays are borrowed from others, anyway. Everyone knows that Pesach usurped a pagan pastoral festival of spring. Sukkot was an autumn tradition elaborated from earlier pagan customs. Some have argued it was the model for the first Thanksgiving. And virtually every northern hemisphere religion has some festival of lights around the dark of the winter solstice. Of course, the Christians took over the solstice traditions and made them their own. Where do they think the greenery and the yule log came from?" She was still looking toward me, but her eyes flitted about as if she were studying my aura. "May I ask? Are you observant?"

"You may ask. And the answer is no, but maybe yes, except not in any way that Orthodox Jews would recognize. It's very idiosyncratic."

"That is the way these days, isn't it? And so many of our young people are marrying outside. Oh, I mean marrying out, not al fresco, you know. Two of my grandchildren were raised Jewish, despite my daughter-in-law being Catholic — Sandy is such a dear — but the other three . . . I don't really know what you would call them." She laughed, then giggled. "I don't think they know either. But that is our family, your family. As you probably know, it's complicated."

"Well, actually I don't know. At least I don't know how complicated. I told you I was doing genealogical digging to try and find out."

"Yes, of course. So, perhaps that will help." She nodded toward the package resting in my lap.

"Should I open it?"

"Is the Rabbi Jewish?"

"Okay." I tried to untie the string, but the knots were too tight. I fished in my pants pocket for my ever-present jackknife, but I had just flown from Boston. "Uh, they don't let you fly with a pocketknife these days, so I don't have my Swiss Army special with me. Do you have a scissors or something I could cut this with?"

"Silly boy." She reached for the package, then worked the string over a corner and slid it off. "There. Can you manage the paper?"

My ears burned with embarrassment as I opened the package, extracted the first of a stack of chapbooks, and impulsively started reading the top one. I stopped in mid-sentence, suddenly aware that Elsie was clearing her throat with impatience. "Sorry," I said. "And these?" I held up a sheaf of folded and yellowed newsprint along with a few glossy tear-sheets that had lain in the bottom of the carton.

"He was a writer, as you will see. Journalism here, some short-stories there, mostly under pseudonyms. He won the Midwest Medal of Literature for 'Blueberry Scripture' but, with so many different pen names, never built up any real reputation."

"Fascinating."

"Yes, but there will be plenty of time for you to study all that later. Now you simply must join us for dinner. Marcus is coming by to escort me. And don't worry about anything; you will be our guest tonight. It's all taken care of."

I would have preferred to start reading immediately, and she could see that, but there was no arguing with Elsie. As I learned on the way to the dining hall, she had started teaching in a farm-country elementary school in the prairie lands but finished at an inner-city high school where being the alpha female in the classroom had been mandatory. She was used to getting her way.

At dinner, we shared a table with three other residents whose spicy personalities contrasted with the bland kosher fare we were served. We reminisced about growing up in the Upper Midwest, and when I told them I had gone to high school with Garrison Keillor, we laughed over a retelling of a famed Prairie Home Companion skit about the winter holidays. No one brought up the subject of his fall from grace, and I was content to leave the memories simple and unsullied. From old news of Lake Wobegon, the group moved on to bring me up-to-date on the news from and about all their grandchildren and great-grandchildren, and within twenty minutes, I had become one of their circle of friends.

Truth be told, the brisket was not too terrible, but the whipped potatoes, made without cream, were watery and bland, and the after-dinner coffee, lightened with the artery-congealing beige powder known as non-dairy creamer, was unbearable. Once again, I was reminded of the many reasons for not keeping kosher. I do have my own modern leftist version of *kashrut* that elevates local and organically grown foods but largely ignores a bloated body of ancient rules and over-reasoned elaborations that always struck me as arbitrary and picayune. I have never boiled a kid in the milk of its mother nor drunk blood, but I reject the authority of long-dead rabbis whose arguments would treat Philly cheese steak done rare as the same thing or who would allow salmon in cream sauce but not chicken parmigiana. Neither fish nor fowl can be milked, but that never stopped the obsessive-compulsives or the control freaks from legislating every tiny aspect of daily life.

The simple truth is, I love good food and good wine, whatever its ethnic origins or ingredients. I have deep respect for the Boston-area rabbi who issued his own ruling that all wine is kosher because forbidding wine handled by a gentile is a form of racism. I am self-righteously reassured by recent surveys that show how few self-identified Jews keep kosher these days, and my conscience is further assuaged by how many of my fellow New England Jews love lobster and have been known on occasion to savor a cheese omelet with a side of bacon. One of my cultural and culinary heroes is the renowned Boston-area rabbi and author who once wrote about saying *mohtzi*, the blessing over bread, before biting into his ham-and-cheese sandwich. Not much can be more forbidden than that, at least in the food department, nor nobler in the realm of genuine gratitude for the fare we eat.

At dinner that night, though, I generously joined in the appreciation of the glat-kosher meal. And over the coffee, which I pretended to sip, the conversation finally turned to what had brought me to Minnesota and the Chai Residence. The other couple and the quiet woman with the ruby-red neck scarf — as I said, I didn't remember anyone's names — wanted to know about my books and about writing. They vowed to get the library to order copies of *The Rosen Singularity* and its sequel, *The Millicent Factor*, after I told them these were thrillers about longevity and life extension. It figures. Elsie asked for more details about my amateur genealogy and, when I elaborated, chided me about the undisciplined way I had gone about it.

When it seemed that the twenty questions were complete, I asked Elsie how exactly she had tracked me down. "You, it was easy. Once I knew your name and your connection to Jakob's writing, no problem. There are only a few Lior Samson's in the world, at least with any kind of presence on the Web, and the other two are a young man and an even younger girl living in Israel. Don't you love the way the Israelis swap names between genders? You, however, have rather the most public persona."

"Do I really?"

"Yes, you do, almost as if you wanted to be found."

"Perhaps I did, perhaps I do."

I took my leave at the first window of polite opportunity and left with my box of treasures tucked under my arm. On the drive back to the motel near the airport, I stopped at a Starbucks for a triple-shot grande latte. That night, I sat sipping my potent milky coffee at the shallow desk in my motel room and read Jakob's memoirs for the first time. Between the caffeine and the revelations, I slept little, and when I did, I dreamed of icy water and searing fire and of crowded ships and long journeys by train.

On the plane home the following morning, I booted up my laptop and began to write this book. And now, at last, I reach the end, starting as I began, by plagiarizing my grandfather's words with his closing paragraphs, written that last day, as he lay in the hospital.

And now I see the dark at the end of the tunnel. In the fading light I hold onto the once-bright image of your face, the now clouded-over sunlight of your smile, enigmatic to me as always, yet clearest of the ever briefer flashes of memory that scintillate before me. My steps slow as I approach the gloom. Still, it is not fear but reluctance, and longing, that retards my advance, though by too little margin to note or to matter. We all walk this path, this singular road from first dawn to final dusk, and we all arrive.

I no longer grant either credence or authority to any divine judge who might await me at the far end, now so palpably near. I am, of myself, judge enough, at once harsh adjudicator of my failures and shortcomings, not the least with you, and generous dispenser of leniency, of forgiveness. I have learned — slowly, and most cer-

tainly painfully — to forgive others as I would ask others to forgive me, to do unto others, that is, the New Testament inversion of the lone rule on which Hillel the Elder once so nobly and wisely stood.

If by some chance I am wrong, and an afterlife lies ahead, surely, surely a just God will have you waiting, arms outstretched, face radiant, to welcome me into the World to Come. And if there I fail to make the grade because I was of the wrong tribe, the desert people whose ancient faith keeps us in perpetual anticipation, ever waiting for HaMashiach, the Messiah, the Christ of your faith, then so be it. I have already, because you were in my life, endured Hell, and with it Heaven.

I almost wrote just now that life without you was an eternity, but then I realized that life with you was that as well. The moments repeat, locked in a cycle of recall that lasts for all time, all the time that I know, all that I shall ever know. The images, the eternal you, still float before my eyes. You are forever in my arms and forever gone. I am —

-30-

Acknowledgements

This is a work of fiction, but some things are fact: demonstrable, documented, and demanding to be acknowledged. My father was Frank Samson, born on February 23, 1910, to Maggie Samson, in the Bethel Home for Women in Duluth, Minnesota. She was sixteen at the time, an unwed mother. She gave him up for adoption, and the decree became final on January 27, 1912. He died of cancer, chronic myelogenous leukemia, at the age of sixty-two, continuing the legacy bequeathed him in his genes.

Over the decades, many have helped me and encouraged me in my pursuit of the past and in my quest to unearth the story of my origins. This book is not that story but a cousin to it. Part of our human heritage is our genius at invention, part our endeavors to ensure that something of what came before may someday be recovered. Nevertheless, much of our invention and equal measure of our reality remains forever beyond the reach of those who follow. So be it.

I am grateful for the support and the material contributions of so many people over the decades of detective work and the five years of writing. At the top of my list are my parents, who left me mysteries and unanswered questions, but also signposts by which to start my personal archeology. There were many others who have helped point the way or applauded my efforts along it: Lucy Lockwood, Tovah Lockwood, Jeremy Beutel, Joy Constantine, Heather Reardon, Liz Cole, Linda Kuhlmann, Shirley Nellen, Lorie Brewer, Cynthia Broadwell, Patricia O'Sullivan, April Taulbee, Sami

Barth, Miriam Weinstein, and Ruth Budelmann plus Benjamin Schwab, Dr. Herbert Brettl, and Professors Bob Martens and Herbert Peter in Austria, as well as Frank Paukowits, Tom Steichen, Fritz Königshofer, Margaret Kaiser, and others of the online Burgenland Bunch. The Minnesota Historical Society, The Children's Home Society of Minnesota, and the School Sisters of Notre Dame must be thanked collectively for their many-faceted assistance. And, of course, there are others whose anonymity here in no way diminishes either their importance or my appreciation. The final hand goes to my ever faithful and effective copyeditor, Janet Lemnah, who rescues my words from my ineptitude.

I must also acknowledge the Minnesota Family Court judge — prudence prompts me to omit her name — who ruled I could not obtain an unredacted copy of my father's original birth certificate, even though the events were more than a century past and all parties to the occasion were long since dead. Instead, I received a redacted document sporting transcription errors and fabricated on a form that was not even in use in Minnesota until decades after my father's birth. And so, in the end, I must thank her for wielding the goad that ultimately led me to stop waiting for the arrival of revelation and simply to proceed, equipped only with the creative imagination granted me, and to write this story.

It will surprise no one that I am particularly indebted, beyond words, to my father, who chose not to know his story or even his name, but who bequeathed to his son the unquenchable urge to dream and to know. In the end, how much does it matter, what came before? We are what we are, we do what we do. *Yitgadal v'yitkadash sh'mei raba ...* Amen....

About the Author

Lior Samson is the pen name of a former university professor who has won awards for both fiction and non-fiction writing as well as for his innovative work in industrial design. He has more than two dozen published books, including eleven novels and a collection of short fiction. As a consultant and teacher, he has traveled the world, lived in Australia and Portugal, and served on the faculties of two international universities.

He resides in Massachusetts with his family, where he cooks creative fusion cuisine and composes serious choral music. He describes himself as a full-time novelist, part-time journalist and photographer, and full-time support system for the three students in his life — and readily acknowledges that his time sheet does not add up.

The readers who write with questions, kudos, and criticism are vital parts of the dialogue he seeks to spark through his writing. He enjoys hearing from readers and appreciates those who take the time to post reviews on Amazon and elsewhere. He can be reached by email at: lior@liorsamson.com

Appendix
Questions

Below are some questions for study and possible group discussion. Please feel free to pose your own.

SPOILER ALERT: These questions reveal important plot elements.

1) Modern parents often try to devise unique or distinctive names for their children. The nineteenth and twentieth century families in this book, especially in "the old country," commonly stuck to a relatively small number of standard or conventional names, especially those of Biblical origins, and children were often named after their parents. As the result, there are many characters named Mary or Joseph in the story. How did this affect you as the reader and your understanding of the narrative? What impact might this practice have had on people living in those days and communities? How might they have experienced having the same name as many others around them? In light of the fact that writers are often counseled to avoid name confusion, what do you think of the author's choice of remaining consistent with the historical naming tradition and the actual real-life names of many of his characters?

2) Both Miriam/Mary and Magdalena were faced with simi-similar choices about abandoning, for reasons of love, the religion in which they had been raised. What do you think of their decisions, and why do you think they chose

differently? Can you ever imagine yourself in a compa-
comparable position, and how do you think you would
resolve the matter?

3) Belief, faith, and fidelity are core themes in the book. All
four of the central characters — Miriam/Mary, Magdalena, Josef, and Jakob — examine and question their
own faith and beliefs? How was this process different for
each of them, and what did they have in common? In
what ways were each of them true and not true to their
religions? To their beliefs?

4) Mary Samson had seven children, only three of whom
lived to become adults; Sadie Oster had many preg-
nancies but only one carried to term. Such outcomes
were not uncommon in their times. How do you think
these experiences affected them personally and pri-
vately and in relation to their children? How do you think
being surrounded by other women who had many more
children might have affected them?

5) In the late nineteenth century, Austria and the United
States had very different official, sanctioned approaches
to religion. In actuality, what were some of the simi-
larities and differences in the real lives of various faith
communities?

6) How might Jakob's loyalty, pursuit, and preoccupation
with his Lena, the love of his life, be interpreted differently through a contemporary lens than from within
the society in which he lived? Would you or would you
not consider him a stalker or obsessed, and why?

7) In what ways were the life choices of Magdalena and
Jakob similar? In what ways different?

8) In some parts of the contemporary world, religions and
cultures intermingle or mix to varying degrees; in oth-

others, each are concentrated in communities largely of their own kind and kept separated. Consider and con-contrast the American notion of "the melting pot" and assimilation with the realities of today's distinctive neighborhoods and the attitudes within groups toward "others" and "outsiders." How is the contemporary land-landscape different from nineteenth century Austria-Hungary and turn-of-the-century America? What has changed little?

9) The modern model of a love story generally includes a happy ending. In this book are two love stories in two centuries with very different outcomes. In what ways did each end happily? In what ways would you say each did not have a happy ending?

10) The author draws on a number of techniques of post-modern fiction, including (1) non-linear narrative, in which the story is told out of sequence and switches among locales and timeframes; (2) metafiction, in which the story is also about the writing of the story; and (3) the blurring of boundaries between fiction and reality, be-tween history and invention. In what ways did this or other techniques used by the author enhance or dimin-ish your experience as a reader?

11) The novel focuses on two women, but both the narrator, Jakob Oster, and the point-of-view character in the his-torical thread, Josef Samson, are male. What do you think about this choice by the author, and why do you think he made it? What does it say about the lives and the times of the characters?

Made in the USA
Middletown, DE
10 April 2019